# The Write Time

## Allie Samberts

Editing by Cindy Ray Hale

Cover Design by Jillian Liota, Blue Moon Creative Studio

alliesambertswrites@gmail.com

www.alliesamberts.com

For my husband.

None of these stories exist without you, but Ben and Jenny are especially ours.

# Author's Note

Writing Jenny's story was a very different experience for me than writing Mac's in *The Write Place*. On one hand, I deeply relate to the feeling of being adrift that Jenny experiences in this novel as everyone around her seems tethered to something. On the other hand, Jenny's humor and unabashed pursuit of pleasure are characteristics I wish I could exude in my daily life. In that way, I'm proud to have created her.

When I set out to write Jenny, I always knew I wanted her to be more than just Mac's funny best friend. I wanted her to be as important to Mac in *The Write Place* as Daniel was. It didn't take me long into the writing of that book to realize that Jenny deserved her own happily ever after—that she deserved, as Ben says, to be the protagonist of her own story.

Jenny and Mac are best friends, but they are very different people. As such, this book is very different from—though hopefully no less poignant than—*The Write Place*. This might also be a good time to add that, while you don't need to read *The Write Place* before you read *The Write Time*, the action of this book takes place two years after *TWP*, and there are references to it. Jenny's past is also a little darker than Mac's, which means I need to warn you about a few things you'll find in these pages before you start. In *The Write Time*, you'll find:

- multiple explicit, on-page sex scenes (Chapters 16, 23, second half of 25, and a little part at the end of Chapter 8)

- descriptions of a car accident, death, and grief

- lots of alcohol consumption and over-consumption by Jenny, and a hint that a side character may be a recovering alcoholic

- cheating/adultery by a past boyfriend (never by Ben!)

- domestic violence (one of the past characters throws a dish at a wall during a fight, which is a clear show of violence, though it doesn't go further than that)

- one-night stands talked about but not described in detail

- feeling alienated by a friend

- an emotionally difficult parent

- profanity

If any of these things might be triggers for you, now might not be the right time for you to read this book. Take care of yourself first and foremost. Jenny and Ben will be here if and when you're ready.

Jenny and Ben's story is one that is close to my heart for so many reasons, and I hope you enjoy it, too.

# Prologue
## Two Years Ago

*I RUN MY HANDS up his muscled back and over his broad shoulders, my eyes squeezed shut to enjoy the feel of him. He shudders beneath my touch, and the realization that I made him tremble like this sends a rush of warmth to my core. I press myself closer to him, and his big hands move from my waist to my hips, pulling me even closer. I can feel the hard planes of his muscles beneath his shirt, and the only thing I want in the world is to drag my palms over his warm skin.*

*He kisses me like he's never tasted anything as good as me. Like he could never possibly get enough. His lips bruise mine, and I draw his bottom lip into my mouth, nipping it slightly with my teeth. He groans into my lips, and his body melts further into mine. My heart skips about ten beats trying to catch up with itself.*

*I pull my hands up over the back of his head, through his cropped hair. I tug a little at it, and he breaks the kiss enough to sigh into me.*

*"Jenny," he breathes. "You're going to undo me."*

*"That's the idea," I tease, my eyes still closed, and he chuckles. The sound of it sends another wave of warmth through me, and my knees weaken a little. He feels it and grips me closer to him, steadying me. He makes a sound that is pure desire, and our lips meet again. His tongue sweeps over mine, and he tastes of hot, sweet coffee and apple cider donuts.*

*I can't help myself. I run my hands down his sides to the hem of his shirt and lift it slightly to get my hands underneath. I flatten my palms against his lower back as one of his hands comes to my cheek. He threads his fingers into my long brown hair and curls into it, angling my head to deepen our kiss even further. I raise my hands along his back, and he shudders again. "Jenny," he says my name a second time. His voice sounds like decadent chocolate, like he is physically and mentally unable to finish that thought, and he presses his forehead to mine as if he can transfer whatever he is thinking by osmosis. We are both breathing rapidly, our breath mingling in the limited space between us.*

*I open my eyes to find his already open, their deep brown smoldering with desire. It shouldn't surprise me to meet Ben's gaze. We have been making out, but it's still a revelation to see his eyes—ones that I meet each day in the hallway at the school where we work—looking at me like he wants to devour every inch of me. This is a far cry from the professional niceties we exchange between classes or after school.*

*I breathe in deeply, the comforting scent of him mixing with the earthy, mossy scent of the... where are we, again? The corn maze at the pumpkin patch? I have no recollection of how we got from chasing each other through the maze to being pressed together amongst the corn husks, but I'm not complaining. This is easily the best kiss I've ever had. And I've had a lot of kisses.*

*Ben's breathing returns to almost normal, but he doesn't move his forehead from mine, and he doesn't break eye contact. "I've been waiting so long for this," he whispers.*

*My heart trips over itself again. "I..." I trail off. My mouth suddenly feels like cotton. I can't seem to form words or even coherent thoughts. Everything is jumbled.*

*Ben frowns deeply, and I can't tell if he's hurt or concerned. I swallow hard, but that doesn't help clear anything up. He pulls his head away from mine. "Jenny?" he asks, but he sounds far away. I close my eyes and shake my head as if to clear it, but when I open my eyes, he's gone.*

And that's when I wake up, taking in big gulps of air as the silence and loneliness of my apartment press in on me.

It was a dream.

Earlier today, Ben was chasing me through the corn maze at the pumpkin patch while my friend, Mac, and her newest obsession, Daniel, made out in there. *They* were making out. Not Ben and me. Not by a long shot.

I touch my fingertips lightly to my lips, but the bruised feeling and the taste of him have disappeared into the dream world. *Are Ben's hands really that warm? Does he really taste like coffee and chocolate?*

I rock my head to clear the intrusive questions. I can't be going back to school on Monday and seeing Ben with those thoughts in my head.

But my fingertips are still on my lips, and I smile lightly at the memory of dream-Ben's mouth pressed against mine. I let myself linger in the warmth of it for just one more minute.

# Chapter 1
## Present Day

MARK'S LIPS ARE ON mine. Or is it Mike? In my defense, my local hangout, Tony's, is loud and dark, and I'm so sick of this whole scene I can hardly stand it. I used to enjoy going out and meeting guys, and I've been in a dry spell for almost a whole year, but ever since I started helping my best friend plan her wedding, meeting guys at bars feels cheap. And dark. And surprisingly wet.

Not wet in the fun way. Wet in the way where Mark/Mike's mouth is opening and closing kind of like a fish, and his sloppy tongue is licking at my lips, kind of like a dog. The fish/dog situation is cringey enough that I pull back to look at him, twist my grimace into a smile, pat him on the chest, and yell something about finding the ladies' room. This isn't worth it, even if a lack of a partner in my life is starting to feel stifling.

I don't find the ladies' room. I don't even find the friends I came with—Kylie and Ava, two younger teachers at the school where I work. I find the exit and walk straight outside. I pause in front of the door to take a deep breath of the humid August air. The silence after the blaring music is welcome. Tony's has been a favorite hangout for a long time, but the loud music tonight is new, and it's almost unbearable.

I check my watch, and it's still relatively early in the evening, but I'm not going back in there and risking another run-in with Mark/Mike the fishdog, so I text Kylie and Ava to let them know I'm headed home and start walking. My best friend, Mac, has a condo very close by. She still spends about half of her time there, even though she's been engaged to her fiancé, Daniel, for about a year, and he has a sprawling house in the next town.

Mac and I actually used to be roommates in this condo. It was always hers, but I paid rent and lived in the other bedroom until we both grew up a little and I decided I needed more privacy. I still have a key. I have one to Daniel's house, too, much to his chagrin, but Mac insisted. I wasn't going to argue. Mac and I are sort of a package deal. We've been friends since high school, we went to college together, and we got jobs together teaching English at the same school. She couldn't get rid of me if she tried.

When I near the condo, the living room light is on, so I let myself in. Mac is cuddled up on the couch with a red-and-black plaid blanket looped over her red hair like a hoodie. She's holding a steaming mug of tea in one hand and a book in the other. It's an interesting choice for late August. When I walk in, she barely looks up, and when I close the door behind me, she says, "Well, well, well, Jenny. I hate to say I told you so."

She does not, in fact, hate to say I told you so. But she did, in fact, tell me so earlier today when she declined to come with us and warned me that the loud music Tony's is trying out was going to be more suited to a younger crowd. I had responded that thirty is the new twenty, but she wasn't buying it.

I roll my eyes and lean over to unbuckle the straps on my high-heeled sandals. I kick them off and make my way to her room where I grab some olive-green joggers and a white t-shirt from her dresser. I pull off my tight tank top and miniskirt and toss them on her bed. I put on the borrowed clothes, knotting the shirt at the hem, and make my way back to the living room. She hasn't moved, so I flop on the couch next to her with a sigh. She closes her book and tosses it on the coffee table, then shifts the blanket so it covers my legs, too. I lean back, propping my feet on the table. "I think I'm sick of Tony's," I whine.

Mac gasps. "I never thought I'd see the day," she says, clutching fake pearls at her neck. I cock an eyebrow and roll my head to glare at her, not breaking contact with the couch cushions.

"To be fair," I say tersely, "It *used* to be fun when my bestie would come with me, but now she's engaged, so she'd rather read books under a blanket like a goblin on Friday nights instead of hanging out with me." I flick the blanket at her head and make a noise of disgust.

She swats my hand away. "To be fair," she parrots back to me, "I have *always* wanted to read books like a goblin on Friday nights. Daniel has nothing to do with that. You dragged me to Tony's, thinking I'd find love or something."

"To be fair," I counter again, "you did find love at Tony's. Technically, you and Writer Boy met there first."

"But *Writer Boy* loves me for who I am," she argues pointedly.

"Sure, but I love you in spite of who you are, which is arguably more meaningful." I shrug and she smacks my arm, laughing. I snicker. "Where is the famous Daniel Evans, anyway?" I say it sarcastically, but Daniel is, actually, famous. He wrote a runaway bestseller when he was only eighteen years old, and all his other books have sold equally well over the past decade. After he and Mac met at Tony's—and we found out who he really was—he ended up shadowing her as research for his latest novel. He was only supposed to be in Leade Park for six weeks, but he moved here to be closer to her and proposed a year later. Their love story is sickly sweet, and thinking about it gives me a little stab of jealousy that I quickly shove deep down.

Mac grimaces. "He is working on a new book."

"Why that face?"

She scrunches up her nose. "Apparently," she starts slowly, "when he's working out particularly difficult passages, he has this ball that he bounces off the wall. Repeatedly."

"No," I say, horrified.

"Yes. Jenny, I don't know how I'm going to survive this marriage."

"Good thing Evans is rich because you'll have to keep this condo forever." I laugh. She winces. "What?" I ask when I see her face.

"I accepted an offer on it today," she says apologetically. "I close at the end of September, just before the wedding."

I try to keep my face neutral, but I can't. I can feel it fall as my mouth opens in surprise. I knew it was on the market, but I never thought she'd actually sell it considering how much time she still spends here, and considering Daniel has enough money to pay the mortgage on five of these places and still live comfortably.

I look around the living room, taking it in. Memories bubble up, but I shove those down, too. I swallow hard and look back at her. She still has a look of remorse, so I try to smile. "That's..." I trail off. "Great. It's great, Mac."

"You're sad." She frowns deeply, her forehead bunching dramatically between her eyebrows.

I shrug. "It's not my condo."

"Your name might not be on the mortgage, but it's always been as much yours as it is mine," she insists. I don't know what I expected; she's marrying Daniel in a little over a month, and it doesn't make sense for them to keep this place only for nostalgia. Or noise control.

"There's a lot of memories here," I say meekly, and I kind of hate how sad I sound.

"Yeah." She sighs, looking around. I think she's a little sad, too, so I sling my arm over her shoulders, pulling her close to me.

"Hey." I squeeze her, and she rests her head on my shoulder. I muster up the most positive attitude I can. She's moving and getting married and, as her best friend, it's my job to keep things from getting too melancholy. "It's good. This is good. Change is hard, but it's necessary."

I'm not sure that last part fits the uplifting vibe I'm going for, but it seems to work as Mac relaxes a little and huffs.

"I'm going to have to build him a soundproof office," she moans.

"Yeah. You are." I laugh. "And speaking of change..." I trail off, shooting her a sharp look.

She groans. "I suppose I'm also going to have to kick it into gear and actually finish some stuff for this wedding," she muses, more to herself than to me, but I squeeze her again. Mac is a planner by nature, but she also hates being the center of attention, and is definitely not a frilly person. The only real things she's done are book a venue, send out invitations, and buy a dress that she doesn't actually like. She's been at odds with the idea of planning a huge wedding ever since she and Daniel got engaged last fall after an author event she coordinated with him and a former student of hers, Isabel Hernandez. She leveraged his fame to host a fundraiser for the school and help promote Isabel's debut book. He proposed to her that night, and it was perfect. He had me set up candles and roses and the works right here in her condo. Another twinge of loss hits me at the thought of this condo belonging to someone else, but I shove that down.

"If you want to get married, yeah, that's probably a good idea."

"I've been meaning to talk to you, anyway. Daniel and I are at an impasse regarding who is going to officiate the wedding. I still want you to do it, but he thinks we are both going to cry too much to get through the ceremony."

I tilt my head back and forth, considering. "He has a point."

She rolls her eyes. "We are professionals in front of students every day. We have had a lot of practice not crying in front of people."

"Teaching a class of teenagers is not the same as performing your best friend's wedding," I insist.

"Do you not want to do it?"

"I want to do whatever you need me to do, Mac. You know I got my internet ordination, but you and Daniel need to decide if it's right for you," I say, and I mean it. It won't bother me, whatever she decides, as long as she's happy. She nods and chews on her bottom lip thoughtfully.

"Are you sleeping here tonight?" I change the subject so she doesn't spiral too far into indecision.

She nods. "He has a deadline, so he'll be at it for a while. You want to stay? Last weekend of freedom before school starts." If I'm not mistaken, I hear a note of hope in her voice. I smile at that.

"Of course I want to stay." I stand up and walk toward the kitchen. "I'll get the wine."

# Chapter 2
## Present Day

I WAKE UP THE next morning and groan. It's time to face reality. School is starting in a day, and we need to get our classrooms in at least passable order before the students descend this week. I go back to my apartment and get together some haphazard materials and toss everything in boxes. Most of my stuff hasn't moved since I brought it home when school ended in May, so it's not too difficult to find what I need. When Mac comes in, she helps grab some things, and we are able to make it out to her car in one trip.

As we're puzzling how everything will fit with her stuff in her trunk, I'm struck by how much different it feels to start our ninth year of teaching than our first. I remember that first year—first few years, if we're being honest—feeling completely overwhelmed. We had so much. We brought bulletin board materials, paper and markers, binders full of idealistic lesson plans and curriculum ideas, and so many second-hand novels for our classroom libraries. We each spent about a week beforehand setting up. Now, most of our school supplies live in our classrooms, and we only have to set up a few things that we bring home or acquire over the summer. It only takes a few hours, but it's nice to get back into the building and get psyched for a new school year.

We fit everything into her trunk, and I climb into the passenger seat of her car. It's tradition to go into school together before the year starts, and I'm glad she's not too far into wedding indecision to continue it with me.

She rolls the windows down on the way and blasts her favorite summer playlist. It's mostly nostalgic songs from the '90s, which is not my favorite genre, but it's her car, so she gets to pick. We sing along, our hair blowing in the sultry summer air. It feels good, having this moment with her.

When we park at school, we get as close to the door nearest our classrooms as possible. We grab as much as we can and drag it up the stairs. I only have to make one trip, but she has to make a few more, so we part ways for a while, agreeing to call it quits before lunch so we can get food on the way home. I unlock my classroom door and start kicking some boxes just inside so I don't have to lift them again, already tired from moving them up the stairs, when the door next to mine squeaks open. I look up to see Ben Allouer grinning from ear to ear and waving at me.

"Hey, Ben." I wipe my grimy hands on my jean shorts and lean against the edge of my open door.

"Howdy, neighbor," he says in a terrible cowboy accent as he tips a fake cowboy hat.

"Did they move your room?" I ask. Ben, Mac, and I have been in the same rooms since we started teaching, and Ben's used to be farther down the hall.

"Yeah," he says excitedly. "Richard got a job somewhere else, and this room is huge, so I asked if I could snag it."

"Cool." I smile. "Welcome to the neighborhood."

He walks into the hallway toward me and stacks two boxes from the floor on top of each other then lifts them, his biceps rippling as he does so. "Let me be a good neighbor and help you out," he says. Ben is the school's wrestling coach, and he is, for lack of a better word, jacked. The man spends at least an hour at the gym every day and can easily move these boxes in half the time it'd take me. I'm not too proud to let him help me out, so I hold the door open wider and motion him inside. He gets all the boxes in my room, and then I direct him to move them where I need them.

He drops the last box on the floor, then brushes his palms against each other. "Did these just sit in your closet all summer, collecting dust?" He studies the gray film on his hands.

"Pretty much." I shrug. "I wasn't trying to think about school this summer."

"Sounds like you probably had some fun, then," he says.

I nod. "It was okay. I didn't go anywhere but the pool, and I've mostly been prodding Mac to make some decisions about her wedding, but it was relaxing, at least. How about you? Did you and Faith take any romantic trips anywhere?" Ben and Faith have been an item since late last fall when they met at a wrestling meet. She was there cheering on her cousin, and they saw each other and hit it off.

"Um." He awkwardly rubs the back of his neck with his palm, leaving a streak of gray dust. He doesn't quite look at me as he says, "Faith and I broke up."

"Oh no," I say sympathetically. "What happened? You two were pretty hot and heavy for a while there."

"Yeah. She, uh... well, this sounds stupid, but she didn't want kids. Like absolutely would not change her mind on it, which is fine. It's her body and her life, you know, but I want kids someday so..." he trails off again and shrugs.

"Oh, Ben, that sucks." I sag a bit in commiseration. "I'm really sorry. She seemed nice."

"Yeah," he repeats, and doesn't continue. For an English teacher, Ben has always been a man of very few words.

I half-smile at him and tilt my head. "You want to talk about it?" I ask, on the off chance that he is cutting himself off, thinking I don't care.

"Nah." He shrugs. "It's okay. It wasn't meant to be."

"Okay, well, if you change your mind, you know where to find me." I wave a hand around, indicating my classroom. "Pretty fun we'll be neighbors. It'll be nice to actually have someone to talk to, unlike Richard the hermit."

Ben chuckles. I forgot over the summer how much I liked the sound of his laugh. It's always warm and over-eager, as if anything less than a full laugh isn't worth his time.

"I liked that guy, but I'm glad he got out." He rubs his hands against his pants again to dislodge more dust.

"He was definitely not happy here," I agree. Ben nods, and we stare at each other in silence for another minute. He never talks a lot, but this is feeling a lot more awkward than usual.

Just when I'm about to ask if he's okay, he takes a deep breath. "You need help unpacking stuff?"

I shake my head. "It'll only take me about an hour to get set up. My ninth year, and I finally feel like I know what I'm doing," I joke, and he gives me a half smile. "I'm not the one who moved entire classrooms. Do you need help?"

"No, I was on my way out when I saw you, actually. I'm ready. Or, as ready as I'm going to be."

"Okay. I'll see you tomorrow, neighbor."

He smiles broadly at that, gives me another little tip of his fake cowboy hat, and I laugh. His smile somehow gets bigger, and he leaves. I stand in the middle of my room looking at my door for a second, and then I shake off the awkwardness of the conversation and get to unpacking.

I finish in about an hour, and I'm sitting at my desk sorting through copies of get-to-know-you activities and icebreakers for the week ahead. Everyone hates these types of activities, but I have to get to know my students somehow, so they're a necessary evil. Mac bursts through the doorway and crosses the room to my desk, flopping into a student desk in front of me.

"I've hardly seen anyone all morning. Do people walk here on day one of school and wing it?" she asks incredulously.

I tap the edges of a pile of papers on my desk to even them out. "Yeah, I think a lot of people do." I place the pile of papers on a corner of my desk. "I saw Ben, though. They moved him next door."

"Oh yeah? That'll be fun. What happened to Richard?"

"He got another job somewhere else."

"That's good. He wasn't happy here." She mulls this over for a second, then smirks. I do not like the look of that smirk at all. "So, how's Ben?"

I narrow my eyes at her. "Fine." I press my lips into a tight line, hinting that the conversation is over. Her smile widens, and I know where this is going. Mac has been almost comically invested in my friendship with

Ben since we met. He may have shown some interest in me a time or two, but that was years ago. We are both definitely over it by now.

"How's Faith?" She's almost giddy, and I can tell she already knows exactly how Faith is from the way she says it.

I narrow my eyes further. "Fine, I'd assume."

Mac continues grinning at me like a fool and waiting for me to elaborate, but we are teachers who are well-versed in using wait time when students don't want to answer questions. I know from her ludicrous grin that she'll crack first, so I continue to stare straight-faced at her.

It only takes another few seconds before I'm rewarded for my patience. She sighs and rolls her eyes dramatically. "You win. I saw him in the hallway earlier, and we chatted a bit. He told me they broke up."

I lean back in my chair, satisfied. "Do not suggest what I think you're going to suggest, Mackenzie Milcrest." I use her full name so she knows I'm serious, but she waves it away.

"We are thirty years old, Jenny. Grown women, more or less. I'm basically almost married. I don't have the time or inclination to meddle in your love life anymore."

I raise my eyebrow and slowly shake my head at her. "You're ridiculous."

"I am," she admits, "but I'm told you love me in spite of who I am, which is the most meaningful kind of love. Now let's get out of here and get some lunch. I'm starving."

# Chapter 3
## Nine Years Ago

"Holy shit," I say, bending to rest my hands on my knees and panting like I just finished a PR cross country race. "If I have to move one more box up those stairs, I'll pass out."

"Those stairs... are not... normal..." Mac wheezes. She leans against the lockers and wipes sweat from her forehead.

"You two go running together like every other day. There's no way you're this out of shape," Mac's older sister, Eleanor, says as she rounds the corner.

"I think I'm having a heart attack." I clutch at my chest. "Thanks for getting me an interview here, Ellie. Unfortunately, they're going to have to replace me, as I will be hospitalized from carrying boxes up these awful stairs."

"Same." Mac feebly raises her hand about halfway, then weakly drops it at her side.

"You are both so overdramatic." Ellie frowns at us, and then she takes in the masses of boxes strewn on the floor. "How do you have so much *stuff*?"

"English teachers have to have the cool classrooms, El." Mac eyes her sister sardonically. "Not like the boring math department."

Ellie folds her arms and cocks a hip. "At least my class is useful. Not like English. Oh, two more lady English teachers. Walking stereotypes, you two." This argument has been a joke between them since Mac declared her major in college. Ellie, at four years Mac's senior and her de facto parent since theirs moved to Scotland shortly after Mac left for school, had tried to convince her bookworm sister to study something "more practical and feminist," like math or science. It was a lost cause.

We hear off-key whistling come from down the hallway and turn to see Ben walking jauntily toward us, fresh as the morning dew. He's one of the new teachers we've been locked in a room with during new teacher orientation for the past week, and the three of us immediately hit it off. "Oh hey, ladies." He is painfully cheerful, and he looks as if this August heat has had absolutely zero effect on him. He takes in our pathetic scene. "Uh... do you need help?"

"Yes," Mac and I say together, immediately straightening up at the prospect of not having to move all these boxes to our respective class-rooms by ourselves.

"And you call yourselves feminists," Ellie scoffs.

"Feminism has nothing to do with upper body strength," Mac counters.

"Yeah, I'm cool sacrificing my pride on this one," I agree. Ben stands there, hands on his hips, looking between us a little wide eyed. Finally, he turns to Ellie and extends a hand.

"Hi, I'm Ben. I'm teaching English here this year."

Ellie shakes his hand, a gleam in her eyes. "Nice to meet you, Ben." She picks up a box and starts to walk toward Mac's room. "A male English teacher. Now there's something less stereotypical."

"Are you kidding me?" Mac is incredulous. "There are male English teachers all throughout literature and film, and everyone loves them."

"Not everyone. I don't know a single one."

"That's because you don't read..." Their voices trail off down the hallway. When they are out of view, Ben raises his eyebrows at me. "They like to egg each other on." I shrug and grab a smaller box that's full of desk supplies. He stacks a few on top of each other and lifts them as easily as if they were full of tissue paper, even though I know those particular boxes carry all the novels for my classroom library. He's barely straining, though I can see his biceps clearly working through the sleeves of the Leade Park Lightning t-shirt they gave all the new teachers at orientation. Together, we are able to move the rest of my stuff into my classroom pretty quickly. He starts opening boxes and placing books on shelves without my asking, but far be it from me to turn down any extra help I can get.

"Are you excited for the kids to start tomorrow?" He makes small talk as we work.

I put a bunch of pencils in a cup on the corner of my desk. "I think so. Anything is better than a week of new teacher meetings."

"No kidding. I almost fell asleep more times than I can count. I'm ready to actually start teaching."

"Do you know what you're doing tomorrow?"

"Probably some icebreakers or something. I'm kind of icebreakered out from all those meetings, but I don't know how else to learn their names." He shrugs.

"Same," I say, though I don't tell him I'm actually very good at learning names quickly, and I will probably only need a day or two before I have them memorized. It feels like bragging.

"Are you ready for all of this?" he asks, and I shrug.

"I don't know. Maybe?" I'm trying to be confident, but the closer I get to the actual first day of school, the less confidence I feel.

"My mom was a teacher for thirty-five years before she retired. She has a super-secret tip for success that she told me. I can tell you, but you can't repeat it to anyone else. Do you want to hear it?" A smirk plays at his lips, and my eyes catch the movement. When I meet his gaze again, it's a little more intense than it was before.

I clear my throat. "Sure."

He leans in a little conspiratorially and says, "Fake it till you make it." He winks, grinning fully now, and I laugh.

"Excellent advice," I say between my laughter. He is still leaning in close to me, and I can feel his body heat. It's not unwelcome, even though the air conditioning in my classroom is having a hard time keeping up with the sweltering August weather. I can't stop smiling.

"You have sophomores?" He must notice how close he is to me because he takes a small step back, and I nod. He grimaces. "I have seniors. That's going to be a trip, being only five years older than them."

"I'm glad I have the younger group for that reason," I admit, just as Mac and Ellie burst through the door of my classroom.

"All right, Green. Time's up," Ellie announces. "Let's go grab some dinner."

Mac's eyes gleam, standing there with her arms crossed and a thin layer of dust coating her brown sandals. "Do you want to join us, Ben? We're going to a place down the street."

I go completely still and glare at her. Her smirk doesn't waver, and she doesn't move her eyes from Ben. I continue to try to bore holes in her brain from across the room, and my words are clipped as I say, "Kyle is meeting us there."

His face falls slightly at the mention of my boyfriend, but he recovers quickly. I told him about Kyle when we were all exchanging introductions during orientation, so his existence is not a surprise.

"Perfect! You won't be the only guy." Mac's smile is brilliant now, and she finally deigns to look at me. She gives a little faux-innocent shrug because she knows that's not what I meant. I *meant* that Ben should stay away, not that he would be outnumbered. Kyle and I have been dating since high school. We've all known each other for a very long time, and both Mac and Ellie are well aware of his attitude when there are other guys around, especially guys who are attractive and friendly toward me. This is what I get for trying not to be rude.

His eyes flick back and forth between us. "Uh." He clearly knows there's a right answer, but he's unsure what it is. "Yeah. Sure."

Wrong answer. "Great, we'll meet you there." My voice is over-eager and too bright as I practically shove Mac and Ellie out the door before they can say something even worse. Leave it to Mac to poke the beast, so to speak. She has never liked Kyle, not since we started dating seven years ago. I'm sure she'd much rather see me with a guy like Ben, but it's not up to her. I love Kyle, and that's that.

I walk quickly outside with them trailing more slowly behind me. Once we approach the cars and I look around to make sure Ben isn't anywhere around, I whirl around to address them. They stop their giggling when they see my face.

Mac immediately raises her hands, palms out. "I was trying to be nice."

"Liar. I can see Ben's interest in me just as plainly as you can." I point a stiff finger at Mac. "You started this, and I'm not going to be rude and tell him not to come, but I would really like to be friends with our new coworkers, so please, *please* do not make this uncomfortable. Kyle is—"

"Jealous?" Mac interjects.

"Overbearing?" Ellie suggests.

"Suffering from a Napoleon complex?" Mac tries hard not to laugh at her own joke. Kyle is the same height as me and asked me one time—*one time*—not to wear high heels to a dance, and she still likes to bring it up. I give them both an exasperated look.

"Come on," I plead.

Mac raises her hands in surrender again. "Okay, okay. But if those two start fighting for your affection, my money's on Ben."

"Definitely on Ben," Ellie repeats. I narrow my eyes at them, but I don't say anything else. There is absolutely no talking to them when they get like this.

Mac and I get into her black sedan, and Ellie climbs into her tiny orange two-door. We drive over to the restaurant, arriving just before Ben. Kyle is standing right outside the door, waiting. He's wearing an old band t-shirt, black jeans with holes ripped all over them, and dark boots. His black hair is slicked back. He is using his tongue to toy with his lip ring, and when he sees us arrive, he pointedly checks his watch.

When Kyle and I started dating, he was definitely my type. I was completely infatuated with the brooding musician in him. He was different with me than he was with anyone else—so loving and attentive—and I felt special with him. But over the past few months, things have gradually changed. He's become slightly snippier with me, and a little more evasive. But, we survived long-distance during college, so I know this is simply a little bump in our relationship. If we can stay together after being so far apart, we can do anything.

"Sorry we're late." I flash my most dazzling smile to soften his irritation and kiss his cheek. He doesn't scowl at me, but he doesn't smile back.

*Okay, it could be worse,* I think. "Moving those boxes took a lot longer than we thought it would."

"Definitely could have used another pair of hands," Mac mutters, plainly referencing the fact that we asked him to help, and he couldn't. He's the manager at a local guitar store, and he said he had to work today, but she wasn't buying it. Kyle looks like he's about to say something, but just then, Ben jogs up to join the group.

"Hey everyone." He extends his hand. "You must be Kyle. I'm Ben." He smiles warmly. As they shake hands, I'm struck by the difference between the two of them. Kyle is all cold, dark shadows and hard edges. Ben is warmth personified. I couldn't write two better foils if I tried.

"Ben is also a new English teacher," Mac is saying when I snap back to the conversation.

"Cool." By Kyle's tone, this is anything but cool. "Can we eat? I have to get back." Ben stiffens ever so slightly, and Mac and Ellie exchange glances. I pretend not to see any of it as I take Kyle's hand and lead us into the restaurant.

Once we are all seated and have ordered, we sit in silence for a while. Kyle dropped my hand as soon as we sat down and hasn't touched me since. Ben, who is seated across from Kyle, is pushing around the condensation on his glass of water and glancing at me every so often. Mac, seated next to Ben, keeps making faces across the table at Ellie, who is seated on the other side of me. They're clearly speaking some silent sibling language. So, I guess it's up to me to start the conversation.

"First day with students tomorrow!" I fake some enthusiasm. Fake it till you make it, indeed.

"Are you finally ready, babe?" It almost sounds like Kyle's faking some interest, too, though I don't love his emphasis of the word "finally."

"Yeah, we were able to get her whole room set up today." Ben gives me a little smile. I smile back, and Kyle's eyes rapidly fire back and forth between the two of us. Mac and Ellie go still.

"We?" Kyle asks, forcing calm.

"I had a lot to do, and Ben was nice enough to help." I try to remain chipper, but even I can hear the frustrated edge creeping into my voice.

"I'm glad you had someone *nice enough* to help you." Kyle glares at me, the sarcasm practically dripping off his tone.

"That's not what I meant—" I start, but Kyle cuts me off.

"No, I get it. I have to work overtime to try to start saving up for a house or whatever it is that you want, but Teacher Boy over here with his weekends and summers off can take all the time in the world to set up your classroom."

Ben holds up his hands. "Hey, man, we're all friends helping each other out here. Nothing more to it."

"Sure." Kyle's eyes slide to him. "Like I don't know how this ends. I get to work a dead-end job that will never pay me enough to keep up with this one's champagne tastes"—he jerks a thumb at me—"while the college-educated golden boy swoops in like a knight in shining armor."

"Kyle, shit. Calm down. We literally just met this guy." Ellie is clearly trying to be the older voice of reason, but I tense. In my experience, when people are told to calm down, the opposite usually happens.

Sure enough, the tips of Kyle's ears start turning red. I've known him long enough to know that's the start of an explosion, so I try to step in. I put my hand on his arm, but he tenses immediately. I see a muscle in Ben's jaw tick.

"Hey," I say soothingly. "Babe, it's fine. Everything's fine. We all had a long day, and we're a little nervous about the students starting tomorrow, right?" I look around the table for support. Ellie and Mac nod. Ben eyes me, then nods once as well. Kyle doesn't miss the way Ben looks at me, but I feel him relax slightly underneath my touch. He grumbles something I can't make out but seems calmer. I leave my hand on his arm. Mac catches my eye across the table, and I shake my head slightly. She purses her lips and looks away.

Shortly after that, our food is delivered, and the teachers make small talk about the upcoming school year. Kyle stays mostly silent, offering a few half-hearted smiles and laughs here and there. No one tries to include him in the conversation, but no one sets him off again, either. We eat faster than normal, and when we are waiting for the check, Kyle goes to the bathroom.

"Are you staying with Kyle tonight or going back to our place?" Mac asks.

"Back to our place." I make sure to toss enough money into the middle of the table for both Kyle and me. "But can you maybe circle the block a few times so I can talk to him?" I know it's a lot to ask after a long day, but I have to be sure he's calm before leaving him. She looks at Ellie, who nods once, then tosses her keys across the table.

"Take my car. Ellie will drop me off." She smiles a little sadly. I take the keys gratefully, then I look at Ben.

"I'm sorry," I start, but he shakes his head.

"No, don't apologize for something you didn't do." His eyes have that intensity again. I open my mouth to respond, but Kyle slips into his seat, and Ben looks away.

After we've settled the check, and everyone has left, Kyle and I hang back. As soon as they're out of earshot, he turns to me.

"I'm sorry, baby. I feel so left out when you all start talking about your teacher stuff." His tone is soft and genuine now as he takes my hands in his, threading his long fingers through mine.

"I know, but you flew off the handle in the first five minutes of dinner," I say, and he tenses again.

"That guy is obsessed with you." His voice is menacing, and I can't help but shudder a little.

"Hardly." I try to keep calm.

"He is. It's written all over his face. You can pretend not to see it if you want, but it's there. I don't like the thought of some all-star football guy moving in on my woman."

"Wrestling."

"What?"

I probably shouldn't have corrected his assumption, but it feels important. "He's the new wrestling coach."

Kyle raises an eyebrow at me. "That's not better."

"It's not?" I ask.

"No. He's good looking, *and* he could definitely kick my ass," he grumbles.

I huff and meet Kyle's gray eyes. It's clear he's joking, but is at war with his insecurities. Not feeling completely secure about school starting tomorrow, I can sort of relate. I soften a bit and give him a gentle smile, looking up at him.

"He's not my type," I assure him. "I'm much more attracted to dark and mysterious musicians than golden boy coaches."

He half-smiles at that, then leans in to kiss me. It's a chaste kiss, but it still feels nice. "You want to come to my place tonight?" There's a note of hope in his voice, but I shake my head.

"I can't tonight. Mac and I are driving in together tomorrow morning, and I still have a lot to do to get ready."

He searches my face, and for a second, I'm worried he's going to get angry again, but he just purses his lips and pulls away.

"You have a way to get home?" he asks. It doesn't escape me that it's not quite an offer to drop me off, but I decide not to push it.

"Mac left with Ellie. I have her keys."

He nods again, then pushes away from the table to stand. "Have a good night, then." He starts toward the door. I stand, too, to walk out with him, but he's halfway across the restaurant when he turns around and, almost as an afterthought, adds, "Good luck tomorrow." Then he's gone.

I stand next to the table, a little dumbfounded before making my way to the bathroom to gather my thoughts. I finish up in there, then walk out to Mac's car. I unlock the door and start to get in when I notice Ben in his car a few spaces down. He's staring at his phone, so he doesn't see me until he looks up and smiles sheepishly. I walk toward him, and he rolls down his window to give me a little wave.

"Hi," he says slowly, as if he has been caught.

"Couldn't get enough of the food here?" I tease.

He blushes a little. "I..." He hesitates like he's searching for what he wants to say, and I frown at him. He sighs. "I was waiting for you."

"For me? Why?"

"I wanted to make sure you were okay. Kyle was a little volatile in there."

"Oh." I'm not quite sure how else to continue. I'm touched that he thought to wait to check on me but embarrassed that Kyle was so nasty that Ben was concerned.

"You good?" His eyebrows pinch together, and I blink a few times to clear my head.

"Yeah, I'm fine. Kyle gets that way sometimes when he feels left out or insecure." I shrug. "He apologized. It's all good."

Ben studies me for a moment, then smiles. His smile is genuine and warm, nothing like the cold, half-smiles I've been getting from Kyle today.

"You need a ride?"

I swallow hard against the feeling of shame that started bubbling up when Kyle left me in the restaurant. It's coming on even stronger now. I'm tired of trying to be cute and funny and chipper to diffuse the tension, so my voice is weak and sad when I say, "No. Mac left me her keys."

"Okay." He eyes me up and down again, assessing. He doesn't look satisfied, but he starts his car, anyway. "See you tomorrow. And if you need anything, you know where to find me."

"Likewise. But I think I'll be okay. Fake it till you make it, right?"

Ben laughs a deep belly laugh. The sound is contagious, and a real grin starts to spread widely across my face.

"Right." He puts his car into drive and waves to me as he pulls away.

# Chapter 4
## Present Day

I ARRIVE AT SCHOOL early the next day. I don't have a lot left to do to prepare for the students to arrive, but I couldn't sleep anyway, so it makes more sense to head into school than to toss and turn uselessly in bed. Even nine years into teaching, I still get nervous to meet the students, apparently.

A few minutes before the bell rings to signal students should start moving to their classes, I prop my door open and step into the hallway. Ben is already standing across the hall from his door. He's wearing a light green button-up shirt and a green-and-gold striped tie with neatly pressed black pants. It's a total cliché for teachers to dress up on the first day of school, especially in green-and-gold spirit colors, but he looks nice. I give it a week before he starts with his khakis and wrestling t-shirts.

The back of his nice shirt is straining slightly against his broad shoulders as he bends over, looking at a student's schedule. The kid is a freshman based on her huge backpack and wide eyes. He straightens and points down the hall, smiling comfortingly at her. She shuffles anxiously on her way.

He turns his bright smile to me. "Howdy, neighbor."

"Is this greeting going to be a thing now?" I raise my eyebrow and cross my arms.

He shrugs. "I'm trying it out. What do you think?"

I pretend to consider, then scrunch up my nose. "Eh. Not my favorite."

He laughs his belly laugh, and I can't help but smile again. Students are passing between us in the hallway, a few of them peeling off the mass to enter our classrooms. I turn around to peek behind me into my room and see the desks are about half full. Most of the students are looking at their phones or have their heads down.

"Not a very lively crowd this morning." Ben's voice is close to my ear. I don't hear him move across the hallway, so he's closer to me than I expect. I startle a little at his closeness before looking up at him. His brown eyes are sparkling. I linger in that twinkle for a second, but I'm quickly torn away by a student shouting behind us.

"Coach!" We turn to see Josh McNamara, a student I had in class two years ago, standing in the middle of the hallway. "I got you for English!"

Ben reaches out, and they do the hand-slap-back-clap that's cooler than a handshake and manlier than a hug. "Yeah, man. I saw you on the roster. It's gonna be a great year!"

"Yeah it is," he says, then he turns to me. "Hey, Miss Green."

"Hi, Josh. How was your summer?" I ask.

"It was okay. This guy here had me working out a ton to get ready for this season." He indicates Ben, and I raise my eyebrows.

"Did you join wrestling?" I say, surprised. Josh has grown up a lot since I had him two years ago, but he used to be one of the smallest kids in his grade.

"Last year." He grins in the way of teenagers who are extremely proud of themselves. "Best thing I've ever done."

"Josh is one of our most talented wrestlers," Ben adds, and Josh flushes at the compliment. "Going to be even better this year if he keeps up the workout plan I made for him."

"I will, Coach. I'm getting to State this year," Josh says earnestly as he makes his way into Ben's classroom. We both smile at his exuberance.

A few more students filter into my classroom as the five-minute warning bell rings. As I'm directing another freshman student to their classroom, two more of my former students—Noah Bell and Javier Sanchez—walk into Ben's room holding hands. My gaze follows them, and I must have a skeptical look on my face, because Ben chuckles.

"They're an unlikely couple," I say under my breath so they can't hear me. "Is Noah still the valedictorian?"

"As far as I know, and from what I've heard from the coaches, Javier's still mostly trouble, but has tried to clean it up for Noah."

"Huh." I shrug. "I guess opposites do attract. Are they both in your class, or is he walking him here?"

"They're both in here." Ben raises his eyebrows, indicating he's expecting issues. "This class will have a strict seating chart, and those two will not be next to each other."

"Smart."

The bell rings to start class, and Ben takes a deep breath, letting it out slowly.

"Here we go," I say with feigned excitement.

He bends to look behind me into my classroom, where most of the students still have their heads down or their noses in their phones.

"Good luck in there, Green."

"I think you've got your hands full yourself, Coach." I tilt my head toward his classroom.

"Wouldn't have it any other way!" He says it sardonically, though I don't think he's totally joking as he pulls the door closed behind him and I hear him shout, "Welcome to your last first day of high school, seniors!"

I face my room, say a quick prayer to whoever is listening that I'll be more interesting than their cell phones this week, and step into my room to start the year.

At the end of the day, I'm completely beat. My cheeks hurt from smiling approachably, I can feel new wrinkles starting to form on my forehead from over-exaggerating my expressions, and my feet are killing me because of the heels I stupidly decided to wear today to make an impression. I do love this job, but the first day never gets easier. I feel out of shape, like I need to rebuild my stamina for teaching.

I flop in my desk chair, slouching back so far that I can tilt the back of my head against the back of the chair and look up at the ceiling. I kick my heels off under my desk and let my arms hang lifelessly on top of the armrests. I only get a minute, though, before my classroom door opens. I assume it's Mac without looking, and I groan in greeting, fully out of words after a long day of introductions and classroom expectations.

"I guess I don't need to ask how your day went." Ben's voice comes from near the doorway. I half-sit up, surprised. He comes fully into the room, allowing the door to close behind him. "No need to cheer up on my account."

"I'm not upset. It was a good enough first day, just exhausting." I wiggle myself so I'm sitting up, but make no move to put my shoes back on. "How about you?"

"My first class is definitely going to be my most interesting one, and I have a section of juniors thrown in there this year, which will be something different, but it was fine. Can't complain."

The door opens behind him, bumping into his back. He jumps out of the way, and Mac pokes her head in, her red hair already in a messy bun on top of her head. Her eyes dart between Ben and me a few times, and I can tell she's trying to fight a devilish grin. I look at her knowingly.

"Should I come back later?" she asks.

"No," we both say in unison. She can't help herself from smirking at that, but she steps inside and quickly corrects her face. She grabs a seat in a student desk, but Ben remains standing.

"So, how was everyone's first day?" She uses her teacher voice—a mix of cheery authority and forced interest. Sometimes I wonder if she has a hard time turning it off at the end of the day, which then makes me wonder if Daniel likes her teacher voice in private. I shake my head a little to clear those thoughts away.

"My sophomores are all more interested in their phones than me. I've been up here putting on a song and dance all day to get their attention, so that was fun." I fold one foot under my thigh and use my toes on my other foot to play with my shoes under my desk.

Ben shrugs. "My classes are basically what you'd expect from seniors."

"They've got senioritis already?" Mac asks.

Ben nods. "Pretty much."

"Well, I can assure you my juniors did not read one single book this summer." She's incredulous, and not in the fake way. She truly can't believe it.

"I can't blame them. I didn't either," Ben says as if this is perfectly reasonable. When we both stare at him in disbelief, he adds, "What? I was busy. And speaking of busy, I have to get down to the weight room for conditioning. See you ladies tomorrow." He tips his fake cowboy hat at each of us in turn and leaves.

As soon as the door is closed, Mac turns to me with a sly grin on her face. "Should I draw your attention to the fact that Ben came to check in on you after your first day?"

"I was here. I'm aware."

"Jenny, that man has carried a torch for you for nine years, and you know it." Mac crosses her arms as if this proves her point.

"I know nothing, and if I have to listen to you play 'Emma the matchmaker' every day for the rest of the year, I'm going to lose my mind."

"Okay, fine," she concedes, then adds, "What about every week?"

"Mac." I use my best warning teacher tone.

She surrenders, standing. "Fine, I'll keep my thoughts on this to myself. Are you free to come to my dress fitting this Saturday?" She changes the subject before I can get too annoyed.

"Yeah, no problem."

"Great." She rests one hand on the doorknob. "See you tomorrow!"

She bounces back into the hallway, and I check my piles of papers to make sure I have what I need for tomorrow and make a few changes to my plans before packing up my things. When I finally leave, it's late enough that I think I might catch Ben in the hallway, but I'm the only one around. Even Mac's classroom is dark, which isn't like her, though I guess it's more motivating to leave when you have someone to go home to every night. As I turn out my lights and lock the door, I'm not sure if the little ache I feel is jealousy or disappointment.

# Chapter 5
## Present Day

MAC IS STANDING IN the bridal boutique wearing a deep frown and the poofy dress her mom persuaded her to buy a few weeks ago via video chat. Or, rather, the dress is wearing her. I tilt my head to the side, standing behind her and looking at her in the mirror. I'm trying to school my face into complete neutrality as I look her reflection up and down.

"This is a monstrosity." Her matter-of-fact tone belies her facial expression, which has me thinking we are about five minutes from a complete meltdown.

"It's not," I say slowly, considering how I want to proceed.

"It absolutely is. It's huge." She takes a fistful of tulle and pulls it from her side, letting it fall. It takes a comically long time to float back down to skirt-level, and I cover my mouth to stifle a laugh.

"This isn't *me*, Jenny," she whines.

I have to agree. "Well," I start cautiously, not wanting to upset her further, but then I can't help myself. "I hate to say I told you so?"

Her shoulders slump as she hides her head in her hands. The skirt presses into the ground as she shortens herself, letting out a *woosh* as it settles. Her whole body starts to shake, causing the tulle to make little swishing noises, which makes her shake even harder. I eye her sidelong, not quite sure what kind of reaction I'm dealing with yet. I'm hoping I didn't make her cry, even though I did tell her this dress wasn't her style a few weeks ago. She was so eager to please her mom that she talked herself into loving it.

She drags her hands down her face and neck, looking up at the ceiling with a groan. It's clear she is laughing now, but there is no humor in it. This is good, though. Laughing is good. I can work with laughter, even if it is desperate. She pulls the tulle skirt up so she can descend the small podium in front of the three full-length mirrors, and she flops into the loveseat I had been sitting on while waiting for her to leave the dressing room. She raises her hands and lets them fall dramatically on top of the tulle, causing the skirt to flare out forcefully at the sides as the air underneath fights for somewhere to go. She hangs her head in defeat and groans again. I make my way to the loveseat, moving the skirt carefully out of the way so I can sit next to her. As soon as I'm seated, her whole body flops into me and she rests her head on my shoulder. I give her what I hope is a reassuring hug.

I can see her signature doom spiral starting now. "Talk to me, Mac. What's going on in that brain?" I squeeze her shoulders a little. She huffs and leans farther into my side.

"This whole *thing* isn't me, Jenny. I never wanted a huge wedding. I hate it when people stare at me. All this happened so fast. I mean, I know a year is a decent length for an engagement, but it's a lot of pressure to plan this thing. I put everything off, and I feel like it's gotten out of control. And now, all of a sudden, I have five weeks to fix this dress, finalize all the plans for this huge ceremony and reception, and start the school year. And Daniel is at home banging balls against his office wall over and over and over again." She cringes. "Don't say it. I heard it as soon as it came out of my mouth."

I stifle a laugh, but a snort escapes against my will, despite the pang of jealousy I feel in my gut. If anyone had asked me eight or nine years ago, I would have been sure I'd be married with kids by now.

And I would have rocked the hell out of this tulle, too.

But that wasn't in the cards for me, and today isn't about me, anyway. It's about Mac and her latest crisis, so I squeeze her closer to me, rubbing a hand up and down her arm. At that moment, the woman who sold us this dress the last time we were here—Kelli-With-An-I—bounces over. When she sees us on the couch, she looks at us with over-exaggerated sympathy.

"Oh," she pouts with her voice. "What's going on?"

I don't let Mac go as I look up at Kelli-With-An-I. "I think we need to do some more alterations." I keep it simple, hoping she'll take the hint that now is not the time. The woman works at a bridal shop; surely, she knows when a bride is about to have a meltdown and can take a hint to leave us alone. She doesn't, though. Instead, she claps her hands together in excitement.

"No problem! I'll get the seamstress." Kelli-With-An-I practically bounces off to find her. Once she is out of earshot, Mac slumps farther into the seat as if she's trying to hide herself. She almost can in all this tulle.

"I don't think there's any fixing this dress," she groans, and I can't help but laugh.

"The only way to fix it might be to buy a different one." My voice is low so Kelli-With-An-I doesn't hear. Mac groans again, putting her head back in her hands. I grab her wrists and pull them away from her face.

"I can't go through that process again." A note of true fear edges Mac's voice, and I breathe a sigh through my nose.

"It was grueling," I agree.

"So bad." Mac looks up at me with wide eyes. "Please get me out of here."

"I can't," I say. As her best friend, regardless of what Mac decides my roll in the wedding will be, it's my job to get Mac over the finish line. "We need to at least see what the seamstress can do. But I'll hold your hand through the whole thing, and if you feel like the only answer is to rip it apart, we'll get Kelli-With-An-I back here and start over, okay?"

Mac sighs deeply, but she drags herself up when the seamstress arrives, and we make it through the rest of the appointment without any tears.

An hour later, she is back in her jeans, flat sandals, and a gray t-shirt I'm pretty sure she stole from Daniel. Her red hair is slightly mussed from the dressing room, but she looks much happier and in her element as we make our way through the doors of Tony's.

It's the afternoon on a Saturday, and Tony's isn't known for its excellent food, so the place is mostly empty. We order drinks at the bar—a beer for her and wine for me—and take them to a table toward the back.

"I don't want to poke the bear," I say when we are seated, "but we should probably come up with a plan for that dress."

Mac winces as soon as the words are out of my mouth, and I give her a look that I hope is apologetic. She takes a long swig from her beer bottle before responding.

"Do we have to?" She sounds like a petulant child. I give her my best teacher look that I usually save for when my students are getting out of line.

"Yes, Mackenzie Milcrest." I try to add some gravity. "You cannot get married without a dress you're happy with." She glares at me. "At least one you can tolerate," I amend. Especially in the spectacle of a ceremony that has come together over the past year. I think Mac thought putting everything off would ensure that it was casual and small, but the reality of it is that she hasn't had time to think things through, and so it has kind of blown up against her better judgment. It doesn't help that Daniel's family is very wealthy and his mother has expected a certain level of pageantry for her only child. It also doesn't help that Mac is very eager to please her future mother-in-law.

"Fine, Jennifer Green. I'll get a plan together about the dress." She scrunches up her nose in disgust, and just as I'm about to remind her that I'm not the one in danger of getting married in a paper bag, her eyes shift to something over my shoulder, and her face brightens ever so slightly. I know without looking that Daniel has walked in, but I twist in my seat to confirm. He spots us immediately and comes straight to our table, sliding in next to Mac and putting his arm around her. He is dressed far too nicely for a dive bar on a Saturday, but, then again, I've never known him to wear an outfit that costs less than a grand, so this isn't even him being flashy.

"Hello, ladies." He gives Mac a squeeze. She looks like she's about to dissolve into him with relief, and I get yet another little jealous pang. I hope it doesn't show on my face as I eye him over my wine.

"Evans." I raise an eyebrow. He looks at me a little apologetically.

"I hope I'm not interrupting. This one"—he squeezes Mac again—"texted me and told me to meet you here. How did the dress fitting go?"

I snort into my wine and give Mac a pointed look that suggests this is her problem to explain, not mine. She sighs and slumps into herself even farther. Daniel gives me a questioning glance, but I shrug, sipping my drink.

"Not great," Mac finally offers, but she doesn't expand on this statement. Daniel looks at me again, then back to Mac, waiting for her to elaborate. She grumbles a little, then fidgets in her seat. "I'm not sure about the one I picked out," she finally says.

He tilts his head, catching her eyes with his. As he searches her face, her shoulders relax ever so slightly. "So, get another one." He's entirely sincere, but she rolls her eyes dramatically.

"It's not that easy. I hated dress shopping the first time and everything else is so..." she trails off, looking at me helplessly.

"Big? Fluffy?" I try. "Expensive?"

"You know money isn't an issue," he says quietly, and Mac seems to shrink even more. She's been a woman with a career since she graduated from college. I know she doesn't like spending Daniel's money, even if it is for a wedding he has had a major hand in planning.

"I know. It's not that, exactly. It's just that none of it is... they don't fit me." She looks down at her hands and starts to rub her right thumb over the plain gold band she wears on her pointer finger. The ring used to belong to her sister, and it's something of a comfort object for her when she's feeling overwhelmed.

"You can have it tailored," Daniel suggests gently, and he genuinely seems to think this is helpful. My laugh sounds harsh and loud in the quiet bar.

"She doesn't mean they literally don't fit her, Evans," I correct him. "She means they're not her style."

His lips make an "O" shape as he realizes what we're talking about. Just then, the door to the bar opens. Daniel and Mac look up. Mac smiles, and Daniel gives a little wave. I twist around again to see Ben enter the bar. He returns Daniel's wave, then his gaze falls to me, and his expression turns a little more intense. I feel it even from across the room, and my cheeks heat a little. I hear Mac clear her throat behind me. I turn around to scowl at her, only to find her and Daniel both trying to hide sly smiles, neither of them looking at me. They meet each other's eyes, and the lovey-dovey look on their faces has my third-wheel radar on high alert. I stand, muttering something about going to say hi, but I don't think they hear me or care.

Ben is facing the bar and leaning against his forearms, and I can't help but let my eyes rake over him in a way that would be inappropriate at work. His broad shoulders stretch his green t-shirt in all the right places, and his jeans aren't Daniel's $300 variety, but they still flatter his shape nicely. His dirty blond hair is cut close to his head, and as I approach, I can see his biceps flexing a little to support himself against the bar.

I slide into a seat next to him, and his brown eyes turn to me. His face lights up into a smile, creasing the corners of his eyes and bracketing lips. I smile warmly back, giving him a little air-toast with my wineglass.

"Howdy neighbor," he says. The man is committed to this horrible greeting, I'll give him that.

"Hey there," I return. "Funny meeting you here."

"I came to grab some wings," he says.

I cringe. "You're a brave soul to eat the wings here." I shudder. He laughs his belly laugh, and I start to feel a little warm. This wedding talk is really getting to me.

He winks at me. "I have a strong stomach."

I chuckle, though his wink ticks my heart rate up a few notches. *Get it together, Green*, I coach myself.

"I was working at the cross country meet," he continues, clearly unaware of the effect he's having on me, "and I'm too lazy to make anything for lunch. What are you doing here? Besides day-drinking on a Saturday, I mean."

"We finished round one of wedding dress alterations for Mac today." I take a deep and telling pull from my glass of wine.

He shakes his head in sympathy. "'Round one' suggests there will be a round two."

"Probably rounds five, six, and seven the way this is going."

"The wedding is in five weeks." He frowns, and a little crease appears between his eyebrows. "My sister had her dress bought and tailored, like, months beforehand."

"I know." I sigh, looking back at where she and Daniel are seated. They have their heads tilted together and are so focused on each other, it's like the rest of the bar doesn't exist. "Girl's got a looming deadline, to say the least."

Ben follows my gaze. "Well, if all else fails, they'll be married in the end, right? That's the most important thing."

I huff incredulously, still looking at Mac and Daniel pressed together in their booth. "That's the altruistic thing people who have never planned a wedding say."

He shrugs noncommittally, leaning back against the bar. His arm is close to mine, and I can feel the heat radiating off him, which is no surprise. He's always so warm—literally and figuratively. His brown eyes are like hot chocolate, and I've seen his smile and belly laugh take the chill off many tense situations.

I sense him watching me—another warm sensation I wasn't expecting—and I slide my gaze to him. Sure enough, he's studying me intently, and I blink rapidly in surprise when I notice. He smiles a little, then looks away. He takes a breath as if to say something, but the bartender brings out his order, and whatever he was going to say is lost.

He holds his to-go box and nods at me. "It was good to see you, Jenny." Suddenly, he looks for all the world like he needs to escape this place as quickly as possible, probably because he's starving. I almost ask him if he wants to join us, but the last time I had wings from this place, I had my head in a toilet for a day and a half, so I wave instead.

"You too, Ben. See you Monday."

"Yeah, see you Monday." He leaves quickly. I watch him leave, then I push myself off the bar and turn toward where Mac and Daniel are sitting. They both look at me as I cross the room with broad, teasing smiles. I shake my head in disbelief as I walk back to the table. I should have known their interest in each other was a cover for spying on me. I sit back down against my better judgment. Daniel is leaning his elbows on the table, likely hiding a grin behind his hands. Mac isn't hiding anything; she's smiling like a maniac. "So," she teases, "how's Ben?"

"Fine," I say, wondering how long and how often we need to play this game. When I don't offer any more information, she grumbles and lightly smacks the table in exasperation, her slight engagement ring making a metallic sound against the top of the table.

"That's it?"

"He was here getting wings for lunch after working the cross country meet." I sip my wine. Mac and Daniel both grimace. "And that's *it*, you fools. Stop giggling every time you see me talk to him. It's getting weird.

And besides," I desperately try to change the subject, "we need to focus here on you two, and we need a plan for this dress."

# Chapter 6
## Eight Years Ago

"You ever think maybe you're not cut out to be a teacher if you have to spend so much time in that building prepping and grading?" Kyle hurls the question at me. I'm not entirely sure how we got here, only that his anger over my job has been building for weeks. We tried to do a trial run living together. Or, at least, I have been treating it like a trial. My bedroom at the apartment I shared with Mac hasn't changed, which is fortunate because, based on how he's been talking to me this week, he either wants me around more often, or can't stand the space I take up when I am here.

"You ever think maybe I'm not coming home because you treat me like shit when I'm here?" I yell back.

"I treat you like a damn queen, Jenny, and I always have. I'm buying you everything you want all the time and making sure there's dinner on the table when you feel like showing your face around here, even though it should be the other way around."

"What the hell is that supposed to mean?" I shout. "You want dinner, Kyle? You want me to put on an apron and pearls and keep house for you? Is that why you asked me to move in here?"

"Don't put words in my mouth." He narrows his eyes at me.

"Then why? Why do you want me here if you're just going to point out everything you don't like about me all the time?"

"I don't do that," he insists, and his tone is softer now, like maybe I struck a nerve, but I'm not done being angry.

"Yes, you do! Every day, it's something else. I stayed too late at school, or I woke you up when my alarm went off in the morning, or I burned the pizza, or—"

"You burned the pizza because you were grading essays and not paying attention!" He's yelling again and flailing his arms. His placating mood was very short-lived. "It proves my point, Jenny. You're hardly ever here, and even when you are, your mind is somewhere else."

"I'm trying to do a good job! I have over a hundred students depending on me to teach them something every day. What I do is important."

"Oh, and what I do isn't important?" He picks up a plastic bowl sitting on the table and hurls it across the room. I jump when it hits the wall. He didn't throw it anywhere near me, but it's a clear display that he could physically hurt me if he wanted to.

When he turns to me, his eyes are wide, like he even surprised himself. He opens his mouth, but I grab my purse and keys. "I'm leaving." My tone is cold and quiet, and I give him a wide berth as I make my way to the door.

"Where are you going?" he asks just as quietly.

"Mac's. I'm staying there tonight." I turn back to face him, my hand on the doorknob. "I love you, Kyle, but asking someone to walk on eggshells in their own home while having bowls violently thrown around is a lot to ask of anyone."

He doesn't say anything, so I walk out and don't look back.

I let myself into Mac's apartment. She doesn't ask any questions, and I don't give her any information. She's a smart woman; I'm sure she can figure it out. I walk straight to my old bedroom, lock the door, flop on the bed, and cry myself to sleep. After an hour or so, she knocks once to tell me she's going to bed, but I don't answer. The next morning, I'm awake before her, so I write her a note saying I'm fine and I'll see her at school. Then I leave.

Somehow, miraculously, I make it through the day. Mac doesn't come to check on me. We've done this dance enough times for her to know that I'll talk when I'm ready. My eyes still feel raw from all the crying I did last night, but I teach all my classes without bursting into tears, which feels like a win.

I check my phone. Nothing from Kyle. He really went through all that just to ignore me all day? This is not the person I fell in love with. He's been growing more and more insecure, and with those insecurities comes volatility. I want him to see that we're good together, but he's convinced himself that he's worthless, which has been hard to watch.

I feel a tear escape down my cheek, then another. Without the students to distract me, it's more difficult to escape my feelings. I decide that since Kyle hasn't reached out, I'll stay for a while, grade and plan a bit, and collect myself before doing... something. I wipe my eyes, take a deep breath, and force the tears to stop.

I pull a pile of papers toward me, but I end up reading the first assignment four times before I realize my brain isn't going to register what is on the page. I push the papers away and poke around at some assignments on my computer instead. The more I look at them, though, the more

I want to delete everything and start over. Nothing feels educational enough or fun enough or smart enough, and I start to think that maybe Kyle is right. Maybe I'm not cut out for this.

My phone buzzes from where it's sitting next to my keyboard. My heart skips at the thought that Kyle finally came around, but it sinks when I see the name "Mom" at the top of the screen. I groan audibly. The woman has some kind of sixth sense when it comes to my misery.

She's the last person I want to talk to right now, but if I don't answer, she'll just keep calling. I take a steadying breath, press the green button, and bring the phone to my ear. "Hey, Mom." I muster up as much cheerfulness as I can, hoping she can't detect the desolation that has been crushing me all day.

"You sound awful," she fusses. I should have known better.

"I'm still at school." It's not a lie, even though I am evading. There's no way she's going to take the hint and keeps the conversation short, but a gal can dream.

"Still at school? Jen, didn't your day end an hour ago?"

I cringe at the nickname. She started calling me Jen a few years ago, insisting "Jenny" sounded too immature for a grown woman. I hate it. "I'm trying to finish up some planning, and then I'll leave." I keep my voice as even as possible, but my jaw is starting to hurt from how hard I'm grinding my teeth.

"Kyle is going to start thinking you're avoiding him if you keep this up," she warns. Well, the joke's on her because he already thinks exactly that, but I'm not going to admit it and open myself up to her chastising. Besides, I'm not sure what she knows about keeping a guy around. I've never even met my father, and I'm pretty sure my mom hasn't been celibate since my birth, but I've never met any of the guys she's dated.

I pinch the bridge of my nose and close my eyes, taking in a quiet breath and forcing my jaw to relax. "I know, Mom. I'm almost done here. Did you need something?" I keep my tone sweet so she doesn't think I'm being impatient.

"Do I need a reason to call my favorite child?"

"I'm your only child."

"And if I had any grandchildren, I could bother them instead of you." She returns my saccharine tone, and I know she's on to me.

"Mom, I'm twenty-four." I don't bother hiding the bite in my voice now. There are only so many lines I can stand being crossed.

"And not getting any younger." She practically sings the statement, and I can't help the low growl as my jaw clenches again.

"Right. I need to finish up here so I can get home, but can I call you later?" I will not be calling her later, and she knows it.

"Of course. You hurry up and get home to your man. I'll talk to you soon." She hangs up without waiting for a response, and I toss the phone onto my desk like it bit me.

I stare at it for a second, then I bury my head in my hands and sob. I don't know how long I've been sitting there crying, but I startle when my door opens.

"Hey, what are you still doing here?" Ben pokes his head in. When he sees me, he comes fully into the room and is at my side in a second. He pulls up a student chair and sits near enough to me that I can smell the gym on him and feel the warmth coming off his sweaty skin. "Jenny, what's wrong?"

I try to sniffle inconspicuously, but I have to grab a wad of tissues and run it over my nose, anyway, which I'm sure is red and raw. If there's an attractive way to cry, I haven't figured it out. Not that I'm worried about Ben finding me attractive.

"Are you coming from the weight room?" I look at my hands, the floor, my desk. Anywhere but at him.

"Yeah. We had wrestling conditioning. I saw your light on and was going to make fun of you for staying so late, but something is clearly wrong. What's going on?" He sounds so concerned that I look up at him, and his eyes are kind.

"I don't know if I'm cut out for this." I give him a half truth. I'm not quite ready to admit that Kyle and I had a huge, embarrassing fight or that my mother is delusional and overbearing. "My students aren't very excited to be here, and I'm here all the damn time planning or grading or who knows what else. I can't imagine doing this for the rest of my life. I'm so..." I trail off, looking toward the ceiling, trying to think of how to convey what I'm feeling. I shrug helplessly and look at him again. "Tired. I'm so fucking tired all the time."

Ben looks as if he's considering what I'm saying, and he nods slowly. He scoots a little closer to me, leaning his forearms against his knees. "This is a hard job, Jenny, and it's not for everyone. But you're good at it. Your students love you. A few of them are on my team, and they have nothing but great things to say about you. It won't always be like this."

I give him a teary laugh. "How do you know?"

"My older sister is a lawyer." He shrugs. "She used to call me crying just like this, asking if I thought she was making the right choice, wasting her life away for her career. Now she makes a boatload of money and has the cutest baby you've ever seen and the nicest husband on the planet. She's super happy. Things got easier for her once she figured out what she was doing. I can't imagine teaching is any different."

"That sounds nice." I sniffle again. "I wouldn't mind a cute baby and a nice husband." This is true, despite my resistance to my mother's prodding. I do want what she wants for me, just on my own timeline.

"Don't forget the boatloads of money." Ben winks. He winks a lot, and you'd think I'd be used to it by now, but my heart flutters a little every time.

"Yes. Boatloads of money would be nice." I smile, then I say, more to myself, "I wish I had any of that on the horizon."

"Kyle's not a baby person?" He leans back a little in his chair. He's teasing, though he sounds a little like he's fishing for information. I'm too annoyed with Kyle to give it much thought. I laugh wryly, and Ben frowns.

"Kyle is convinced I'm not cut out for this. He says if I have to work so hard, I'm not very good at it. I'm pretty sure he's got it in his head that he's not marrying or having children with someone who is never home," I admit.

A muscle in Ben's jaw ticks, and his face turns to stone. His expression reveals nothing of what he's thinking. His gaze doesn't leave mine, but he is silent for so long, I'm starting to think I shouldn't have shared that much information.

Finally, he takes a deep, shaky breath. "He said that to you?" His voice is almost menacing, and I shiver slightly, though I don't think it's because he's making me nervous.

"Not in so many words," I say quietly, "but he'd rather I quit and stay home and tend to him or whatever. I refuse to do that unless he shows a little more commitment."

"Is that what you want?" Ben's voice is still low and rumbling, but his expression is carefully neutral.

I blink rapidly, surprised at how taken aback by the question I am. I guess it's been a while since someone has asked me what I want. "I…" I trail off, swallowing heavily.

Ben's expression shifts quickly to one of soft interest. He tilts his head, waiting.

I shake myself a little, trying to wrap my head around the sudden change in his countenance. "No. I want all of it. I want to continue this career I trained for and enjoy most of the time. I want a husband. I want a million babies. I want a good work-life balance."

"And boatloads of money?" He smiles slowly, and the energy in the room immediately changes.

"I don't need boatloads of money if I have the rest of it," I say, smiling back.

Ben leans ever-so-slightly closer to me. "You can have all of that, Jenny," he insists. "Maybe not all at once, and maybe not with someone who wants you to be someone you're not, but you can."

"Kyle has known me almost as long as Mac. He wouldn't want me to be someone I'm not." I pause, taking in a deep, shaky breath. "He knows me," I repeat, and it sounds almost like I'm trying to convince myself.

Ben shakes his head slowly. "Anyone who would try to talk you out of keeping this job has no idea who you are. I've seen you when you talk to the kids. You light up. You're at ease and comfortable. It's clear that you love teaching." I give him a disbelieving look, which he waves away. "Maybe not at this moment, but most of the time, you do. I can tell. It's hard when you first start out. It'll get easier with experience."

I sigh, swiping at my eyes again. "What do I do, then?"

He regards me for a moment, tilting his head as if considering what to say next. "Don't let anyone dim your light, Jenny. You're better than that."

His eyes are intense and warm, and they draw me in. My breath catches, and he swallows in the silence. His Adam's apple bobs up and down, and I feel the heat coming off him. I blink, and a stray tear falls. I groan as I wipe it from my cheek, looking away from him.

"I'm a damn mess," I mutter.

"You're not. You're..." he trails off, and I look at him, waiting for him to continue. He shakes his head. "I think you should start by setting some boundaries."

I'm not sure if he's referring to boundaries with school or with Kyle, but I feel a corner of my mouth tilt up either way, awed at how different this advice is coming from a place of kindness and not derision. "I guess I can start by... going home now?"

Ben's smile is wide and warm, and a little heat flares in my belly, too. "That would be a good start. I'll go get my stuff from my room, and I'll walk you out." He leaves, and I grab my bag from my desk to load up. In the spirit of setting boundaries, I leave all my work on my desk instead of putting it in my bag to drag it home with me. I collect my other things and sling my tote bag over my shoulder. My back is facing the door, so when it swings open behind me, I expect to see Ben when I turn around, but Kyle is standing there, a huge bouquet of roses in his hand.

"What are you doing here?" I ask, surprised.

"I'm sorry, Jenny. I acted like an asshole." He walks toward me, handing me the roses.

I take them and smell them on reflex. Their sweet scent floods my senses. *He loves me*, I think, relieved, but I'm not letting him off that easily. I look at him over the flowers, and hopefully my expression conveys how angry I still am. "I love you, but I love this job, too, and I want to be good at it. It's hard now, but it won't always be. You need to understand that, and you need to stop deliberately saying things to hurt my feelings." I narrow my eyes at him. "And if you violently throw one more thing when I'm around, I'm leaving, and I won't be coming back."

He raises his hands, palms out in surrender. "We've been together eight years, and I've never done anything like that. You know that wasn't like me, Jenny. It'll never happen again."

I narrow my eyes further. "Never."

"Never."

I look him up and down, assessing, and decide that he's right. We've been together for the better part of a decade, and he's never done anything like that, and probably never will again. Living together is hard, too. It's an adjustment, just like teaching, and we'll have to work at it.

"Let's go home?" he asks hopefully.

I nod, cradling the bouquet in my arms as we walk out into the hallway. As I lock my classroom door behind me, I see Ben out of the corner of my eye. I look up, and he stops in his tracks when he registers Kyle is with me. I flash him what I hope is an apologetic look and give him a little wave.

"Have a good night, Ben," I call to him.

I can almost see his face fall. "Yeah, Jenny. Have a good night."

# Chapter 7
## Present Day

On Monday morning, I walk around the classroom handing an old, dusty book to each student. They are thick—probably thicker than what most of the sophomores are used to reading, and I hear some grumbles throughout the room as the students flip through the pages.

"Shakespeare?" Diego Lopez groans. "Why we gotta read all this old stuff?"

"Yeah, Miss Green. Shakespeare is boring," Jayden Roberson chimes in.

I bite the inside of my cheek against the urge to laugh at their predictability. Not once have I started a Shakespeare play without this soundtrack of moans and complaints. "Well," I say calmly, still working my way around the room. "For starters, Shakespeare provides an excellent foundation for all of your future studies of literature."

At that, almost every single student in the room stares at me skeptically, and I do chuckle quietly at their matching expressions.

"Are you saying that we need to read some tragic play where everyone dies in order to do well in the rest of our classes?" Kayla Eaton speaks up, her eyebrows pinched together.

"Ah ha!" I point in her direction, returning to the front of the room. "That's where you've been misled. Not every Shakespearean play ends in tragedy. In fact, this one is called *Twelfth Night* and has a happy ending."

Cecily Brooks rolls her eyes so hard, I'm surprised they don't roll all the way to the back of her head. She lightly slams her book down on her desk. "Well, why would we read it now? You spoiled it."

"It says right on the back here that it's a comedy, Leelee." Kayla leans over to Cecily and points to the synopsis on the back.

Cecily inspects it and frowns. "So, it's funny?"

"Well, yes, but not in the way you would think of a comedy, probably. Shakespeare was very funny in his way, but 'comedy' mostly means that there is a happy ending rather than a tragic one." There are a few more mumbles, so I raise my voice to be heard over them. "And that isn't even considered a spoiler. Not only is it rare for comedies to end with the stage littered with dead bodies, Shakespeare's audience would have known what they were getting when they entered the theater. Outside of the Globe Theatre, there would have been a flag hanging. If it was black, the audience could expect a tragedy. If it was red, they could expect a history. If it was white..."

"It was a comedy?" Jayden interrupts.

I nod. "Exactly. The same way that modern audiences know essentially what type of movie they are going to see when they go to the movie theater, Shakespeare's audiences would have been prepared," I explain.

"Why the colors?" Diego wants to know.

I lean against my podium, book in hand. "In Shakespeare's time, it was usually only the very wealthy who were educated. Most of his audience would have been illiterate, so the colors were necessary for those who couldn't read."

Diego lightly punches Jayden's arm. "You would have fit in back then since you can't read either."

Jayden scowls at Diego and moves to punch him back, but I loudly exclaim, "Hey!" to get their attention. They immediately stop and look sheepishly at me. I put on my best stern look and say, "You don't know me very well yet, but I can tell you right now that we will not have punching or insults in this class. Am I understood?"

Both students mumble, "Yes, Miss Green."

"I thought plays were supposed to be short. This book is huge." Ana, who is usually very quiet, clearly tries to change the subject. The boys seem sufficiently chastised, so I address her.

"They are usually shorter to read than a full-length novel, and this one is no different. What you have here are actually two versions; one side of the page is the text as Shakespeare would have written it, and the other side is the translation to modern-day English."

The class perks up at that, and Cecily asks hopefully, "We get to read the modern version, then?"

"Nope!" I say, overly cheerful, and the class groans in unison again. "In fact, we are going to read this aloud as a class, taking parts. So, who would like to volunteer?"

The rest of the class passes in stilted Shakespearean dialogue and fits of giggles at the new-to-them words. We fall into a rhythm, and I'm heartened by how few students pull out their phones or put their heads down.

When the class ends, I follow the students out into the hallway, propping my door open as I pass it. Ben is already there, smiling at me as I step across my threshold.

"Howdy, neighbor." He tips his fake cowboy hat at me.

I wrinkle my nose. "Are you going to keep that up all year?"

"Probably, since it seems to annoy you so much," he says good-naturedly.

I fold my arms, cock my hip, and give him a playful glare across the hallway as students shuffle past us.

He laughs his full-bodied laugh, which makes me grin in turn, like it always does.

Out of the corner of my eye, I see our department chair, Ken Hastings, make his way toward us through the sea of students. When he sees me notice him, he nods in greeting, his white beard shifting as he smiles. He peels off the mass of students in the hallway to stand next to me, and he smells vaguely of peppermint. It's fitting, since Ken is the school's resident Santa Claus. He looks exactly like Santa, with his round belly and white hair and beard, but he also has a jolly laugh and, today, smells exactly like Christmas.

"Hello, Jennifer. Benjamin." He uses our full names, as he always does for every English teacher in the school. "I trust the school year is off to a good start?"

I raise my voice to be heard over the chatter in the hallway. "I caught my first period class's interest with some Shakespeare this morning, which I didn't expect, but I'll take it."

Ken claps his hands together, his beard twitching in excitement. "Wonderful! Which play did you decide to teach this year?"

"*Twelfth Night*," I reply. I hear Ben snicker across the hallway, and I snap my head in his direction. "What?"

"A comedy? Why not a classic like *Hamlet* or *King Lear*? Something with some drama and excitement." He folds his arms across his chest and leans back against the wall. The bell rings to end the passing period, and the students who had been lingering in the hallway all quickly make their way inside the classrooms.

I roll my eyes, lowering my voice as the hallway noise dims down. "There's drama and excitement in love too, you know. Plus, the comedies are fun and accessible. Perfect for sophomores. Not that I need to defend my choices, Mr. *In Cold Blood*."

"Hey, that's a great text, and the kids love it." His shoulders sag a little, but his tone is playful.

Ken laughs his jolly laugh, rubbing his beard between the fingers of his right hand. "They are both excellent choices by excellent teachers, and I'm sure your students will love studying them. Speaking of books, I have a request to ask of you, Jennifer, if you would be so kind as to indulge me for a moment?"

"Of course, Ken. What's up?" I ask as Ben slowly makes his way toward his open classroom door. He lingers, though, like he wants to hear what Ken has to say.

"As you know"—Ken turns to face me—"Mackenzie organized a fundraiser last year with Mr. Evans and our very own Isabel Hernandez. We raised a good deal of money."

I nod slowly. "Yes, I was there."

"Well, as you also know, Mackenzie was very specific as to how these funds were to be used, and we just finished collecting requests from the English teachers for novels they want, per her direction."

"Yes. I put in a request, myself." I'm not trying to be short with him, but I can hear my class starting to get loud behind me, and I need to get in there to get them started before it becomes too difficult to settle them down. Ken never taught before becoming a school administrator, and sometimes he forgets that teachers and students thrive on rhythm and routine.

"Right. Well, I asked Mackenzie if she would like to go over the requests and allocate the funds for which novels to purchase, but she has declined because she's too overwhelmed with wedding plans. Of course, the next person who came to mind was you. Would you be able to go through the requests and allocate funds in the next few weeks so we can get these books ordered for next semester?" His eyes are slightly wide in anticipation. I know he loves the idea of brand-new books for the school, and I also know he likes it when teachers take charge on projects like this, but as I'm mentally flipping through my calendar, I'm not seeing where I could possibly squeeze this in. I have been attending every wedding appointment right along with Mac, and I feel booked solid with that and the start of the school year.

Ken is so hard to say no to, though, with his eager eyes and twitchy beard. And if I do this, I can ensure that my books get purchased. I've been using the same dingy Shakespeare books for years; it would be so nice to have a crisp, new novel on deck for next semester.

Ben must sense me hesitate, because he takes a step back into the hallway, leaning into our conversation. "Not to intrude, but I'd be happy to help if you want, Jenny. I know you're busy with wedding duties, too, but we could work on this together."

My shoulders relax from their position by my ears in relief. I can certainly do this with help, and Ben is a great work partner. He always pulls his weight on group projects. "That would be amazing." I flash him a grateful smile, and he grins warmly back at me.

Ken claps his hands again. "Wonderful! I will share the requests with both of you. I know it's a quick turnaround, but if you could process the requests, price the books with links to purchase them, and have the results back to me in three weeks, that would be fantastic."

"Sure, Ken. No problem," Ben assures him, and Ken continues on his way down the hall.

"Thank you," I whisper to Ben, and creases form on the edges of his brown eyes as they settle on me and don't move.

"My pleasure," he says quietly, and there's something about the way he says it that has me feeling a little giddy.

Just then, a loud crash comes from inside his classroom, and he snaps his head toward the sound. "Hey!" he yells, entering his room fully and letting the door close behind him. I stare after him as I wonder what the heck that little exciting feeling was just then. I look at his door for an extra second, frowning slightly.

My own students are starting to get restless, too, so I take a deep breath. Time for more Shakespeare, and if I'm going to sell it to this group, too, I need to bring my A game.

# Chapter 8
## Present Day

On Thursday, I'm packing up my things at the end of the day when a loud boom of thunder sounds. Outside the window, the sky suddenly opens up in a torrential downpour. I frown at the rain dripping down the windowpanes and the ominous, dark sky that only promises more rain. This weather is pretty common for early fall in the Chicago suburbs, but I wasn't expecting it to rain today, and Mac and I had planned to go for a run after school to hash out some wedding planning.

As if she knows exactly what I'm thinking, my door clicks open and her mess of red hair pops into the room.

"We're going to have to take a rain check on this run, I think." She comes fully into the room when she sees me, letting the door close behind her.

"You think?" I ask, incredulous, as another flash of lightning lights up the room and the clap of thunder sounds not long after.

"Unless you believe running in the rain is good for the soul," she jokes.

"Running in a storm is good for tearing your soul from your body." As if punctuating my thought, another flash of lightning and quick thunder rumbles. It's so loud, I can feel the vibrations through the floor. The lights flicker overhead. Mac looks up, then shifts her eyes to mine, eyebrows raised.

"We should probably wait this one out here," she suggests, and I agree. I'm not trying to even walk to my car in this.

I flop in my desk chair, disappointed. "I was looking forward to this run, too," I pout. "I feel like we haven't spent much time together these past few weeks."

She sighs as she lowers herself into a student chair across from me. "I know. The start of the year is always rough."

I wrinkle my nose in what I hope she interprets as an agreement that the start of the year is icky, but, in reality, it's not the start of the year that has kept her from spending time with me. She has been spending almost all her free time with Daniel. I don't blame her, but I did think that our relationship probably wouldn't change too much, even despite her getting married.

She sits up straighter in her chair as the lights flicker again. "But good news. I found some motivation and scheduled a ton of wedding appointments. So, we are going to get to spend approximately one million hours together in the next few weeks. And, I hope you're not offended, but Daniel and I decided to go with a different officiant that we are all going to go meet. You'll be only maid of honor instead. Is that okay?"

She doesn't sound like this is exactly good news, but if she wants to try to fake some excitement, I'm not going to talk her out of it.

"It's great." I match her tone.

She snickers as the lights flicker again, then go out completely. The dim emergency lights in the hallway flood into the room through the window in the door. Mac and I eye each other with our eyebrows raised.

"It figures this wouldn't have happened in the middle of the day so they'd have had to let us go home." I frown up at the dark ceiling.

"Which is worse: storm outside or a power outage inside?" She winces.

"Not a great choice." I laugh humorlessly. "We could go to the gym. Do a quick run if they have power?"

She stands, shaking her head. "I'd rather take my chances with the storm than the dreadmill. You know how I feel about those things." If I didn't know already, her use of the nickname would have made it plain, as would the disgusted expression on her face. She runs a hand through her hair and drops it at her side, shrugging.

I glance at my gym bag in the corner near my desk and back to her. "Rain check, then."

"Literally." She chuckles as she makes her way toward the door. "I'll send you the calendar invites for the appointments, okay? If you can't make some of them, that's fine." She says it like it would be anything but fine.

I smile as reassuringly as I can. "I'm sure it won't be an issue. What the hell else am I doing?"

Her shoulders relax a little as she grins brightly. She gives me a little wave as she makes her way into the dimly lit hallway.

I look at my gym bag again, pursing my lips in thought. I don't love the treadmill either, but I'm feeling antsy. The run today wasn't only about talking to Mac; it was about working off some of the beginning-of-the-year energy that has been building over the last week and a half. I grab my gym bag and my school bag, and once outside, I all-out sprint to my car in the rain.

About twenty minutes later, I'm in my hot pink leggings and sports bra, my navy running shoes laced up and my long brown hair pulled into a high ponytail. I'm holding a hand towel and standing in front of the bank of gym treadmills, trying to talk myself into getting on one. *Thirty minutes*, I tell myself. If I can just run for thirty minutes, then I can stop if it sucks. Sufficiently persuaded, I put my headphones in, start my music, and step on the deck, hitting the start button on the machine and my running watch. I start slowly, then click the speed up a few points once I feel warmed up. I settle into my easy pace as I check the timer on the treadmill screen. Three minutes have passed, and I groan inwardly. How has it only been three minutes?

I raise my eyes from the screen, thinking that if I stare at the clock, it'll only feel longer. I look around the gym, hoping I can do some people-watching to pass the time. The rain has driven a lot of people inside, but no one on the bikes in front of me is all that interesting. I sweep my eyes across the gym. Through the windows of the exercise room, I can see an aerobics class in full swing. Two young women shake their hips ridiculously, then look at each other and burst out laughing. Mac and I used to try out all the group fitness classes when we were in high school, and we used to laugh like that, too. I click the speed up a few more points against the little twinge in my chest.

I check the timer again. Five minutes. Honestly, Mac had the right idea. This is unbearable.

I look to the weight room on the other side of the gym. A bunch of bulky guys are there, and thankfully I can't hear their grunts through the music blaring in my headphones. One of them loads a large plate onto a barbell, then looks up, meeting my eyes from across the room. He lifts the corner of his mouth, then waves, and it takes me a second to realize it's Ben. I blink a few times, then wave back, blowing a long breath out of my mouth. His eyes linger on me for a moment, then he leaves his weights and starts walking toward me. As he approaches, I pause the treadmill and my watch. I take an earbud out of one ear as he steps up to the side of my treadmill. He rests his forearm against the handrail and leans into it.

"Please don't say 'howdy, neighbor,'" I greet him.

He chuckles deeply, his brown eyes meeting mine. "Hi, Jenny," he says instead, and the way he says my name while looking at me like I'm the only person in this place has me feeling a lot hotter than my warm-up would suggest I should. All day, we chat across the hall during passing periods, and it never feels like this. They really need to kick the air conditioning up in this place.

I smooth a hand over the top of my head and drag it down my ponytail. He watches the movement and swallows, his Adam's apple bobbing. Beads of perspiration sit under his hairline, and he makes no move to wipe them away. I can feel a drop of sweat trail down from my neck into my sports bra, and I shiver slightly.

"No conditioning today?" I ask, trying to escape this building tension.

He looks at my shoes, then back to my eyes, still leaning against the treadmill. "Power stayed out for longer than five minutes, so we called it. Weren't you and Mac supposed to run together?"

Did I tell him that? We talked a little during each passing period today, and I was excited about my run time with Mac, so I may have mentioned it, but I can't remember. I'm surprised he does. "Yeah." I smile a little sadly. "The storm hit, and we called in a rain check. She hates the treadmill, so she went home."

"Can't blame her for that. I heard someone call these things 'Satan's sidewalks' once, and it felt apt." He stands upright and pats the front of it.

I giggle, and his eyes find mine again. I glance back at the timer on the screen, which still reads slightly over five minutes. "I thought a run on the treadmill would be better than nothing, but this is torture. I'm at five minutes, but it feels like fifty."

He regards me for a moment, chewing on the corner of his mouth as if considering something. "You could come lift with me instead."

"Lift?" I arch an eyebrow. "Next thing I know, you'll be selling me protein powder."

He smiles as if I've just challenged him. "It's more fun than running in place, and strength training will make you a better at your sport in the long run."

"Was that a pun?" I ask, bemused.

"Maybe." He ticks his head toward the weights. "Come on, Green. I'll spot you."

I take one last peek at the treadmill screen and decide I cannot possibly continue on this hamster wheel. From the look on his face, he already knows I've made up my mind, but I purse my lips and narrow my eyes slightly, pretending to think about my options.

"What's in it for me?" I cross my arms over my chest. His eyes dip, but he quickly meets my gaze again.

"You'll get stronger?" he suggests. I raise my eyebrow, skeptical. He tries again: "Better running form?" I tip my head back and forth in a maybe-maybe-not motion. "The best coach at LPHS as your personal trainer?"

"Hmm." I look him up and down. "I did always want a personal trainer."

His grin turns dopey and earnest, and he looks like an eager puppy ready to play. I shove my phone in the pocket on the side of my leggings and step off the treadmill.

When we approach the weights, I look around, a little lost. One of the guys in a muscle shirt doing bicep curls and staring at his own muscles in the mirror as if he's only flexing to show off for himself gives me the side eye like I don't belong in his domain. I pinch my eyebrows together and look him up and down with my best "you aren't as impressive as you think you are" look, and he quickly looks back to his own reflection. He seems the type to prefer the look of himself over anything else, anyway.

I meet Ben's eyes in the mirror, and by his proud half-smile, he watched that entire interaction. I shrug a shoulder. "Okay, Coach. What's first?"

He puffs up slightly, then grabs some plates off a smaller barbell. His biceps ripple with the effort, but unlike Mr. Flex over there, he's not intentionally showboating. It's much more attractive.

Ben places the plates on a nearby rack and hands me the empty barbell. "Lunges. Unilateral exercises are going to be the most important for your running. If you think about it, running is a one-leg sport since you're only on one leg at a time, so these types of exercises are going to be the most helpful."

"You've always been a little nerdy about exercise, but this is next level. How do you know so much about workouts for runners?"

"I've been friends with a couple of runners for the better part of a decade." He looks at me pointedly, then he helps me situate the barbell behind my neck.

"Have you been holding on to information about running form since you met us in the hopes that we'd ask for your help one day?" I tease.

A corner of his mouth tips up, but he avoids looking at me and changes the subject. "Okay, let's start with your right leg behind you. About two inches more between your feet. That's it. Now, brace your core and lunge. You can get lower than that, Green. Your knee should be just above the ground. Yeah, like that. Now back up. And down again. Good. Do eight more of those."

"Eight?" I twist to look at him incredulously, taking the barbell with me and almost swiping his face. He catches the end of it and uses it to turn me back toward the mirror.

"Watch what you're doing with that thing," he warns. "Yes, eight. Then the other leg. And then you're going to do this leg again. We're going to work these muscles to the point of fatigue."

"Who's 'we?' I don't see you lunging," I grumble as I dip to the ground and back up a few times.

"I'm commiserating with you." He is looking at my body intently, studying my form.

"Your wrestlers buy that shit?" I grunt, lowering and raising myself until I get to ten reps.

He laughs a deep laugh. "Not usually."

I situate my legs so the opposite leg is in front. "Funny. Me neither." I try to lower my knee as close to the ground as I can, but I wobble a little. I'm able to catch my balance, but Ben reaches a hand out just in case. He pulls it back when I've righted myself. "This side is harder," I remark.

"It's pretty common to have a weaker side. That's another thing lifting will help. You'll not only notice your weaknesses, but you'll also be able to work on correcting them."

"Hmm," I murmur, now fully focused on not falling over as I finish my ten reps and then switch my feet again. I whisper-count to ten on that side, then switch to the other. Ben senses that I'm concentrating and follows my lead, not talking except to offer a few encouraging words.

When I switch back to my weaker side, I am able to do about five more reps, but my quads and glutes are burning. I try to get my knee as low to the ground as possible, but I tip again, and this time I almost fall completely over. With an agility that belies his build, Ben steps behind me and reaches his hands out to catch me. His big hands cover almost my entire waist, and the feel of his touch on my bare skin sends a shock of warmth through me. I inhale sharply, but his hands remain on my waist. I focus on the floor a few feet in front of my shoes. Mr. Flex side-eyes us again but has the good sense to avert his eyes back to his reflection.

"You okay?" Ben asks, his hands still on my waist and his breath tickling my ear over the barbell.

I swallow hard, forcing myself to meet his gaze in the mirror. His brown eyes are molten, and his gaze immediately finds mine. I take a steadying breath, unable to look away from him. "Yeah," I choke out. "I guess this side needs a lot of work."

He huffs, the sound quiet and just for me. I fight the urge to shiver. Then, he steps back a safe distance, and even the hot gym air feels cold against my bare skin. I blink rapidly a few times, hoping he's attributing my rapid breathing to exertion and not something else.

I finish the set, and my burning legs are grateful when he takes the barbell from me and puts it back on the rack. He hands me two dumbbells and walks me through some arm exercises. I watch myself in the mirror, and though my biceps aren't the size of Mr. Flex's, they look pretty good. I catch Ben looking, too, but based on his corrections, he's checking my form. By the time we've finished, I feel like I imagined whatever happened with those lunges.

Ben takes a long sip from his water bottle while I check my phone. There are no fewer than twelve calendar invitations from Mac on my screen, and a groan slips out.

"What's going on?" Ben asks, wiping his mouth with the back of his hand. We start to make our way toward the locker rooms.

"Mac decided she actually wants to plan this wedding, and I'm along for the ride." I turn my phone to show him the notifications.

He grimaces. "I guess now isn't the time to ask when you want to get started on that project for Ken?"

"Let me sort all this out first. I don't want to double book myself." I wince apologetically. We stop in front of the locker rooms.

"Sure, no problem. Just let me know." His gaze turns warm again suddenly. "This was fun. We should do it again, maybe."

I bask in his warmth for an extra second before I reply. "I'd like that."

His smile looks like he won the lottery before he turns and enters the men's locker room. I watch him disappear inside before I walk into the women's side to get my bag.

Back at my apartment, I draw a hot bath. I set up my wooden bathtub tray with a candle, a glass of water, and my book. This book is about as hot as the steaming water filling my bathtub, and I'm ready to ease my sore muscles and distract my brain for an hour or so.

I slip into the tub and sigh as the warmth seeps its way into my aching quads. I shimmy myself farther into the water so my shoulders are almost submerged and keep my hands out of the water so I can hold my book.

This book is just starting to get really spicy. The main characters can't keep their hands off each other, and they're currently the only ones in their office building. He has her undressed and open to the floor-to-ceiling windows of his penthouse office. I read a few more pages, but the warmth from the tub and the descriptions in the book are only making me think of Ben's hands on my waist and his breath in my ear. Another warmth floods my core, and I moan quietly at the feeling. I haven't slept with anyone in a while, and I'm sure it's the dry spell making me laser-focus on the feel of Ben's hands, but I shift slightly and the feeling between my legs elicits another moan. I close my book and drop it outside the tub, reaching a hand under the water to cup between my legs. I rub a finger over the sensitive spot with gradually building pressure, then dip a finger inside myself as my breathing quickens. I can't help but wonder what Ben's hands here would feel like, and the thought of it has me gasping.

I finish while thinking of him, and as I relax fully in the pleasant water of the tub, I have the vague notion that something has shifted. I take a long sip of my drink, then swirl my hands around, studying the pattern they make on the surface of the water of the tub. I sigh deeply, looking up at the ceiling. This isn't the first time Ben and I have toed the line between friendship and something more, but if it hasn't turned into anything in nine years, I have a hard time believing it ever can.

My phone buzzes again, and I tilt my head to look at the screen. Another calendar invitation from Mac. She hasn't texted or called me all night, but these notifications keep coming. I sigh again, rolling my head against the edge of the tub. I'm even more grateful for Ben's friendship now that Mac and my relationship has become almost transactional. Anything more than friendship with him, and I'd risk that collapsing, too, which is not something I'm willing to chance.

My phone buzzes again, and I shift my eyes to the screen, dreading another appointment. But it's not another calendar invite. Ben's name lights up my screen.

*Good work today, Green.*

I bite my lip and smile, wiping my hands on a towel so I can type back: *It helps when I have the best coach at LPHS as my personal trainer.*

My phone doesn't buzz again for the length of my bath, but I can't stop smiling even after I dry off and climb into bed.

# Chapter 9
## Seven Years Ago

"YOU CAN STAY HERE as long as you need." Mac's voice is gentle and tentative. My voice still isn't reliably steady, so I nod. I don't want her sympathy right now, so I don't look at her. I stand just inside the door of her new condo, my overnight bag dropped carelessly at my feet, as I take in the space. There is a small living room with a couch across from a television set to my left. Across that space, there is a breakfast nook by the window next to a galley kitchen with a bar-height counter and a couple of stools pushed up to it. Down a short hallway are two rooms and one bathroom. I know from having toured this place with her before she bought it that the bathroom has two doors, one that opens to her bedroom, and one that opens to the hallway. There's a guest room—my room now, I suppose—that is on the other side of the hallway.

She only moved in a few weeks ago, so everything still looks new and shiny. There aren't any boxes anywhere, I'm sure. Mac likes a cozy space, so I know she probably started and finished unpacking in the same day. I hadn't been around to help because my life had been falling apart while hers was taking shape in the form of this very permanent real estate purchase—a sure sign that she knows she belongs in Leade Park. I, on the other hand, am now completely adrift. A piece of debris floating on an ocean.

*"I can probably get away tonight." Kyle's voice is coming from the bedroom, and it sounds like he's on the phone. I'm standing in the hallway, my school bag still over my shoulder. I had come home right after school to surprise him, so I'm waiting for him to come out and see me.*

*"I know, baby." Baby? "Not much longer... Yeah, I don't want to piss her off. You know how she can be... You're my spice. I love spice, and Jenny is boring... You've been there for me through all this, and she's never around. You know that. But I need to do this my own way. Trust me, baby."*

*"What?" I yell. It figures that I'd show up at exactly the wrong time and overhear this conversation.*

*"Oh, shit. Baby, I've got to go."*

Tears start to well up in my raw eyes again, and I don't bother interrupting their twin paths down my cheeks.

"I'm not a violent person, but I'll kill him," Mac is saying, her voice taking on an edge I haven't heard yet. My gaze finally skates to her, and she's looking at me with a burning hatred on her face, her eyebrows low and darkening her eyes, the corners of her mouth turned down.

I shake my head, blinking to clear away the tears. I swallow and take a huge, shaky breath, then let it out slowly. "He doesn't deserve your jail time." My voice is almost a whisper.

Mac looks doubtful, but she leans over to grab my bag off the floor. She frowns when she realizes how light it is and how little I brought with me. "When can you get the rest of your stuff?"

"He works tomorrow afternoon, so I figured I'd go over there and get in and out while he's gone."

Mac nods approvingly. I know she'd probably hide his body if I asked her to, but she'd rather avoid seeing him at all. "El and I have cleared the entire weekend, so we'll come with and help." She walks with my bag down the hall, leaving me standing in the entryway to process this information. I all but ignored them while Mac made this huge life decision buying this condo, and they cleared their schedule at the drop of a hat. For me.

*"You can fuck right off with that shit, Kyle. I'm so sick of hearing every single way I'm not good enough for you."*

*"Grow up, Jenny. Did you honestly expect that we wouldn't ever sleep with anyone else but each other? Was it your dream to have vanilla sex once a month until one of us dies?"*

*"You... you slept with her because I'm boring in bed? Because we don't have enough sex?"*

*"I don't know why I did it, but I'm not sorry I did."*

*"We were going to be a family,"* I whisper, and I hate myself for how pathetic I sound.

He laughs bitterly. *"Don't lie to yourself, Jenny. You never had time for a family."*

My breath catches in a half-sob as the door bursts open behind me, and Ellie barges in, a greasy paper bag clutched in her right hand and a bottle of white wine in her left. She sees me and raises the bottle of wine triumphantly over her head. "You probably aren't ready to hear this, but I've been saving this bottle for exactly this moment."

"Geeze, El. You're such a jerk." Mac's voice comes from the guest room before she pops her head out into the hallway to scowl at her sister.

"A jerk with good wine," Ellie corrects. I laugh wetly. She swings the arm with the paper bag around my shoulders, and the scent of cheeseburgers wafts up to greet me. My stomach growls loudly. When was the last time I ate? Probably yesterday, but I can't remember.

Ellie huffs. "Let's get some food and wine in you. It won't fix anything, but at least you won't be hungry anymore."

Mac comes into the room, grabbing the bottle of wine and moving to the kitchen to find her corkscrew. Ellie sits on the floor of the living room next to the couch and pulls out three cheeseburgers and cups of fries, spreading them on the ground. I join her, resting my back against the seat cushions of the couch. I grab a handful of fries and jam them into my mouth. Mac brings the bottle of wine over to us and hands it to me before taking her place on the floor on the other side of Ellie. I take a long swig directly from the bottle and pass it to Ellie, who does the same and passes it to Mac.

It's a strange tradition, eating cheeseburgers and fries on the floor while drinking directly from a bottle of wine, but it has been the way we've acknowledged every heartbreak since we were seniors in high school and came home to find Ellie on the floor, shoving red meat and wine into her face after a particularly difficult breakup. She didn't let us have any of the wine that first time, but we eventually talked her into it once we were in college, and it has been the way we've started processing grief ever since.

We eat and drink in silence for a while, and once my stomach stops growling, I look at the two of them and am filled with an overwhelming sense of gratitude. I can feel the hot sting of tears yet again.

Mac catches me looking at her, tears in my eyes. "What's up?" she asks around a mouthful of cheeseburger.

The tears start falling in earnest. "I..." I trail off and quickly swipe at my eyes with my sleeves. "I've been too busy for you for weeks. You bought and moved into this whole place, and I was so worried about trying to salvage my failing relationship that I didn't bother helping you out. Yet, here you both are, schedules cleared and cheeseburgers in hand with almost no notice." I bury my head in my palms, feeling my body being wracked by sobs. "I don't deserve you," I choke out into my hands. I feel Ellie's arm around me, then I hear a cheeseburger hit a wrapper, and Mac scoots her way to my other side, putting her arm around my shoulders, too.

"Oh, kiddo." Ellie squeezes me tight. "You're family. You don't have to do anything to deserve our love."

"Yeah, Jenny. We're here for you. Always. No matter what."

I start to cry harder. There's something about the kindness of others that always turns me into a weeping mess. But the harder I cry, the harder these two hold on, tethering me to the shore, and after a while, it feels good not to be so adrift anymore.

My mother and her sixth sense call me the next day, insisting she be allowed to cash in her quarterly lunch date with me. Mac insists on coming with for moral support, and I don't have enough energy to deny either of them. So, on Saturday, I find myself seated in a booth next to Mac and across from my mother at a local chain restaurant, picking at a chicken sandwich and sweet potato waffle fries.

"You'd better keep running if you're going to eat that garbage," my mom says as she stabs a leaf of lettuce with her fork. I try to decide if it's my imagination that she forked it harder than necessary. Probably not.

Mac reaches over and grabs a waffle fry from my plate. "Sweet potato waffle fries are a gift from a higher being," she says as she pops it into her mouth and grins stupidly at me. I press my lips together in an almost-smile.

Mom hums as she chews a piece of grilled chicken. I catch her eyeing my fries with a hint of longing, and the self-satisfaction I feel at having ordered something delicious despite knowing what she would say about it is enough to motivate me to grab two and shove them both in my mouth at the same time.

Mom grimaces, then turns to Mac as if I'm not worth her conversation. "What are you up to these days, Mackenzie?"

Mac straightens in her seat. "I bought a condo. It's really cute. Now that Jenny's living there, you should come see it sometime."

I tense and Mac's mouth makes an O-shape when she realizes the bomb she just dropped. My mom looks from Mac to her salad. She pushes the lettuce around a bit, chewing on the inside of her bottom lip. Mac and I both sit there stiffly, like two small children waiting for a punishment.

"Couldn't make it work with Kyle after all?" she finally asks.

She could have said worse. I let out a puff of breath. "He was sleeping with someone else." My voice is meek, but not shaky.

She sighs deeply, still clearly avoiding meeting my eyes. "Oh, that's too bad."

Mac's eyebrows shoot up her forehead, and she looks like she's one more thinly veiled comment away from jumping across the table. I shoot her a warning glance, and she presses her lips together.

"He was such a sweet boy," Mom says. Mac can't help herself from snorting at that, but Mom continues as if she hasn't heard. "He brought me those flowers that time, do you remember that?" She sounds like she's reliving the good old days, her voice just this side of inappropriately dreamy.

"Mom, that was when we were in eleventh grade." And he did it after he and I had a fight. He was worried my mom would take my side, and he wanted to soften her up. Little did he know, I can't remember the last time my mom took my side on anything, and it wasn't any different then. I probably should have seen that red flag from a mile away, and I mentally curse myself for having been so young and stupid.

Mom hums as if the time that has passed since then is inconsequential. She finally looks at me and my almost-untouched plate. "You'd better eat something, Jen. Men don't like waifs, and now you're on the market again so you have to think about that."

My head spins from the complete about-face she's done regarding my eating habits. I shove a few more fries in my mouth to avoid saying something that would get me in even more trouble and start counting down the minutes until this awful lunch can be over.

Three weeks later, I'm standing in front of the full-length mirror in my bedroom at Mac's place, studying my reflection. I'm wearing a very short, very tight black dress, my hair curled in brown waves that fall over my shoulders and down my back. My eyeshadow is dark, and my eyeliner is darker. I'm wearing black high-heeled sandals that are as impractical as they are sexy.

Mac cautiously opens the door, leaning in. When she sees I'm dressed, she comes fully into the room. She's wearing slightly nicer jeans than she wears on spirit Fridays and a royal blue tank top. She looks me up and down and takes a breath as if to remind me that we are only going to Tony's, not a ritzy nightclub, but she thinks better of it and closes her mouth, pressing her lips tightly together. This is my night, after all, and I'll dress up if I want to.

Cheeseburgers and wine, then three weeks of wallowing, followed by drinks. That's the tradition, and we're sticking to it.

"Ellie's here," Mac announces. "You ready?"

I look at myself in the mirror again. No, I'm not at all ready. Three weeks isn't nearly enough to mourn an almost-ten-year relationship. I sigh deeply at my reflection. *Fake it till you make it*, I tell myself. I turn to face Mac and nod.

Ellie is waiting for us in the living room, sitting on the couch and flipping through a magazine. When she sees us, she gives me the same exact expression Mac did when she saw my outfit, and, just like Mac, she presses her lips into a thin line to stop herself from critiquing it. It's eerie how similar they are sometimes.

She tosses the magazine on the cushion next to her and stands, making her way out the door. Mac rolls her eyes and sighs, then grabs the magazine and places it at a perfect right angle to the corner of the end table. She shakes her head in dismay and follows Ellie out. I glance at the magazine, and a side of my mouth turns up slightly before I knock it off-center and trail them out the door.

The walk to Tony's is short. If given a choice, I probably would have chosen somewhere besides the local dive bar, but I know Mac and Ellie want to unwind with a few drinks, too, so it makes sense to go to the place that we can walk home from. As soon as we're inside, I make my way straight to the bar and order a shot of tequila. The bartender places it near me with salt and a lime wedge. I ignore everything but the alcohol and knock back the shot, pounding the glass on the bar and grimacing as the sour liquid hits my bloodstream. I motion to the bartender for another, pretending to ignore the look the sisters share over me. Another shot appears in front of me. I down that one, too, and motion for another.

"Uh, no. Three beers, please." Ellie gives the bartender a cautionary look, and he nods curtly, message received. No more tequila for me, I guess. That's fine. Beer will do the job, too, just slower. Ellie opens a tab with her credit card, then hands a bottle to Mac and one to me. I take three huge gulps, then belch, covering my mouth with the back of my hand.

"Lovely." Mac glowers at me. I shrug, taking another swig of beer.

"Okay." Ellie draws the word out and searches the bar for a distraction. "Let's step away from the bar for a bit, shall we? Let's play some pool."

I roll my eyes dramatically, already feeling a little fuzzy. "You're so responsible all the time. Don't you ever get sick of it?"

"I'm only responsible around you two." She plucks the beer bottle out of my hand, and I make a little noise of protest. She carries both our drinks to the pool tables, and I follow, if for no other reason than I want my beer back.

There is one empty pool table, and Ellie grabs two cues. Mac starts racking the balls. I pick up my beer from where Ellie left it on the edge of the table. She glances sidelong at me, and I take an overly dainty sip, being sure to stare at her the whole time. Apparently satisfied, she holds out a cue. "Who's first?"

Mac and I look at each other. I tilt my head to her, taking another sip of beer. "I'm not in the mood. You start. I'm going to make a round."

Mac looks like she's about to protest, but I walk away quickly, not wanting to hear it. I enter the bar area again, and as I do, the door swings open. Ben and two other coaches from school walk in. One lightly punches him in the arm, and they all erupt in raucous laughter. As if sensing my presence, Ben's head swings in my direction, and his eyes snap to mine. I don't bother smiling because I'm not in the mood for that either, but I raise my beer to him in salute. He dips his chin in acknowledgement, his face suddenly serious. His buddies continue to razz each other behind him, but he doesn't seem to notice them anymore. Since he found out Kyle and I broke up, it's been like this. He looks at me like he either wants to devour me or fold me into his arms and not let me go. As it turns out, though, I'm not in the mood for *that*—whatever that is—on top of everything else, so I pivot on my heel and walk to the other side of the bar.

I find a dark table in a corner and down the rest of my beer. When a waitress walks by, I order another and put it on Ellie's tab. I can see Ben across the room. He doesn't look at me again, but by his stiff shoulders and straight back, I can tell he is probably acutely aware of my exact location. He's never made a secret about his interest in me, though he's never said it outright. But I'm not blind. The problem is that he's a nice guy and a good friend, and he deserves better than the mess I'm pretending not to be at this stage of my life, so my plan is to steer clear of him as much as I can. So far, it seems to be working.

I'm about halfway through my third beer when a shockingly attractive man slides into the seat across from me. His jaw is practically chiseled onto his face, and he wears a fitted navy shirt that shows off his very nice arms. He has wavy brown hair that is scooped into a perfectly messy man bun. How is it that men can always get the perfect level of mess with those buns? It's completely unfair.

"A beautiful lady like you shouldn't be sitting alone." His dark eyes glint in the dim light of the bar.

I take a casual sip of my beer, playing unimpressed. "Good thing you're here, then." I cock an eyebrow at him, and he lifts a corner of his mouth. "I'm Alex."

"Jenny." I reach out a hand for him to shake, but he takes it and turns it over, lowering his head to brush a kiss on my knuckles. I laugh.

"What are you drinking, Jenny?" He releases my hand, and I show him the label on my bottle. He signals to the waitress for another round. I bat my eyelashes in my best attempt to flirt, but I'm feeling a little woozy, so I'm afraid it might come off as creepy. He doesn't seem to notice.

"So, what brings you to this fine establishment?" I ask.

"A couple of my buddies live nearby. We were bored. What about you?"

"My two friends dragged me out. Well, not dragged, but..." I trail off. "Anyway, they're playing pool over there." I tip my chin toward the pool tables. He twists in his seat as if he can see them, which he can't because of the wall. I catch Ben's eye over his shoulder. He sees me looking at him and Alex sitting with me, and his face goes stoic. He faces the bar and his friends again, his back to me.

Alex is talking, and I turn my attention to him. "Well, I'm glad they did. It's not every day I get to talk to someone so gorgeous at a dive bar," he's saying.

I bite my lip and give the best coy smile I can muster. The waitress delivers our drinks, and I do my best not to take too big of a gulp. I'm feeling nothing for this man aside from an acknowledgement of his objective attractiveness, but if he wants to buy me a few drinks, who am I to say no?

Mac walks out and scans the room. When she sees me sitting with Alex, she wisely decides not to interrupt. Ben waves her down, and they talk for a minute or two while she waits for another drink at the bar, then she goes back to the pool room. Ben doesn't turn around to look at me again.

Alex and I chat through this drink—is it my fourth or fifth?—but it's clear to both of us that it's going nowhere. His buddies find him and ask if he's ready to leave, and he's nice about it, but we say our goodbyes. When he walks past Ben to the door, Ben straightens a bit. He finally turns to look at me as I gulp down the last bit of my drink and plunk the bottle down on the table. I stand, and as soon as I do, I wish I didn't. The whole room tilts, and I grab the edge of the table. I have the vague sense that Ben has jumped to his feet and is coming toward me, but I make a beeline for the restroom and lock myself in a stall.

No sooner am I safely inside the stall do I fall to my knees and hurl my guts up into the toilet. Luckily, there's no one else in the bathroom, or this would be truly embarrassing. And as soon as I think about how mortifying it is that I've retched in the filthy toilet at Tony's, the waterworks start. Even though it's disgusting, I lean my head back against the side of the stall and stare up at the ceiling, my body shaking with sobs.

I hear the bathroom door open, but I don't care enough to try to stop at this point. Through my tears, I see Mac's brown hippie sandals and her unpainted toenails under the stall door. She taps lightly. "Jenny?" she asks quietly.

I groan, then gag into the toilet again.

"Oh boy." Ellie's voice comes from farther away. "We probably should have kept a closer eye on her."

"Last time I saw her, she was flirting with the hot man bun we saw walk in, so I figured that was better than wallowing." Mac sounds like she's shrugging, and I start crying even harder. "Okay, Jenny. Time to go, huh?"

"No." The word has a whining, moaning quality to it that I don't remember intentionally adding. I try again: "No. I'm fine. Go have fun."

"Are you for real?" Mac doesn't sound angry, but she doesn't sound happy either. Leave it to me to ruin everyone's night. I didn't think it was possible, but I start crying even harder. Loud, shameful sobs echo off the tile walls of the bathroom, which only makes me cry more.

"I don't think you should be in here," I hear Ellie say, and then heavier footsteps sound. I see men's shoes next to Mac's, then hers step back.

"Jenny. It's me." Ben's deep voice fills the room, and I don't know why, but my sobs calm a bit at the sound of it. "Let's get you home."

I sniffle, then wipe my nose with the back of my hand. "I don't think I can walk home." My voice sounds pitifully small and slurred.

Ben's shoes shuffle a few inches closer, and he sounds like he is right next to the stall door. "You don't have to, sweetheart. I've got you. Open the door for me, okay?"

I swallow hard. My mess of a self doesn't deserve the attention he's giving me, but there's something gently commanding in his tone that makes me feel like letting him in is truly the best option I have. I reach up and release the latch, letting it swing open. Ben's shoulders fill the stall door. He immediately crouches down so he's eye level with me. The room is still spinning, but I force myself to focus on his warm brown eyes. "I'm going to carry you out of here, okay, Jenny? Can I do that?"

I should be humiliated by this, but his kind voice shows no sign of judgment or annoyance, and the sadness that had rocked me a few minutes ago is still too big to leave room for anything else. I nod, and he smiles softly. "Good girl," he whispers, just for me. And then one of his arms is under my knees and the other is behind my back and I'm being lifted off the floor. His hands are broad and warm, almost covering my whole back and easily holding me up, and I sink into the feel of him. "I've got you," he murmurs into my ear. I hold around his neck and rest my head against his chest to try to stop the room from spinning. I close my eyes, but that's worse, so I open them again and stare at an empty spot on the wall.

"We walked here." Mac sounds apologetic, but Ben shakes his head.

"I drove. We can get her in my car, no problem."

The music is blasting in the bar, but all I register is the soft, slow, steady beat of Ben's heart against my ear as he moves quickly and almost effortlessly outside. I bury my head even farther into his chest, and I swear he lets out a little contented sigh, but everything is still muddled and spinning, so I can't be sure.

The next thing I know, I hear a car door opening. "I'm going to put you in the back seat with Ellie, okay?" Ben's voice is quiet and gentle, but I whimper, tightening my grip on his neck. He chuckles, and I feel the sound through my chest to my toes. "Okay, sweetheart. I'll stay with you." He shifts as he lowers us both into the car, then I hear keys jingle. "You good to drive, Milcrest?"

"Yeah, I only had one." Ellie must grab the keys and start the car, because I can see Mac in the front passenger seat. I feel a little guilty because I know they were trying to have fun tonight, too, but Ben runs his hand comfortingly up and down my back, and I focus on that sensation instead.

It only takes a few minutes to get back to the condo. Ben lifts me out of the car and carries me up the steps and inside. Mac points out where my room is, and he brings me back, setting me gently on the bed. He unbuckles my shoes and pulls them off, then covers me with the throw blanket from the chair in the corner. He squats so he is eye level again and brushes a strand of hair out of my eyes.

"Thank you," I manage to whisper, and I hope my breath doesn't smell too bad.

He swallows, then smiles softly, his gaze never leaving mine. "Don't mention it. Take care of yourself, Green. I'll see you Monday."

He lingers for a second longer, and I close my eyes. He stands and leaves, shutting the door softly behind him.

# Chapter 10
## Present Day

"HOLD ON." JAYDEN INTERRUPTS me for about the fifth time in the first ten minutes of class. "You mean to tell me that Viola thought it would be a good idea to cross-dress to get into Orsino's court?"

"She's not cross-dressing, exactly. She's pretending to be her brother," I clarify.

"But she's a woman dressing as a man. That's cross-dressing," Jayden insists.

I notice Diego has put his head down in the back of the room, and his breathing has deepened. As I talk, I move slowly toward his desk. "Okay, sure. Keep in mind, though, she is a woman alone in Shakespeare's time. Shipwrecked. She doesn't have many other options." I place my hand gently on Diego's shoulder, and he starts awake, then looks at me apologetically. I simply continue my lap around the room. He works late at his parents' auto shop sometimes, and I know it's hard for him to get enough sleep.

"Someone's gonna notice," Kayla chimes in. "She can't look all that much like a guy."

"Yeah. Doesn't she still sound like a girl, too?" Cecily is also unconvinced.

"Well, she's not trying to pretend she's a grown man." I've had almost this exact conversation with students every time I've taught *Twelfth*

*Night*, so their incredulity is nothing new. "She's pretending she's a eunuch. Regardless, this is a good time to talk about this nerdy literary thing called 'suspending your disbelief.'" I lean a hip against the bank of windows at the side of my classroom.

"What's a eunuch?" Jayden asks, and Ana snickers.

"Something to look up later." I wink at Ana, and she giggles. I continue, "More importantly, suspending your disbelief means that you let go of your expectations of reality in order to enjoy a book or play, or even a movie or television show. Not everything is going to be plausible—in other words, not everything in fiction could actually happen in real life. In fact, probably none of *Twelfth Night* could have actually happened, so you should let it go and enjoy it."

Kayla squishes up her face. "That sounds a lot like the way my mom explains away things she doesn't want to bother explaining."

I laugh heartily, and right as I'm about to respond, the bell rings to release this class. The students toss their books into their bags and stand, shuffling out of the room. I take a moment to get my things in order to reset my classroom for the next class, then step out into the hallway, still laughing to myself about Kayla's comment.

Ben is already there, and his fresh-faced grin is a far cry from the intense looks he was giving me at the gym last night. It almost makes me feel embarrassed about the way I was thinking about him in the tub. Almost.

"How was class this morning?" he asks, seeing my residual smile.

"Good enough. How about you?"

He raises his eyebrows ominously. "Trouble in paradise. Noah and Javier are not even speaking to each other. They were working together in a group, and I had to switch kids around so they'd actually get some work done."

"What happened to keeping them far apart?" I fold my arms across my chest and lean back against the wall.

He shrugs. "I let them pick their groups for this first project while I get to know them."

I tilt my head to one side and look at him pointedly. "Rookie mistake."

He chuckles and nods. "Yeah, well. Live and learn. Hey, did you get all those appointments with Mac sorted out? When do you think you want to get started on this thing?"

I groan loudly and slink lower on the wall, dropping my hands at my sides. "I didn't even look at my calendar yet. It's all so overwhelming."

"When she decides she wants to do something, she goes all in."

"You can say that again. I promise I'm going to get everything organized today at lunch, but I think I have an opening next Sunday, late afternoon? It sucks to work on a weekend, but I know you have conditioning during the week—"

"Next Sunday is perfect," he cuts me off, almost over-eager. "My house?"

"Sure. Text me your address again, okay? I know I have it somewhere, but I'm too lazy to look for it."

"No problem." He pulls out his phone, and a second later, mine buzzes in my pocket. "What about another lift? I was serious about helping you become a better runner."

"I am an excellent runner, thank you very much," I protest. He simply raises an eyebrow at me and waits. I narrow my eyes at him over the few students still making their way through the hallway. "Ben Allouer, if I didn't know any better, I'd think you were trying to find ways to spend more time with me."

He doesn't say anything, but his gaze intensifies in the same way it did at the gym last night. It's only for a second, but it's unmistakable. So, I didn't imagine it, then.

I raise an eyebrow slightly, and then his expression turns chaste again. He shrugs as the bell to start the next class rings. "I'm in the weight room every day after school. Come on down any time you want."

I wrinkle my nose in disgust. "With the students? Ew. No thank you."

He shrugs again, walking back across the hallway to his classroom. "You're right. Your gym attire is completely inappropriate to work out in front of the students." His voice is about an octave lower than it usually is, and he raises his eyebrows suggestively.

Suddenly, my mouth goes dry. Without waiting for me to respond, he winks, then pulls his door open and enters his classroom, leaving me to my stunned silence.

I decide to eat lunch in my empty classroom while I force myself to open each of Mac's wedding appointment invites and get them into my calendar. As I go through the mind-numbing task of accepting each and every invite so it shows up in my phone, then setting reminders for all the appointments so I don't forget, I can't help but replay the interaction with Ben in the hallway after first period. We often flirt. It's kind of our thing, but it's mostly just friendly, and always—*always*—outside of school or, at least, never when students are around. We have never discussed it outright, probably because we've never actually talked about the flirting in general, but there has always been an unwritten rule that we will be professionals in this building. His heated gaze from across the hallway and his suggestiveness about my workout clothes were definitely him crossing an invisible line, and I'm not sure how I feel about it. If I'm being completely honest, I think I kind of liked it.

I bite my lip and scroll through the next few weeks on my calendar. I open up next weekend and hover my finger back and forth between Saturday and Sunday. Which day did Ben and I decide? I can't remember, but both late afternoons look free; Mac only scheduled morning appointments those days. I type it in for Saturday and make a mental note to ask him later, then glance at the clock. Fifteen minutes left to devour my deli meat sandwich and yogurt. I put my phone away and get my lunch out, not wanting to waste any more time.

At the end of the day, I practically follow my students out the classroom door and make my way to Mac's room. When I walk inside, she already has her feet propped up on her desk, her green-and-yellow spirit shoes wiggling back and forth as if they're taunting me. I hate those shoes. She got them off the clearance rack years ago, and I told her they were on sale for a reason. Once, I tried to throw them in the garbage, but she must have picked them out of the trash because, the next Friday, they were back on her feet.

"Classy," I say sarcastically, lowering myself into a student desk in front of her. She crosses one ankle over another and puts her hands behind her head as if this is the most relaxing position for her to be in on a Friday afternoon. She tips back so far in her seat that I think she might fall over, but she doesn't.

"I know, I know. Not everyone can exude Leade Park Lightning spirit every Friday. It's burden I must bear alone." She sighs and leans back farther, and then her chair almost does tip, forcing her to plant her feet on the ground and lean forward to right herself.

I snort. "Serves you right, tormenting me with those awful shoes."

She scowls at me, leaning her forearms on her desk. "I know you didn't come in here just to complain about my shoes."

"Your shoes are objectively disgusting, but no, I didn't. I came in here because it's Friday, and you and I missed some friend time this week, so I'm making you come out with me."

She groans heavily and bangs her forehead on top of her desk. "Do I have to?" Her voice is muffled by her hands.

"We don't have to go to Tony's if you don't want to, but we have to do something that's *not* wedding-related. I saw those calendar invites, Mac. It's going to be nothing but wedding from now until the end of the month. While that *is* an opportunity to spend a lot of time together, I'd like to spend some time with you not centered around tulle and floral arrangements."

She lifts her head, then sits up straight and tilts it to the side, considering. She's going to agree to hang out with me. I know I had her at "we don't have to go to Tony's," but for some reason, she needs to make a show of weighing her options.

"Pasta night at the condo?" she says, finally.

"Oh, yes please." I practically moan in delight. "Pasta and meatballs sound so good right now."

"Okay. I'll meet you there in an hour. I want to go home and change and say hi to Daniel."

It takes me a second to realize that when she says "home," she no longer means the condo. The realization brings with it that now-familiar sadness, but I shake it off. Mac and I are going to hang out, like we used to, and that's exactly what I wanted tonight. "Sure thing. I'll make the meatballs and be there by five." I stand to leave.

"Can you bring the wine, too? We've been packing stuff up at the condo, and Daniel and I may have drunk whatever was left."

I eye her over my shoulder. I didn't know she had already started packing up the condo. Not that I expected her to wait forever, but it would have been nice to be able to help, or at least be somewhat useful. That pang of loneliness I'm starting to become all too familiar with lodges itself in my chest. I rub my sternum as if that could take it away, but it's useless. Mac is moving on, and I'm left to watch from the sidelines.

I put on my best smile and say, "Sure, no problem," and try to smother this nagging sorrow as I make my way out.

# Chapter 11
## Present Day

WHEN I GET BACK to my apartment, I pull on my black sweatpants and a light pink tank top and get started on the meatballs. I pull a bottle of wine off the wine rack on top of my refrigerator and set it by my shoes so I don't forget it.

Mac and I have been having regular Friday pasta nights since our high school cross country days. It's not a hard schedule, but we try to have one at least once a month. I dump the ground meat, some fresh herbs, salt and pepper, and breadcrumbs into a bowl and start mixing it up with my hands. There's something soothing about the process of making these meatballs. It was my grandma's recipe, and I have it memorized. I make them for every pasta night, and it feels like one small thing I'm sure I know exactly how to do. It's steadying, and it's a connection to both my past blood family and my current chosen one.

I roll the meatballs and put them in the oven, cleaning up the kitchen while they bake. Once they're done, I take them out and cover them with tinfoil. I check the clock as I'm pulling on my shoes, and it's a few minutes past five. I scowl, knowing that Mac will poke fun at me for being late yet again.

I drive as fast as I can to Mac's condo, the bottle of wine snug in my cupholder while I steady the glass tray of meatballs in the passenger seat with my right hand. She opens the door before I can and leans against it, an eyebrow raised. "I swear, Jenny, you'll be late for your own funeral." "I'm disappointed in you, Mac. That joke is old. You don't have anything new?"

"I've been occupied lately. Not a lot of time to come up with new material." She shrugs, still standing in the doorway.

"If I'm too late, I can always take these meatballs back to my place and eat them myself." The tray is flat against my palm, and I raise it slightly. She quickly moves out of the way to let me in. "I'm not ever going to turn down your meatballs," she says as I walk past her.

I make my way across the living room to the kitchen and immediately open the preheated stove to put the meatballs inside to keep them warm. "Not even after you're a married woman, settled in your domestic bliss?"

"Especially not then. Apparently, you can take Daniel out of New York, but you can't take New York out of Daniel. If we eat takeout one more night this month, I might puke. If I want anything homemade, I have to make it myself."

"How feminist of him, keeping you barefoot in the kitchen." I raise my eyebrow, and she huffs.

"I'm working on him. We're taking a cooking class together next Saturday night."

"Dammit, that's adorable." I soften a little and lean my elbows against the counter. "I think cooking with someone you love might be peak relationship goals."

"You obviously haven't seen Daniel try to cook. It's more like cooking with an angry toddler than a grown man."

I giggle at the image, which makes Mac laugh, too. This feels so normal that I almost don't notice how empty the living room is without books on the bookshelves or throw pillows on the couch, but it registers in my brain without permission. My face falls.

Mac sees, and her smile fades, too. She looks behind her, then back at me. "I know." She sighs deeply, like her whole soul was in that breath. "I'm not ready for it, either."

"Doesn't feel like that long ago that I was moving in here," I say quietly, letting the kitchen counter support me.

Mac raises her eyebrows pointedly. "Or that you were moving out."

I hum noncommittally, looking at the empty couch behind her again. "We've been through a lot in this place."

"We have. But, you know, I hope we'll keep going through it in the new place, too. Just with more space." The look on her face is hopeful.

I didn't expect this evening to get so dour so quickly. "A lot more space." I widen my eyes, trying to pivot the conversation, and she laughs. Good. Laughing is good. "Is Evans building you a library for all your collective books, or what?" I'm joking, but she looks a little sheepish, and my eyes just about pop out of their sockets. "A whole-ass library? Are you serious?"

"Well..." She trails off, looking up at the ceiling, then back to me. She shrugs. "We have a disgusting amount of books when we put them all together. You know what I had here, and he shipped in about double that from New York. A lot of them are author copies of his own books he keeps around. He has an entire box of proofs that he keeps for sentimental reasons. And then he gets so many advanced copies to blurb and stuff." She shrugs again. "It made sense. Right now, it's just a bunch of boxes, but he's going to hire someone to create built-in shelves after the wedding."

"Damn, Mac. A whole library." I can almost bet it'll be in the front office. It's a huge, empty room to the right when you walk in. Mac had tried to get him to set up his writing desk in there, but then realized that he is a complete, unorganized mess when he is working, and decided she didn't want the first thing people see when they come in to be his chaos.

I look at her grin and smile slyly. "I'll have to add a few of my favorites as a housewarming gift."

Her expression turns borderline horrified. "You can't hide erotica in our collection."

"I can, and I will. You, of all people, should know that a book is not less important because there's sex in it."

"It's not, but it would be really awkward for his writer friends to come over and find some random guy with a six pack among all these award winners." She's almost pleading. She knows I'm serious.

My grin turns almost feral. "All the more reason to do it." I raise my eyebrows suggestively, and she looks so scared that I burst into a fit of laughter, clutching at my sides.

"You seriously wouldn't." She's trying to hold back her laughter now, too.

I calm myself and eye her over the counter. "I would, and you know it. But," I add when I see her frown again, "I probably won't."

"Probably?" Her expression is pleading again, but I just chuckle.

"Probably. Now, can we eat? I'm starving."

She eyes me a little skeptically, but her hunger must be winning out, too, because she nods once and walks into the kitchen. She grabs a stack of paper plates off the counter next to the stove and hands me one. "Sorry, we have to use these. All my regular dishes are packed up."

I turn the plate over in my hand, looking at it, and that's when it hits me. This is probably our last pasta night in the condo. A lump rises hard and fast in my throat, and I'm suddenly not hungry at all anymore.

Mac is studying me, but I can't look at her. I'm still staring at the paper plate. She lays a hand on my arm. "I know," she says quietly.

I swallow hard and drag my eyes to hers. Her hand is still on my arm, and her lips are pressed together in sympathy.

"Shit. I didn't expect to be this sad." I shake my head slightly and clear my throat. "I'm fine. I'm sorry."

"Don't you dare say you're sorry," Mac scolds me. "We've been through a lot here. Even when you didn't live here, it was our home base. You're allowed to have feelings about this. I sure do."

I nod silently and look around. I can't think about how many pasta nights we've had or late-night movies we've watched or post-Tony's breakfasts we've cooked in this place, or I'll burst into tears. I don't want to be sad tonight; I want it to be Mac and me being friends like we used to. I shove all these thoughts way down and smile as brightly as I can. "Pasta now. Feelings later. Deal?"

Mac smiles and moves her hand from my arm, grabbing the big spoon that's sitting on the counter next to the stove. "Deal," she says.

I take the meatballs out of the oven and put them on top of the stove next to the pot of pasta. She opens the lid on the pot, stepping back as the steam releases. For a second, I wonder how she's planning to get spaghetti out of the pot with that spoon, and then she dips it in and shovels some pasta on her plate.

"Penne?!" I ask incredulously.

"I'm sorry, okay?" She says it quickly, as if she knew exactly what I was going to say before I said it. "It's all I had left, and I had already asked you to bring the wine, so I didn't want to ask you to bring the pasta, too!"

"Penne and meatballs? Who eats penne and meatballs?"

"It's the same pasta in a different shape! Carbs are carbs!" She knows that, when it comes to pasta, none of this is true for me, but my stomach growls loudly, and she points the spoon at me in victory.

"Fine," I concede. "Just this once, I will lower my standards. But only because I am too hungry to protest any further." I scoop some pasta and sauce on my plate, then add some meatballs with my fingers. I grab a plastic fork and make my way to the couch with Mac trailing behind me.

"I promise to have ten boxes of spaghetti in the new house at all times," she says, sitting cross-legged and balancing her pasta on top of one knee.

"You're going to need it if Evans is that bad at cooking." I slice a meatball in half and spear it with my fork.

"I wouldn't even trust him with the boiling water." She scoops some pasta onto her fork, then pokes a piece of a meatball and puts it all into her mouth. She chews for a second, then grimaces as she swallows. "I hate to admit you're right, but spaghetti is better with the meatballs."

"It's an objective truth." I take a bite of my own pasta and meatball, and we chew in silence for a few minutes.

"I'm having a hard time thinking of things to talk about that aren't wedding-related," she admits. It wasn't meant to be a hard-and-fast rule not to talk about wedding stuff, but I'm touched she's trying.

"My life is painfully uninteresting," I say around a mouthful of meatballs.

She eyes me sidelong, then looks back to her pasta. "I heard you and Ben got a little cozy at the gym last night."

My jaw drops, and some pasta almost falls out of it before I shut it quickly and swallow my food. "Who told you that?"

"I'm not disclosing my sources." She smiles slyly, still avoiding eye contact.

"I'm your best friend. It's not disclosing sources; it's telling me who is talking about me behind my back." I'm starting to get a little angry. I don't need the LPHS rumor mill firing off about who I talk to at the gym.

Mac shifts so she's facing me, a placating look on her face. "Okay, okay. I ran into Ben before school this morning. He suggested I join you two for regular lifting sessions. Something about becoming a stronger runner." She can't stop the grin from spreading. "I added the stuff about getting cozy myself, but you definitely didn't deny it."

I can feel my cheeks getting red, so I scowl to try to hide it. "Why are you so invested in this all of a sudden?"

"I've always been invested in this. I've watched you two circle around each other for the better part of a decade."

"We don't 'circle around each other,'" I insist, but my heart skips a beat at the thought of other people noticing the things I've been seeing this week.

"Yes, you do. Every time both of you are single, you flirt like teenagers. When he sees you outside of school, he looks at you like you're the only person in the room. Even when he was with Faith, he knew where you were at all times."

That is not entirely true, but this isn't the time to argue semantics. I look at her skeptically, playing ignorant with my lips pursed and an eyebrow raised. I take another large bite of pasta, slowly chewing it. She mimics me, never breaking eye contact.

"He told you himself," she says after she swallows her food.

"That was years ago." Six years, to be exact, but I'm not counting.

She waves this away as if it's an insignificant detail. "He didn't suddenly change his mind."

"Mac, be serious. We've both been dating other people since then. It's harmless, useless flirting."

"It's definitely flirting, and it's all the time. Why not see where it goes?"

She shoves a whole meatball in her mouth, and I'm surprised it all fits. I laugh at her chipmunk cheeks. "Why do you care so much?"

She shrugs, then finishes chewing and swallows. "I want you to be happy, Jenny. Ben is a good guy."

"Are we forgetting about finding him talking about you to Marty and Edgar after school that one time?"

She waves this away, too. "That was years ago," she mimics, giving me a pointed look. "He apologized and made amends. Why are you so resistant to this?"

"We work together!" I say it as if it's obvious. "You may remember how against Daniel you were because you were working together when you met."

She rolls her eyes and points her empty fork at me. "Yeah, and look at us now. Domestic bliss and all that."

"Ah, yes. The blissful sound of his balls banging against walls late into the evening and a man whose idea of cooking is dialing a new takeout number every night."

"Don't forget the library, though." She waggles her eyebrows at me.

I chuckle. "Ben wouldn't build me a library."

"I have a feeling Ben would give you anything you wanted and then some, but whatever helps you sleep at night."

I glare playfully at her over my pasta, but my heart has been tripping in my chest during this entire conversation, and I've been fighting the blush I know is still creeping up my cheeks. I am well aware that Mac sees it, but she graciously hands me the remote. "Your turn to pick the movie, I think."

I take the remote from her and browse through the various streaming services, eventually selecting a rom-com. We each get another serving of pasta and settle in.

I feel a little shake on my shoulder and open my eyes to the blue light of the television. The credits are rolling, and I scrub my hands over my face. I don't think there has been a pasta night at Mac's that I haven't gone into an immediate carb coma and fallen asleep before the movie ended. Usually, she lets me sleep on the couch, but she's sitting next to me, her hand dropping from my shoulder as I sit up.

"Sorry, Jenny." She does sound apologetic. "I know you could let yourself out, but I didn't want to leave you here alone."

"You're leaving?" I yawn and shake myself, trying to wake myself up.

"I was going to go home to Daniel." She says it like it's the most obvious thing in the world. I guess it kind of is.

"Yeah. Right. Of course." I stand up and start collecting my empty meatball tray and my shoes.

"But tomorrow you're coming to taste the cake with us, right?" Her eyebrows are raised, and I can see how wide her eyes are in the light from the television.

"Don't you think that's something you and Daniel should do alone?" I ask.

"I want you there." Her tone is determined, and I'm not sure why she sounds like she needs me there, but I'm also not going to argue with a bride a few weeks before her wedding.

"Okay, sure. I'll be there." I pull my shoes on and grab my keys and purse in one hand while holding the empty tray in the other. Mac also pulls on her shoes and follows me out the door. We wave to each other and get in our respective cars. She wastes no time pulling out and driving away, but I linger, looking up at the familiar building.

I pull out my phone. No messages. I open the message thread with Ben, and the last message there is his address from this morning. I look up at the dark windows of Mac's condo, then back to my bright phone screen. What would I say to him, anyway? *Hope your Friday night was fun? Enjoy your sleep? Just had a whole conversation about you with Mac. Hope that's not creepy?*

I click my phone off without typing anything and throw it on the passenger seat. Then, before I can think better of it, I open it again and type: *I'm going to copy and paste all the book requests into a spreadsheet tomorrow so things will move faster next weekend.* I hit send and click my phone off. I drop my forehead to the steering wheel and groan. What a stupid thing to send. Who cares about work on Friday?

But before I can think too hard about it, my phone lights up in my lap. *You want me to come over and help?*

A smile plays on my lips. Do I want him to come over and help? What is there to even help with? *I think I can handle some CTRL + C/P.*

The three dots instantly appear at the bottom of the thread, and I sit there, staring at them. They disappear and reappear a few times before his message comes through. *I think you can handle a lot of things, but that doesn't mean you don't deserve help sometimes.*

He's so kind, this man. He always has been. It's part of the reason I didn't date him when he asked me six years ago, and it's probably the same reason we haven't hooked up since. I never wanted him to be just another one-night stand, and after everything, that seemed to be all I was capable of for a long time.

I bite my lip and type: *Thanks, but I'm good. Just wanted to let you know.* I hit send and toss my phone back on the passenger seat, backing out of Mac's driveway and starting my drive home. My phone doesn't light up on the way, and when I finally burrow myself into my bed, I look one last time to find my unread messages empty.

# Chapter 12
## Six Years Ago

THE BEST WAY TO get over someone is to get under someone else.

At least that's what I'm telling myself as I start to literally slide out from under this guy's arm. At least we made it to the bed this time. Last time I went home with a guy, we ended up on the floor. This one—Jake, I'm pretty sure—fell asleep shortly after we finished, and I've been laying under his arm for the past twenty minutes or so, waiting for his breathing to deepen enough that I can make my exit undetected.

He twitches a little when I'm about an inch away from freedom, then rolls over so his back is to me. Perfect. I slip out from under the tangle of sheets, collect my dress, underwear, bra, and shoes, and tiptoe out of the bedroom and into the living room where I hurriedly pull my clothes on. I grab my purse from where I tossed it on the couch, and I'm out the door. One of his neighbors is sitting on a porch swing across the street, holding a beer and clearly gaping at me, so I flash a bright smile and wiggle my fingers before I yank my car door open and get in. If that guy is going to sit on his porch in the middle of the night, he should expect to see some things.

I glance at my phone to check the time and see there's a missed call from my mom. I'm glad it's too late to call her back. I'm a terrible liar, and based on her over-critical nature when it comes to my love life, I'm not exactly sure if she would be proud of me for how many guys I've managed to snag or disgusted by the fact that I only keep them around for one night. I decide to forget about her as I pull out of the driveway. It's none of her business, anyway.

I pull up to the condo and make my way inside. I open the door as quietly as I can, thinking Mac will probably be asleep by now, only to find her on the couch in the living room, under a red plaid blanket, holding a book open on her lap. She doesn't look up when I come in, so I roll my eyes and slip off my shoes.

The clock in the kitchen says it's just after two in the morning. I take a few steps toward my bedroom, then I sigh heavily and turn around to face Mac.

"You're going to be tired tomorrow." I cringe inwardly at how nasty it sounds, but it's too late.

Mac turns a page of her book, not looking up. "So will you."

"You didn't need to wait up for me."

She turns another page. It's clear that she's not actually reading. "Someone had to make sure you got home."

"What would you have done if I didn't come home? You didn't know where I was."

She finally looks up at me, closing her book and putting it on the cushion next to her. "Yeah, Jenny. That's kind of the point. It's not safe to leave a bar with a guy and not tell anyone where you're going. And this isn't the first time."

"Don't slut-shame me, Mac. I'm finally having sex that's not 'vanilla'—"

"I'm not slut-shaming you," she interrupts me, and by the increased volume of her voice, I can tell she's pissed. "I don't care who or how many guys you bang. I want to know that my best friend is coming home and hasn't been murdered or whatever by some creep she picked up at a bar."

She's right, of course. I should be more careful about who I leave with, but short of that, I should at least tell her where I'm going and with whom. I sigh and walk over to the couch. I lightly smack her legs, and she moves them over so I can sit down. Her arms are folded, and she's staring at the coffee table in front of her.

"I'm sorry." I stare at the coffee table, too. "I finally feel free of him, you know? I finally feel like I'm having all the fun I missed out on in college."

"I don't think there's anything wrong with that. Truly, I don't. I hope the sex you're having is amazing and fun and satisfying and all the things it never was with Kyle. I just want to know you're safe." She looks sidelong at me, her shoulders sagging a little. She's lost some of her initial anger, and I can tell she feels bad about this entire conversation. I sling an arm around her shoulders and squeeze.

"The sex is really good." I'm trying to lighten the mood. She rolls her eyes, but a small smile plays at her lips, so I carry on. "Wonderful, actually. I'm trying things Kyle could have only dreamed of."

"Please stop," she begs, but she giggles.

I hug her shoulders again. "I promise I'll let you know where I am from now on. Starting tomorrow at Tony's."

Mac practically sinks into the couch as she groans. "Do we have to go to Tony's tomorrow? I'm so sick of Tony's."

"Yeah, me too, but we told Ben we'd meet him there for a drink after his first wrestling meet of the season. We can't blow him off."

Mac looks at me as if we can, actually, blow him off without guilt, but eventually wrinkles her nose and sags farther. "Okay, fine. But if we are going out tomorrow, we need to sleep. Now." She glares at me, and I half-smile.

"Fair enough." I raise my hands in surrender, and we make our way to bed.

The next afternoon, Mac and I enter the school gym for the end of the wrestling meet. When we get there, we're immediately greeted by loud cheering and screaming. We come around the bleachers to see several mats rolled out in the middle of the gym floor and a few matches are going on all at the same time. Parents, coaches, and other students are standing at the edges of the mats, and everyone is shouting at the tops of their lungs. This isn't the first wrestling meet we've ever attended, but I still haven't gotten used to the chaos.

"One of my students is wrestling over there. I'm going to go watch," Mac yells, and I wave her on. I, on the other hand, hang around the outskirts of everything, scanning the room for Ben.

I spot him on the edge of a mat on the far side of the gym. He's bent over as close as he can get to the two boys wrestling in front of him, and he's shouting something. His words are lost in the crowd, but he is alternating between clapping his hands and gesturing energetically while he yells.

It's strange, seeing this side of him. He's normally so calm and kind. To see him screaming at his athletes is completely different from seeing him interact with students or other teachers in the hallway. It's kind of exciting to see him so animated.

The match ends, and I honestly can't tell from his expression if he's happy or upset about the outcome, but when the ref raises the hand of the kid in LPHS green and gold, it's clear he's satisfied. Somehow, he finds me from all the way across the gym, his smile blazing over the distance between us. I hold out my hands and clap in his direction, and he laughs. I can't hear it over the screaming of everyone else in the gym, but it's a sound I've heard so often, it's like it echoes in my ears.

Eventually, Mac finds me again and we wander in and out of the gym, catching a few matches and watching Ben coach. I don't know how he keeps up his energy through the whole meet, but he never loses his stride. Eventually, the meet ends. Leade Park did well, and Ben seems happy. He finds us almost immediately after a final debrief with his wrestlers.

"Thanks for coming." He smiles broadly and even though he stands relatively far away from us, I can still smell the day-long meet on him. Mac wrinkles her nose slightly, so I know she's thinking the same thing.

"It was fun," she says, and I nod in agreement.

"You still up for drinks?" I ask.

He nods enthusiastically. "I need one after that. These guys kept me on my toes all day." Then, he looks from Mac to me. "From the looks on your faces, though, I should probably shower first?"

"Is it ever an option to *not* shower after this?" Mac waves her hand at the gym with an incredulous look on her face. Ben laughs his warm laugh, then sniffs himself and shrugs. Mac and I both recoil, and he chuckles again.

"I'll meet you at Tony's in an hour?" This, he directs entirely at me, our eyes locking. I give him a simpering little smile, while I'm all too aware of the energy practically radiating off Mac. She's not moving or making a sound, but she senses it. She always does.

"Sure." I look down at the ground, breaking eye contact.

Mac clears her throat. "See you soon," she practically sings, grabbing my wrist and leading me out of the school to her car.

Tony's is... well, it's Tony's. I can't blame Mac for her constant whining about meeting people here, but it's the teacher hangout, and it's so close to our place. We order our usual—beer for her and white wine for me—and grab a table while we wait for Ben.

We don't have to wait too long. He comes in a few minutes after us and orders his drink at the bar before coming over and sitting next to Mac. He looks freshly showered—his hair is still a little wet, and he's wearing jeans and a white t-shirt. I notice how the short sleeves hug his biceps, and while I think he made a poor choice wearing a t-shirt in November, I'm not complaining about the view.

"Congrats on the success today, Coach." I raise my glass in a toast. Mac, Ben, and I clink glasses over the middle of the table, and we each take a sip of our drinks.

"Thanks," he says, then yawns. "Sorry, ladies. Long day."

Mac nudges him with her shoulder. "Hosting an event like that is a lot of work, let alone coaching through it, too. It's special for the team to have their first meet at home every year."

"I'll perk up after this drink." He raises his beer.

I huff. "Yes, because alcohol is known to wake people up." I'm already starting to feel a little sleepy myself after about half of this glass of wine. He shrugs and takes a sip anyway, and I laugh.

He does actually perk up after his beer, and he orders us another round. We spend most of the evening talking about our classes and swapping stories about students we've shared over the years. At one point, Ben launches into a twenty-minute rant about the abysmal state of funding for his wrestling team. Mac and I listen politely, but my eyes glass over at about the fifteen-minute mark. When he pauses for air, I offer to get the next round and make my way over to the bar. Ben says he wants soda since he's driving, but Mac looks like she needs another beer after that diatribe.

The place has filled up since we came in, so it takes a few minutes to get the bartender's attention. No matter what, there is always only one person behind the bar here. It seems like the owner thinks the solo grumpy bartender is part of the dive bar charm, but in reality, it's just annoying.

I stand there, resting my elbows on the counter and drumming my fingers on the bar. A man sidles up next to me and plunks an empty glass down. The bartender looks over at the noise and scowls, returning to his drink-pouring.

"You just bought yourself an extra five minutes' wait time." I lean in slightly and speak over the music. He chuckles, and it's a nice sound. I can see from the corner of my eye that he's very attractive. He's tall and lean, and he has dark hair with the beginnings of a little salt-and-pepper at the temples. He's rocking a five o'clock shadow and a blue button-down shirt that fits as if it were made for him.

I shift my weight to my other foot, still leaning against the bar, but the movement brings me about an inch closer to him. He holds out his hand. "Liam," he says.

I shake his hand in return. "Jenny."

He shifts so he is facing me, one elbow leaning against the bar, and I do the same. "So, what are you drinking, Jenny?"

"White wine, but I'm here to grab another round for my friends over there." I indicate Mac and Ben at the table behind me. Mac is now the animated one, and Ben looks a little glassy-eyed. By their body language, I'm guessing Mac is talking about the latest award-winning literary fiction she's read.

"That's some pair," Liam notes.

"We all teach together. None of us are together or anything."

He looks me up and down and smiles just as the bartender comes over to take my order. I tell him what I need, and he goes back to the taps to pour them. He pointedly ignores Liam, who chuckles again, shaking his head in dismay.

The bartender brings my three drinks back, then begrudgingly looks at Liam. He orders a gin and tonic, and the bartender goes to mix it, doing so painfully slowly. He's practically adding the ice one cube at a time, and a laugh escapes me. Liam makes a small noise of disbelief, then faces me again.

"I don't want to keep you from your friends," he says.

I shrug. "You're not."

He raises an eyebrow and looks over my shoulder. "Judging by the daggers your friend is shooting with his eyes, I'm guessing he either wants his drink or you back at the table."

I twist around to see Ben is, indeed, looking this way, and he is definitely shooting daggers with his eyes. When he notices me looking at him, though, he schools his expression into something a little more neutral.

I face Liam again and laugh a little uncomfortably. "He likes his soda. What can I say? It was nice meeting you, Liam."

Liam nods at me as I balance Mac's bottle of beer and Ben's plastic cup of soda in one hand and my glass of wine in the other. I make my way back to the table and distribute the drinks. Mac excuses herself to the restroom, and I sit, taking a sip of my wine.

Ben is studying me intensely. He takes a breath as if to say something, then changes his mind and lets it out.

I eye him over my wine glass. "Spit it out, Allouer."

His lips become a thin line, and he narrows his eyes at me. "You're not going home with that guy."

I rock back in my chair, shaking my head a little as my eyebrows pinch together. "Why not?" I know I'm not going home with Liam after Ben's display, but I'm not sure what say he has in it.

"Because." The word is its own sentence, as if that explains anything, but Mac plops down in her chair before I can ask him to elaborate. Ben's demeanor immediately changes. He goes right back to his friendly banter with Mac, but I step to the sidelines, only offering a few words here and there.

When we finish this drink, Mac senses that I'm ready to go, so she makes the first move to leave. We all make our way to the door, and when we open it, we are greeted by a cold downpour.

Mac groans. "I do not want to walk in this."

"You don't have to," Ben offers. "I can drive you both. Wait here, and I'll get my car." He doesn't wait for a response before running out into the rain. He makes it to his car quickly, then pulls it up right at the entrance. Mac and I both jump in as fast as we can, and Ben drives us the few minutes to the condo.

When we arrive there, Mac fumbles in her purse for her keys. She triumphantly holds them over her head, then bolts from the car. I hang back a second until she unlocks the door and tumbles inside. Then I rest my hand on the door handle, getting ready to follow.

"Jenny," Ben says, and I turn in my seat to face him. His hair is wet and matted to his head, and his white shirt is almost completely soaked through, but he doesn't so much as shiver. His eyes are molten, like they could heat the whole car when they rest on me.

"Yeah?" I ask.

He opens his mouth, then closes it again. He breathes out through his nose, making a little, frustrated sound, before he says, "Have a good night."

"You too. Thanks for the ride." I push the door open as fast as I can, then slam it shut and run.

Mac is inside, shaking her hair out over the welcome mat. I slide my shoes off, then grab a towel to wipe them down. Before I can, my phone dings. I pull it out of my purse and look at it, frowning.

"What's up?" Mac asks, slipping her shoes off, too.

"It's Ben. He wants me to come back outside."

"In this weather? Must be important."

"Yeah. I'll be right back." I don't bother putting my shoes back on as they'll just get soaked anyway. I run back out to his car, pull the passenger door open, and jump back inside, slamming the door behind me.

When I face him, he's fully looking at me, and he's fidgeting with a crease on his pants leg, a muscle in his jaw ticking slightly.

I giggle a little nervously. "I hope this is critical since you made me come back out here in this." The rain drums steadily against his windshield, and his wipers slide back and forth rhythmically.

"Go out with me, Jenny." It's a plea, not a question, and he says it so quietly, I almost miss it under the noise of the rain and windshield wipers. But there's no mistaking the determined set of his jaw and the heat still in his gaze.

*Oh shit*, I think. It has never been a secret that Ben has had a crush on me since we met, and I'm sure it took him the full year Kyle and I have been broken up to work up the courage to ask me out.

But I can't.

Ben is the nice guy. He's the warm and funny puppy I can see someone cuddled up with in front of a fire. He's hot chocolate on a bad day, or a comfortable sweatshirt after a long day of teaching.

And me? I'm a mess. I'm fighting my own inner battle against "vanilla sex once a month" and the ghost of a volatile and explosive man who dictated the better part of my teens and early twenties. I know it's been a year since I left him. I know I should be over him, and in the most important ways, I am. But I'm still working on myself.

Ben deserves a finished product, not... whatever I am at the moment.

I shake my head slightly, and his eyes instantly turn sad. It's painful to watch, so I study the pattern the windshield wipers are making out of the rain instead. "I can't," I whisper.

"Why?"

"I just can't. I'm not... It's not a good idea."

He huffs. "It's the best idea I've ever had. Let me take you out. One date."

I drag my eyes away from the windshield and meet his again. "You wouldn't be satisfied with one date, Ben."

He looks back and forth between both of my eyes, then drops his gaze to the center console. "You're right. I wouldn't."

"And that's all I've got right now. One date. One night at a time. I spent almost a decade with Kyle, and that's not something I'm looking for again right now. Save yourself the heartbreak and forget about me."

He meets my eyes again. "I could never."

I swallow hard, blinking rapidly. "I'm sorry. Now's not the time."

"Will it ever be the time?" There's a note of hope in his voice, and I can't bring myself to crush it.

"Maybe."

He studies me for a moment longer, then lets out a puff of air. "Okay. I'm not giving up on this, Jenny, but I'll leave you alone about it for now."

I don't want to string him along, but I have a feeling he won't find anything on the spectrum closer to "no" acceptable, so I pull a corner of my mouth up sadly.

"Have a good night, Ben." I don't wait for him to say anything else. I push the door open and run back inside the condo.

By the time I've shut the door and look out the window, his car is already halfway down the street.

# Chapter 13
## Present Day

THE WEEK PASSES QUICKLY as I begin to fall into the groove of the school year. When I'm not teaching, I'm running around with Mac to a million different appointments. When I finally get home at night, I barely have enough energy to shower and crawl into bed. I could really use a run or maybe even a weightlifting session, but I can't find the will to fight with my sports bra, let alone do any kind of physical activity.

Cake tasting had been a disaster. Daniel and Mac couldn't agree on anything, and it ended with Mac in a puddle, crying about how the two of them would last when they couldn't even agree on a cake flavor. Daniel had rushed back inside, ordered one cake in each flavor, and swept Mac away. I was left to give the bakery instructions for where and when to deliver them. This Saturday, I am determined not to have a repeat of last weekend, but today's appointment is to look at floral arrangements, and Daniel will be there again, so it already doesn't bode well.

The appointment is later in the morning, so I get in a run, then shower. Somehow, I am able to make sure I pull up to the flower shop five minutes before our scheduled appointment. I sit on a bench outside to wait for Mac and Daniel. When they walk up, they are both shocked to see me there before them.

"I *can* be on time, you know." I raise an eyebrow.

Mac looks impressed. "Well, let's do this, then." She grabs Daniel's hand like a lifeline and straightens up a little, fortifying herself for yet another appointment she wants nothing to do with.

We walk inside and are immediately struck by the sweet smell of flowers. I take a deep breath in through my nose and smile. I love the smell of fresh flowers.

Daniel sneezes once, and I cringe. He sniffles, and Mac lays a hand on his arm. His eyes are already starting to turn red. "Are you okay?" she asks quietly. A little bell dings above a door at the back of the shop, and a woman about our age walks out to greet us.

Daniel sneezes again three times in a row, then groans. "I'm so sorry." Sneeze. "There must be something in here I'm allergic to."

Mac looks like she's about to lose it again, so I clap my hands with forced enthusiasm. "Okay, Daniel. Why don't you head home? No need for you to be miserable. Mac and I can take it from here, and I'll drop her off when we're done." I start to usher him out the door.

He sneezes again, then says over his shoulder, "No daisies, okay?" He walks outside and to the car, sneezing the whole way.

I face Mac, whose mouth is partially open as she watches him go. She turns to me, a little wide-eyed. I do my best to put on a very reassuring smile.

"Um, hello," the woman finally says behind us. We both whirl around to face her, having forgotten she was there. "I'm Charlotte. You must be Mackenzie Milcrest?" She looks between the two of us, like she's not sure who she should be addressing.

Mac snaps out of her shock and raises her hand a little. "That's me."

"Excellent. And you are...?" She addresses me, trailing off.

"Jenny Green, maid of honor."

"Wonderful. Congratulations on your engagement, Mackenzie. Let's take a look at some floral arrangements, shall we?"

"Yes. Please. But nothing with any daisies, apparently." Mac looks apologetic.

Charlotte smiles comfortingly. "That won't be a problem at all. Come on back. We have some sample arrangements made up, and also some pictures you can look at to get a sense of what you like." We follow her back. "Do you have a favorite flower?"

"Roses," Mac says simply.

"Ahh, a classic choice. We have some lovely arrangements with roses. Do you have a color in mind?"

"Well, Jenny's dress is navy, and we will have teal accents," Mac offers as we enter the back room. It's colder back here, and there are beautiful—and huge—floral arrangements set on various tables throughout the room. Mac looks a little like a deer in headlights when she sees them, as if she's truly afraid they'll jump out and bite her.

"Hmm. We can't do navy or teal roses, but might I suggest a classic white or pale yellow?" She pulls out a huge photo album and flips through some of the pages. Mac politely looks at each picture, telling Charlotte what she likes and doesn't like. She tries to keep a brave face, but throughout the appointment, her shoulders start drooping, and by the end, her eyes are almost completely glazed over. Charlotte takes notes, and after an hour or so, she says she has what she needs to get started and she'll be in touch with photos of what the arrangements will look like.

As Mac is signing the contract and paying her deposit, my phone buzzes. I pull it out to see a reminder that I'm meeting Ben to work in an hour. I give myself a mental facepalm. I had completely forgotten that was today. When Mac finishes up, we walk to the car.

"I'm meeting Ben in an hour to work on spending your fundraising dollars, so we have to hurry."

"Do you want me to get Daniel back here to pick me up? I can wait for him," Mac offers. "Oh, and I forgot that I cancelled tomorrow's appointment with the photographer. We found a different one we like better."

I shake my head. "Oh, I'm never sad about a cancelled appointment. And I can drive you home, no problem. No one lives that far away. I just can't stay and chat."

"I'll tuck and roll when you get to the house." Mac giggles, already perking up a little now that the flowers have been dealt with. I roll my eyes, but I'm glad to hear her laugh, even if the bags under her eyes and lines bracketing her mouth are starting to get deeper than I would like.

# Chapter 14
## Present Day

BY THE TIME I get back to my apartment, I'm already late, so I hurriedly pull on jeans and a school sweatshirt, toss my hair in a ponytail, and drive the fastest over the speed limit I can legally get away with on my way to Ben's house. He lives in the next town over, so it takes me about twenty minutes to get there. I park in his driveway and practically run to the door, ringing the doorbell quickly. A crash sounds from inside, followed by some shouting, and it isn't until then that I look around and see a bunch of cars parked on the street in front of his house.

Then, a few things happen all at the same exact time. Ben opens the door holding a wooden spoon and wearing a bright red apron that says *I'm the FUN-cle* in big, white letters. A small, shirtless child runs past his legs and outside onto the front lawn. And I realize we said Sunday, not Saturday, and I am here on the wrong day.

"Grab him! Grab that toddler!" I hear a woman shout from inside the house.

This feels like a reasonable request, so I take a few steps off the porch, lift the kid from under his arms, and carry him back to the door. I hold him with my arms extended, and he is giggling maniacally and kicking his little legs as if he is still making a break for it. Ben sets his spoon down inside and holds out his arms for the small boy.

"Get over here, you little demon." He scoops the child into his arms and settles him on his hip. The child sees me then, and decides he wants to be a little shy, so he buries his head into Ben's shoulder. He looks completely natural holding this small child, and it takes me a second to realize I've never seen him hold a toddler before. A woman appears at Ben's side and takes the little one from him, disappearing back into the house saying, "You can't run outside without a grownup, Caleb." Ben laughs quietly, shaking his head and scrubbing a hand back and forth over his hair.

"I'm sorry," I say slowly. "I just realized we aren't supposed to meet until tomorrow. I got my schedule a little screwed up with all these wedding appointments." I'm used to being late, but I'm not used to showing up places on the wrong day, and I feel my cheeks start to heat with embarrassment.

Ben smiles in a way that lights up his whole face, and it goes a long way toward making me feel less self-conscious about my mistake. "No worries," he says, and I think he means it.

"Who's at the door, Benny?" I hear another woman call from inside. He cringes at the nickname, and I press my lips together to hide a smile. Suddenly, an older woman is at Ben's side. She is about a foot shorter than he is and has a much smaller build. Her hair is gray and cut just below her chin, but there is no mistaking who she is. They have the same warm brown eyes and the same almost-smile dancing on their lips. This is undoubtedly Ben's mom.

"Mom, this is Jenny. I think I've told you about her. She's in the classroom next door to me, and we are working on a project together."

"Hi." I wave a bit sheepishly. "We were supposed to meet about the project, but I got my days mixed up. I'm so sorry to interrupt."

"Nonsense." She looks at Ben, a stern expression on her face. "Don't let her stand there, Benny. Honestly, who raised you?"

Ben squints at her. "You did."

"And I know I raised you better than to let a woman stand outside on the porch." She turns to me. "Come in, dear. There's plenty of food."

"Oh, no, I couldn't. I truly messed up my schedule. I'll see you tomorrow, Ben." I wave again and, as I turn to leave, I swear I see a little disappointment on his face. Before I can step away, though, Ben's mom grabs my hand and pulls me past him and through the door. My shoulder brushes against his biceps, and I can feel the warmth of him through our shirts as I pass.

"Don't be silly," his mom is saying, though I'm disoriented by both her strong grip on my arm and the feel of him as I brush past, so it takes me a second before I can insert myself back into the conversation. "What's one more? Right, Benny?"

I open my mouth to decline again, looking to Ben for backup, but he shakes his head. "Once she gets an idea in her head, it's a lost cause." He rolls his eyes, and she swats at his arm. She doesn't say he's wrong, though, as she moves away from us, leaving us alone in the entryway of his house.

I look around, taking in the room. We've been work-friends for almost a decade, but he only bought this house a year ago, so I've never been here. Everything is as neat and orderly as it is in his classroom, and it's sparsely decorated. The walls are a light beige—probably the paint color the builder of the house picked out—and there's a long table near the door where his spoon is sitting, along with some keys. Several women's handbags rest underneath. I pick up the spoon, circling it at him and raising a taunting eyebrow.

"Nice getup, Benny," I tease.

His nostrils flare a little, but his eyes are sparkling. "Watch it, Green," he cautions. "Start talking smack, and I'll put you to work."

"Bring it on, Allouer," I return. "I know my way around the kitchen." He laughs his deep belly laugh, and I instantly feel less awkward. He takes the spoon from my hand and motions me into the living room, letting me enter before him. Three women sit on his couches, all with the same chin-length haircut and brown eyes. One of them is his mom, and, judging by the matching brown eyes staring at me, the two others must be his sisters. The toddler, Caleb, is no longer shirtless. He is laying on his stomach with another boy of about seven years old, loudly crashing trucks into each other. A girl, about ten years old, sits curled up in an armchair next to a roaring fireplace, a book in her lap. She doesn't bother to look up at me, but the rest of them do. It suddenly gets silent in the room, and I feel my cheeks starting to turn red.

"Jenny, this is everyone. Everyone, this is Jenny," he says, as if this is nearly enough information. I gape at him incredulously, and one of the sisters laughs, a sound unnervingly similar to Ben's.

"Always had a way with words, this one," the laughing sister says, then starts indicating people around the room. "I'm Ashley, Ben's older sister. This is Chloe, Ben's younger sister. Yes, our initials go A-B-C. Yes, Mom did it on purpose. You've already met Caleb. His brother's name is Brody. His sister, the bookworm over there, is Amelia. Yes, their initials also go A-B-C. Yes, I did it on purpose. And you've met Mom."

"Debbie," their mother chimes in.

"There will be a quiz later," Ben says sardonically.

"I've got it," I insist, and point at people around the room as I rattle off names. "Ashley, Ben, Chloe, Debbie. Amelia, Brody, Caleb." Then I point to myself. "Jenny." Everyone laughs as I continue. "The initials are very helpful. Sorry to interrupt your... meal?"

"You didn't interrupt anything. Ben is still cooking," Chloe says, shooing him toward what I assume is the kitchen. Ben rolls his eyes good naturedly, then turns to me.

"You can sit in here with these she-wolves." They all make offended sounds, but he continues louder to be heard over them, "Or you can come help me finish dinner."

"I do remember you saying you'd put me to work," I offer.

His eyes sparkle again, and he holds an arm out, indicating I should walk in front of him.

The women's conversation resumes as we enter the kitchen. I look around. There is a pot of boiling water on the stove, and various bowls and ingredients are strewn all over the counters. It looks like an absolute mess, but there's no mistaking what Ben is cooking: pasta and meatballs. I practically wiggle with joy.

Ben chuckles behind me. "I take it you're a fan of spaghetti," he ventures.

I nod enthusiastically. "It's my favorite form of carbohydrate."

He laughs a little harder.

"I have the best meatball recipe." There is giddy excitement in my voice as I turn to face him.

Ben looks skeptical but waves at the bowls nearest to the sink. "My mom's recipe is pretty damn awesome, but I haven't started yet. Feel free to give it a shot if you want, unless you need the recipe in front of you."

I shake my head. "This is going to sound morbid, but my grandmother made me memorize the recipe before she died. She said it was the only family heirloom worth passing down." I lift one shoulder. "You don't mind?"

"I'm glad for the help. You saw how useless everyone else is."

"We heard that," one of the women calls from the other room.

Ben rolls his eyes yet again, and I laugh. He makes his way back to the stove where there is a cutting board and some vegetables. He starts chopping, so I roll up the sleeves of my sweatshirt and move to the bowl of ground meat. I look around for the seasonings I need, plus some breadcrumbs and cheese, and get to work.

We cook silently for a while, him putting together a delicious-smelling sauce, and me rolling meatballs and getting them in the oven. As I'm washing raw meat juice off my hands, a glass of red wine appears at my side on the counter. I smile over my shoulder at Ben, and he smiles back.

The smells of the kitchen, the ease of our work together, and the warmth of the laughter and conversation coming from the next room work their way deep into my muscles, relaxing all the tension from the past few weeks. As I wait for the meatballs to finish cooking, I lean back against the counter, folding my arms and watching Ben work over the stove. The sleeves of his lightweight sweater are pushed up, showing just enough of his muscular forearms dusted with dirty blond hair. His apron is still covering the front of him, and it's splattered with red tomato juice. He is wearing jeans, and they aren't perfectly tailored to his body, but they highlight everything all the same. I find myself enjoying this view and this peek into his family life more than I probably should.

His mouth ticks up at the corner, though he keeps his eyes on the sauce he's stirring. "What?" he asks, and I take a sip of my wine for something to do.

"I didn't know you were such a chef," I joke.

He hums dubiously. "I'd hardly call chopping some vegetables and stirring a sauce chef-level cooking," he counters.

I shrug. "Still pretty impressive."

"It's better than hanging in there with all those meddling hens," he says, but there's a note of love in his voice that warms my heart.

"They're not so bad," I insist.

He laughs. "You ain't seen nothing yet, sweetheart."

The air leaves my lungs in a woosh, and I blink a few times, staring at him. His eyes widen slightly as if he just realized what he said. As if it slipped out on accident.

"You've called me that before," I say quietly. "That night at Tony's. When you carried me out of the bar." My cheeks heat at the memory.

His hand that is stirring the sauce stills, and he stares at the spoon as if it is going to jump out at him. His shoulders rise ever so slightly, and he swallows hard. "You remember that?"

"I remember you." The words are out of my mouth before I can think about the implication of them. His eyes fly to mine, wide with surprise. His eyebrows pinch together a little, and he takes a breath as if to say something.

As if on cue, his sisters enter the kitchen, Ashley complaining that the kids are hungry, and Chloe complaining that she's hungry. The oven timer goes off, and I force myself to recover quickly. I bump Ben out of the way with my hip to remove the meatballs, and he stumbles slightly but takes the hint and laughs as if we hadn't just shared some kind of moment right here in the kitchen with his family in the other room.

I put the meatballs on the counter next to the stove, and the women gratefully grab plates and start loading them up. They move to a large dining table in the next room, and Ashley comes back to make up smaller plates for the kids. Debbie shepherds the children into the dining room and gets them set up before coming to make a plate of her own. It all feels like a well-practiced event, where everyone knows their place but me.

Ben and I serve ourselves last, and he lingers in the kitchen, watching me make up my plate. I give him a questioning look, but he just smiles lightly.

We move to the dining table, sitting in the last two seats available, which happen to be nearest to all the kids. As soon as Ben sits down, Caleb comes over and crawls into his lap.

"Hey, buddy." Ben squeezes him and shifts him to sit more comfortably.

Ashley slides Caleb's plate nearer, and Ben gives the toddler a plastic fork. It's clear that this is a regular occurrence. Ben is as comfortable with the boy in his lap as he is without him, and it makes my heart squeeze a little to see this side of him.

Ben takes his own fork in his hand and uses it to slice a meatball. "I'll have everyone know that Jenny has challenged Mom's meatball recipe and insisted on making her grandmother's recipe tonight."

"Hey now," I protest. "I simply said her recipe is wonderful—which it is—and offered to help. It's not a competition."

"It's totally a competition," Chloe mutters, and Ashley laughs ominously. Debbie raises an eyebrow as she cuts a meatball into small pieces, then stabs one with a fork. She stares me down as she lifts it and slowly pops it into her mouth. She chews for a second, then a look of pure bliss passes over her features.

"Oh. Jenny. These are amazing," she almost moans.

I let out a breath I wasn't aware I was holding. Chloe and Ashley both take their own bites and hum their approval, too. Ben looks at me, impressed.

A little of the tension broken, we all dive into our meals. The kids make an absolute mess of their faces, and the adults take turns surreptitiously wiping spots off the table and their little hands. Caleb eats his whole meal sitting on Ben's lap, and Ben eats around him as if he doesn't notice there's a toddler sitting on his leg. Every once in a while, he bounces him on his leg or tickles his side, and Caleb lets out a squeal of laughter. Ashley narrows a glance at the two of them every time, but she doesn't say anything.

The conversation is light and easy. The women ask semi-interested questions about teaching, though it seems they've heard it all from Ben. At one point, I turn to Amelia and ask her what she had been reading.

"A book about Harriet Tubman," she responds, smiling at having been finally directly addressed at the table.

"Do you prefer nonfiction?" I ask, and when she scrunches up her nose, I realize that's probably a question phrased for a high school student, not a ten-year-old. "True stories," I explain, and she nods.

"Yeah. The fake stuff isn't interesting to me," she answers.

"Just like your uncle," I say, and he doesn't look at me, but he smiles softly.

"He's the one who gave me the book," she responds proudly, and Ben's smile deepens. "He always gives me the best books."

A grin spreads slowly across my face. "That's really nice of him," I say, and she nods again. I catch Ashley watching us out of the corner of my eye, and her expression is gentle. I turn back to Amelia, and Ashley catches Ben's eye. It's clear they think I don't notice as a silent sibling conversation happens between the two of them. Ben ends up shaking his head slightly and averting his eyes.

The rest of the meal passes in much the same way, but I'm left with a feeling of warmth I haven't felt in a long time. Eventually, Caleb turns to face Ben and wraps his chubby little arms around his neck, burying his face in Ben's shoulder. Ashley takes that as her cue, scooping him up in her arms and gathering the other children, pushing them gently toward the door. Chloe helps get the kids' shoes on and gathers all their belongings, trailing Ashley outside. Debbie makes a half-hearted offer to help clean up, and Ben refuses, kissing her on the forehead and giving her a one-armed squeeze. This is a choreographed and well-practiced scene, and I'm just a voyeur.

For some reason, I linger after his family has left. Ben closes the door and faces me, his eyes moving over me, leaving a trail of warmth in their wake.

"Thanks for dinner," I say quietly, breaking the silence.

He clears his throat. "Thanks for staying."

"Your family is great. I'm glad I met them."

"They loved you," he says, and then looks immediately like he regrets saying it.

I laugh, maybe a little too loudly. "How could you tell?"

"For starters, my mom has never made that face at a meatball before. It was a little scandalous, if I'm being honest." He grimaces uncomfortably, and I giggle. One side of his mouth ticks up. "Amelia actually talked to you. She never does that."

I scoff, but he takes a step toward me, his gaze heating. I'm used to being the object of men's attraction, so I'm not usually one to feel the pressure of a look like this, but there's something about Ben studying my face that has me fighting not to squirm.

"Hmm." I look around his dining room, trying to change the subject. "Do you need help cleaning up?"

"No." His voice is a little hoarse. "But I can offer you more wine and dessert for your service if you stay."

"Dessert? Say no more." I immediately start to collect plates from the table. He laughs and joins me.

I make several trips from the dining room to the kitchen, rinsing dishes and loading the dishwasher, while he takes care of the pots and pans left on the stove. When we are done, as promised, he presents me with another glass of wine and pulls the tinfoil off a plate of brownies. He sets them on his smaller kitchen table, and we sit. I take a bite and close my eyes at the decadent softness of the chocolate. They are easily the best brownies I've ever had.

"Where were these hiding, and why didn't we eat them after dinner?" I moan.

Ben makes a little strangled noise he tries to turn into a laugh. "My mom brings them to every family dinner, but Chloe is too busy counting calories and Ashley doesn't like the kids to have chocolate too close to bed, so I end up eating them myself when everyone is gone." He pops a whole brownie into his mouth, then smiles, crumbs sticking to his chin. I find myself resisting the urge to wipe them away.

"How often do you do these dinners?" I ask, sipping my wine and taking another brownie off the plate.

"Every few weeks or so. Ashley works long hours as a lawyer, so she likes to bring the kiddos over every so often to give her husband a break."

"It's nice that you have your family close by and you do stuff like this," I say, and he nods. "I really am sorry I barged in."

"You didn't barge in. My mom physically dragged you in. And I'm not sorry. It was nice having you here." He blushes a little at the admission, and I hide my smile in my glass of wine. I take another sip and set it on the table, looking at him. He studies me intently, then brings his hand to my cheek. My breath catches. He blinks a few times but doesn't immediately move his hand.

"You had a crumb there," he says by way of explanation. His hand hasn't moved, and it is warm against my face.

"Did you get it?" I ask, half amused, half turned on.

"I did." His eyebrow ticks up ever so slightly. "Sweetheart," he adds.

He says it like he's teasing or maybe even challenging, but I know he's also trying to recapture the moment from earlier. It's a question he's asking, and it becomes all the more obvious when his brown eyes dip to my lips. His eyes meet mine again, and he holds my gaze. Then, he looks as if he's made up his mind about something, and he leans into me, his fingers sliding to the back of my neck and curling against it. My eyes flutter at the touch, and his lips meet mine.

It's a soft kiss, but not tentative. It's tender and gentle, and he tastes of chocolate. I sink into it, savoring the feel of him, but before I've had enough, he pulls away from me, his eyes searching mine.

"Okay?" he asks, and my heart skips at the thought of him checking in on me.

"Yeah," I assure him, a bit breathless.

He smiles and drops his hand from my face. I feel a chill against my skin where his hand was. He pops another whole brownie into his mouth, and I giggle.

"Good." His voice is muffled by the brownie. He makes no move to kiss me again, though the gleam in his eyes suggests his hope is that this was the first of many to come.

I also take another brownie and stand. I'm feeling a little giddy, and I want to get out of here before I do or say something we can't recover from. "I should probably get going," I suggest. He stands, too, and our bodies are closer together than I had anticipated. I swallow audibly, and he backs away slightly.

"You coming back tomorrow?" he asks. He quickly adds, "To work?"

"If you want me to," I reply.

He nods. "I do."

"Okay. See you tomorrow."

"Yeah. See you tomorrow."

He walks me to the door, and after I get into my car, he waits for me to back away, his broad shoulders illuminated by the warm light from his entryway. He's still standing in the doorway, watching my car, when I turn the corner at the end of his street.

I make it back to my apartment in a daze, and I pull out my phone to text Mac before I even get out of the car.

*I had the day wrong. I was supposed to go to Ben's tomorrow,* I send.

*You're figuring that out four hours later?* she sends back.

*I stayed for dinner. With his whole family. Then dessert.* I run my tongue over my bottom lip, tasting a lingering flavor of chocolate.

*What kind of dessert?*

I only send back a winking face, and I can almost hear her laughing across the distance between us.

# Chapter 15
## Five Years Ago

I'M STARING OUT THE window of Mac's hospital room. The dawn sunlight is streaming in as the sun rises over the neighboring buildings, almost blinding me. Why is it always sunny on the saddest days? It feels like cruel irony. Is that irony, or just something unfortunate? I'm an English teacher; I should know the answer. Right now, I truly don't care.

I've been chewing on my lip so much that I'm starting to taste the iron tang of blood, but the pain feels like something, and right now I'll take something over nothing.

I blink, the sun's negative image on my retina blocking out my vision momentarily. I squeeze my eyes closed, pressing my fingertips into them, trying to massage the dryness from the hospital air out and studying the searing blackness of the sun in my vision. I take a deep breath for what feels like the thousandth time tonight, and my lungs feel like over-stretched muscles after a long workout.

Yesterday, Ellie was here. Now, she's dead.

I haven't cried yet. I'm usually pretty emotionally available, so it feels weird to have not cried, almost like wearing a too-tight, too-itchy turtle-neck sweater for a long day of teaching: an itch right under the high neck that can't be scratched, and red skin from scratching at it anyway.

Mac is still here. She's alive, though I'm sure she'll wish she wasn't as soon as she wakes up. They had to do surgery on her left arm because of a complicated break. She got out a little while ago, and I've been waiting for her the whole time. Her sleep isn't a natural one, but I'm still jealous of the peace she has for now. She knew Ellie was gone before they took her into the operating room. We all knew. She was killed on impact.

I've been sitting in this straight-backed chair all night, my feet propped on the edge of her bed. I haven't slept for even one second. At some point, a nurse told me to go home and get some rest, that they would call her next of kin for me to let them know when they could come get her. I shook my head and told her I'm it. I'm her next of kin now. Her parents are expats in Scotland. Her sister is dead. I'm all she has left nearby, and besides, someone would literally have to drag me from this room kicking and screaming, anyway. I'd hold my arms out and grab the doorframe like some kind of cartoon. My best friend is going to go through the hardest thing she's ever had to endure in her life, and it starts the minute she wakes up. I'm not going anywhere.

I open my eyes and move my feet to the ground, resting my elbows on my thighs and dropping my chin to my chest. I take another deep breath, but I can't get enough oxygen to make my brain feel less foggy. I close my eyes again but am immediately greeted with the sight of Ellie's little orange car, smashed to pieces in the middle of an intersection. My breath speeds up, and I quickly open my eyes again. For a second, I think I'll finally start crying, but the tears don't come.

That little orange, two-door car. So tiny. So impractical. So ugly. The butt of so many jokes. There's nothing left of it anymore, and no one to claim it even if there was.

*"It's so…" Mac trails off and frowns.*

*"Cute?" Ellie asks, nodding encouragingly.*

*Mac's frown deepens, and she shakes her head. "Orange." She says it with awe, as if she's never seen a car this brightly colored before. To be honest, I don't think I have either.*

*"It's a bold choice, El," I say, raising an eyebrow.*

*"I got it to match Mac's hair," she deadpans.*

*"How very Holden Caulfield of you," Mac retorts flatly. Ellie reaches over and ruffles Mac's hair like she used to do when we were kids. Mac swats her arm away, giggling.*

*"I don't know who that is," Ellie says, "but if he bought an orange car to match his sister's hair, then sure."*

*"Red hat. Brother's hair. Seriously, did you read* anything *in high school?" Mac gapes at her, and she shrugs.*

I laugh quietly at the memory, and the pang of sadness that follows is almost physically painful. But I still don't cry.

The door opens quietly, and I don't look up, assuming it's another doctor or nurse coming to check Mac's vitals. The door closes equally quietly, and I don't shift my gaze from where it's fixed on a stain on the tile until I hear the person who entered clear their throat.

I slowly look up to see Ben standing by the door, a small bouquet of wildflowers in one arm and the other hand still on the doorknob. Our eyes meet across the small room, and there is sadness and a desire to protect us written plainly on his face. I see myself through his eyes–pale and rumpled, with dark circles under my brown-almost-black eyes, slumped painfully in an uncomfortable hospital chair next to my best friend's bed. I take in yet another deep breath. It's shaky, and that's when my face decides to crumple, and the tears start streaming unchecked down my cheeks.

Ben is at my side in less than a second. He's agile for such a big guy, which feels like a weird thing to notice while I lose my shit. He gently puts the flowers on the bedside table and kneels on the ground right next to my chair, wrapping his arm around me and pulling my face to his shoulder. I press my eyes into the fabric of his sweatshirt, sobs wracking my body. I'm trying to cry quietly so as not to wake Mac, but it isn't working very well.

As if sensing this, Ben rubs my back vigorously, like he's trying to wake up a limb that has fallen asleep. "Come on," he whispers. "Let's take a walk." I manage to pull it together enough to stand, wiping my nose with the back of my hand. It's gross, but I don't care. Ben doesn't seem to mind, either. It's not like this is the first time he's seen me lose it, I guess.

He opens the door to the hospital room and ushers me into the hallway. We walk in silence for a while through a winding maze of fluorescent-lit hallways. Every few seconds, I swipe a tear from my eyes, but I don't cry again. He leads us to a coffee cart, buys two cups of something that smells awful, and leads us to a couch in a sitting area. It's a small couch, and our knees touch as we sit down. Ordinarily, I'd be thrilled at the contact, but I barely notice it now. I curl my hands around the warm cup, but don't drink. I'm just grateful for the warmth.

Ben doesn't say anything. He's a man of few words usually, so this isn't surprising, but I think he might be waiting for me to start. The coffee cup is starting to burn my hands, so I put it down on a small table next to the couch and say the only thing that comes to my mind.

"I was supposed to be in that car." My voice is hoarse, and tears start falling again. It feels like an admission of guilt. I wasn't there. I was supposed to be there, but I wasn't. I was following behind them, but I had to stop for gas. I didn't see the accident happen. I saw it when I came to the intersection. The crumpled orange car. Mac's red hair, shocking against the windshield. Ellie's blond hair, almost the same color as her sister's from all the blood.

"You couldn't have done anything had you been there," Ben assures me quietly.

"We surely would have been later. I'm always late. One minute and that other car would have missed them. Or maybe my added weight in that tiny car would have changed the impact."

"That's not how physics works," he interrupts gently, but I wave away his logic with my hand. I look at him, and he's wearing that same protective expression. He looks as if he would throw his own body in front of that car if it would save me from this, and my bottom lip trembles.

"I wasn't there because I was going to leave dinner early. I was going to meet you," I whisper. He had finally asked me on a date again last week, and I was going to meet him at a different restaurant after having appetizers with Mac and Ellie. I hadn't told anyone, not even them. They both adore Ben, and all of us working together makes it complicated. I hadn't wanted to get their hopes up or make work awkward in case it didn't go well. Now, I'll probably never say anything about it. Mac won't have the capacity to care about my stupid love life for a long time. I'll never have the chance to tell Ellie.

His expression turns pained, and I think that is the moment we both realize there won't be another chance at a date. Not any time soon, anyway. There is too much to deal with now—too much baggage that needs to be cleared away. The awareness rocks me. It feels almost as awful as the doctor telling me Ellie was dead, which doesn't make sense. Not going on a date isn't nearly as bad as your friend dying. It must be one of those things where even minor inconveniences feel insurmountable after a tragedy.

He schools his face into concern, as if the same thing has just occurred to him, and he puts his arm around my shoulders, letting me lean on him.

"She doesn't have anyone else," I whisper.

He squeezes me reassuringly. "She has you." The vibration of his deep voice through my cheek is oddly comforting. "She has me. She has the whole school. Ken is already putting together sub coverage and having the entire department chip in with emergency lesson plans for as long as she needs. She can take care of everything. You can have time off to help her, too. It'll be okay." He says the last part uselessly, like he isn't sure he believes it, but I'm grateful to him for trying.

I wrap my arms around his torso, pulling myself closer to him and leaning into the reassurance—both physical and emotional—he's offering. I close my eyes and sink into him as he holds me.

I don't know how long I sleep, but when I wake up, Ben is still holding me on this tiny, uncomfortable couch, and he's still gripping a paper cup of foul-smelling coffee in his hand, resting it on his knee. For a second, I'm disoriented, but it doesn't take me long to realize where we are. Hospital waiting room. Bad coffee. Ben's visiting. Mac's out of surgery. Ellie's gone.

I wonder if there will ever be a time when the pain of it won't hit me like a ton of bricks.

I push off Ben, scrubbing at my eyes. My cheeks feel raw from the tears that dried there. He tries to stretch surreptitiously, but I can tell he must have been uncomfortable with me asleep on top of him.

"How long was I out?" I ask.

"Not long. Half-hour, maybe." He checks his watch. I try to give him a little smile, but my face doesn't seem to be working.

"Sorry," I offer instead.

"You needed it," he insists. We sit for a moment in silence.

"I should probably get back."

"Do you want me to stay?" I can't tell if the hope in his voice is hope that I'll say yes or that I'll let him off the hook. I shake my head. There will be too many questions later if he is here when Mac wakes up.

"It's okay," I say. "I don't know if Mac wants to see anyone yet."

He nods, standing and grabbing both of our coffee cups. He chucks them into the garbage. "I guess I'll see you... soon."

"Yeah. Thanks, Ben." I awkwardly half-smile again and wave as I turn to walk back to Mac's room. I try to remember the maze we walked through to get to the sitting area, but I can't. I end up having to stop and ask for directions. A very nice nurse leads me back, and when I open the door, Mac is still in bed but with the back propped so she's sitting up, staring blankly out the window like I was doing an hour or so ago, her head resting against the pillow and her heavily bandaged left arm laying on the blanket over her lap. She looks for all the world like she doesn't have the will or the energy to lift her head. She doesn't even look at me as I come in.

The only thing I can think of is that she woke up, and I wasn't here. My first duty as her closest remaining person, and I failed because I was cuddling with Ben on a hospital couch. As if I was the one who needed comforting. I loved Ellie, but she wasn't my sister. I should have been here for Mac when she woke up, and I wasn't. In a dark corner of my brain, I know it's not Ben's fault, but logic and reasoning aren't winning out today. I'm mad at myself for not being here, and I'm mad at Ben for his presence. I wonder if I'll ever not be mad at everything ever again.

But this isn't about me. I try not to let any of my anger or guilt show through as I move back to the chair next to her bed. She slides her eyes to me without moving her head, and it's a little creepy to see my normally vibrant best friend as this shell of a human in a hospital bed.

"Hey," I say quietly, taking her uninjured right hand in mine. She blinks rapidly a few times, as if she just realizes I'm there. She doesn't say anything, and her expression doesn't change. She doesn't pull her hand away either, so I leave mine resting on top of it. Her eyes slide back to the window.

"She's gone," she croaks, her voice not quite steady after her surgery. I feel hot tears in the corners of my eyes, and I will them not to fall.

"I know. I'm so sorry."

"I miss her," she says shakily, still not looking at me.

That's the last thing she says for twenty-four full hours. The doctor comes in and discharges her. We drive home. I set her up on the couch in our condo. I ask if she wants the television. A book. A glass of wine. A bottle of wine. Ten bottles of wine. She just stares out of the window as if I'm not even there.

Eventually, she falls asleep on the couch, and I decide that if she's still comatose tomorrow, I'll start calling funeral homes and arranging things. I called their parents while Mac was in surgery to tell them, so arranging a funeral can't be worse than that. That's what I tell myself, anyway, as I make my way to my bedroom, leaving the door open. I sleep lightly, waking up often and checking on Mac, who sleeps the whole night on the couch.

In the morning, I wake to the smell of pancakes and the sound of Mac's voice coming from the kitchen. I lay still and listen to her conversation. It's clear she's on the phone with a funeral home, so I wait for her to finish her phone call, giving her the illusion of privacy. When she hangs up, I wait a few extra minutes and then make my way to the kitchen. There's a huge stack of pancakes on a plate next to a vase that's holding the flowers Ben brought to the hospital, and Mac is facing the stove making more. I eye the tower of pancakes warily, and I'm fairly certain even five adult humans couldn't finish all of these. I'm not at all sure how she's done all this with only one functioning arm. I sit on one of the bar stools facing into the kitchen and start loading up my plate.

"The funeral will be in a week. That should give my parents enough time to get here." Mac doesn't turn away from the stove, but her voice is confident and sure.

"Okay." I pour syrup on my pancakes.

"They've recommended cremation because... well, she doesn't look good. But we'll bury her ashes. I think having them here would be... weird."

"Okay," I repeat. She flips the pancakes with a spatula in her right hand.

"I'm not going to work this week," she says quieter, as if she feels guilty for not going into school.

"I think that's a good decision." I want to be what she needs, and it feels like she needs me to validate some of her decisions right now, which I'm happy to do. She nods, still not looking at me.

"Can we have cheeseburgers for dinner?" she asks weakly, tilting her head up from the stove and taking a deep, shaky breath. I can only see her back, but I can tell she's doing whatever she can to remain upright under the crushing weight of her grief. I slide off the barstool and come around to the stove, looping my arms around her waist from behind and resting my chin on her shoulder. She leans back slightly, as if I'm literally supporting her.

"We can have whatever you want for dinner," I say, and she nods, sniffling. Suddenly, she throws the spatula against the counter and turns, grabbing me with her good arm and hugging me tight. This can't be comfortable for her with her bandaged arm smooshed between us, but if this is what she needs, I'm here for it. Her body shakes with sobs as she buries her head in my shirt. I gently rub her back, waiting for the sobs to subside.

As she's crying, I start to smell burning from the stove. I look down, and there is smoke coming from the pancakes in the pan. Mac doesn't seem to notice and doesn't want to let go, so I try to shimmy a little so I can reach the burner. I can't quite get it.

"Uh," I start, cautiously. She continues to sniffle into my shirt. "Hey, Mac? The pancakes."

She looks up at me, confused. "Huh?"

"The pancakes are burning." I finally gain enough range of motion to reach over and flip the burner off. I grab a potholder that's resting on the counter and push the pan off the heat.

"Shit," she says, then buries her head in her hands and starts sobbing again.

"It's okay, Mac. Seriously, it's fine."

"That was breakfast," she wails.

"There are *plenty* of pancakes. Plenty. You could feed a family of twelve with this stack." She goes back to the batter to start stirring, and I grab her good wrist, pulling her to the stools. "Will you sit down, please?" I set her down on the stool, load up a plate with pancakes, drench them in syrup, and hand her the plate and a fork. I dump the burned pancakes in the trash, rinse out the batter bowl, and sit next to her.

She pokes at her pancakes without eating them, but I make a big show of eating all mine and grabbing more.

"Can we talk about something... normal?" she asks meekly.

"Sure," I say, but then we both grasp for a topic. Turns out, it's kind of hard to talk about normal stuff when your best friend's sister has just died.

"Those flowers are pretty." She indicates the bouquet from Ben.

"Ben brought those to the hospital for you while you were sleeping."

"Hmm," she hums noncommittally. "I don't think he brought those for me." She looks sidelong at me, a smirk playing at her lips, but falling just as quickly as it appeared.

It occurs to me that she might be right, and those flowers may have been originally for our date. The regret hits me hard before I can shove the thought out of my mind. It doesn't matter anymore. Everything that matters to me for the foreseeable future is sitting on the barstool next to me. I loop my arm over her shoulders, and we lean the sides of our foreheads together.

"I know I'm not your actual sister," I start, and she huffs a wet laugh. "But you're the closest thing I've ever had to one. I'm here for you, okay? Whatever you need. We'll get through this. I promise."

Tears are falling unchecked down her cheeks now, so I hold her close until the food is cold, breathing in the faint scent of burnt pancakes and wildflowers.

# Chapter 16
## Present Day

WHAT DO YOU EVEN wear to the house of a man who kissed you last night, but with whom you have to work today?

Apparently, that's the million-dollar question as I stand in front of my closet in my lavender cotton underwear and bra, pulling out and putting back every single option I see. I pull on a light sweater and grab my favorite jeans, but then think better of it and swipe my phone open to check the weather. As I suspected, it's unseasonably warm and humid unlike yesterday, when it was cold enough for this outfit. I pull the sweater off and toss it in a corner with a frustrated little noise as my phone rings. I answer without looking at it with a gruff hello.

"Wake up on the wrong side of the bed today?" Mac's amused voice comes from the other end of the line.

"Today is the day I'm *supposed* to go to Ben's to work," I grumble. "I'm headed back over there in a half-hour."

"Jenny Green." Mac sounds positively giddy. "Don't tell me you're worried about what to wear."

"It's not my fault climate change has ruined temperate Midwest autumns from now until the end of time," I whine.

She laughs, but I think it's more at my discomfort than my dark humor. "You've known Ben for, like, nine years. He's probably seen your entire wardrobe at some point. Put something on and don't think twice about it."

She's right, of course, but this feels different somehow. Maybe because he had his tongue in my mouth last night. And maybe because I really liked it. I sigh heavily, pinching the bridge of my nose and sitting on the edge of my bed.

"Did you need something, Mackenzie?"

"I wanted to hear all about you and Ben, obviously. Is he as good at tongue wrestling as he is at actual wrestling?" She's trying very hard not to laugh at her own joke, and I hear Daniel groan dramatically in the background. Great. They're both laughing at my expense. Excellent.

"Rude," I mutter.

"Payback," she says sweetly. She's got a point; I used to tease her about Daniel all the time. I just never thought it would come back to bite me.

"Unless you are planning to be helpful, I need to go get dressed in... something." I glower at my closet. "I'll call you later, okay?"

"Oh, come on," she whimpers. "You can't send me some cryptic message about dessert last night and then not give me every delicious detail." Daniel makes a gagging noise before his muffled voice announces he's moving to another room. I consider giving Mac the details she craves, but this feels different from my other escapades.

"I can tell you it was, indeed, delicious, but I'm not saying more than that until I get a chance to talk to him. Which is fair"—I raise my voice slightly to drown out her protests—"considering you'd feel the same way about coworkers knowing *your* business."

"Ugh. Why do you have to be so reasonable?" she grouses.

I laugh. "It's one of my better qualities."

"Debatable. Fine, I'll put a pin in this for later, but don't, for one second, think I'm letting this go completely."

"I wouldn't dream of it. Now if you'll excuse me, I need to leave in—" I check my bedside clock. "Shit. I have to go."

We say quick goodbyes and hang up, and I hurriedly pull on the nearest casual dress I see—a light blue t-shirt dress with daisies on it—and my sandals. A dress feels easier than trying to decide on pants and a shirt, and it's humid anyway, so it feels like a good, safe choice. I run a hand through my hair in the mirror, deciding it's good enough, and grab my work bag and keys before heading out the door. This is either going to be awkward or sexy as hell, and I'm a little nervous to find out which.

For the second time in as many days, I find myself rushing to Ben's house and pulling in his driveway late, though this time there aren't any other cars escaping my notice. I park in his driveway again and grab my bag, speed-walking to the front door, which opens exactly as I'm about to ring the doorbell. I jump about a foot, white-knuckling the handle of my bag in the process. I must be wound tighter than I thought because it's just Ben on the other side of the threshold, frowning at me. He scrubs a hand back and forth through his hair.

"You're late," he says by way of explanation.

"So, you thought you'd pounce on me the minute I got here?" I respond, breathless, and realize too late this may not have been the best choice of words.

He stares at me for a second, blinking, his expression now completely blank. "I wasn't sure you'd come."

"Why wouldn't I?" My eyebrows pinch together. He continues to stare at me blankly, opening his mouth once and then closing it again as if deciding against whatever he was going to say. Instead, he moves aside to let me into his house. I walk past him, but unlike yesterday, he's pushing himself flat against the wall to make sure I don't brush against him. He'd rather push himself against the wall than touch me. It seems we're going for awkward, then.

He closes the door behind me, and I turn, waiting for direction. He clears his throat as if finally gathering himself, and says, "I thought we could set up at the kitchen table."

The kitchen table. The same kitchen table where he kissed me last night. Right. I purse my lips, determined not to make this weirder than it already is, and walk purposefully into the kitchen, sitting at the table and removing my laptop from my bag. Ben sits at the seat next to me, pulling his laptop to him on the table as I start punching keys to log in.

"I don't think we have much more to do. Ken has already gone through all the survey results and decided which requests were reasonable. We just need to get on the internet and quote some prices, add them to the spreadsheet, and then we should be done. I'll take the first half of the list and you can take the second, and then we can see where we are in the budget," I say without moving my gaze from the screen. When he doesn't respond, I look up at him to find his eyes drilling holes into me. I raise an eyebrow. "What?"

"Should we... I don't know. Should we talk about last night?"

I let out a slow breath and straighten in my chair, dropping my hands to my lap. I narrow my eyes at him and decide now isn't the time to start this. "I'm not usually one to do a post-mortem on a kiss," I say, "and besides, we should get this done."

He nods and turns his gaze to his computer screen, though I can tell he's trying to keep his face blank. I study him for a second, wondering if I made the right choice, and then ultimately decide that what's done is done and it's time to get to work. We search the internet in silence for a while, the only noise between us the occasional clicking of keyboards. Every once in a while, his typing goes silent, and his eyes shift to me. I try very hard to pretend like I don't know he's looking at me. Once, he takes a breath as if to say something, but when I ignore him, he lets it out and starts clicking on his keyboard again.

With all the awkward side-glances from him, it takes a little over an hour to complete my calculations, and I can see from his part of the shared spreadsheet that he's also done. I run a quick formula to add up the total price of all the books, and we are a little over.

"Shoot," I mumble, and Ben grunts. I press my lips into a thin line as I scroll through the spreadsheet, looking at where we can cut a few titles to get us under the budget. My eyes snag on Marty's request, and I snort a laugh.

"What?" Ben asks.

I look at him sidelong. "If we denied Marty's request, we'd break even."

He huffs and rolls his eyes. "You can't cut Marty out just because you don't like him."

"Why not? I don't see him here doing the work. The only thing he ever does is sit and complain."

"True," he says slowly, scrolling through the spreadsheet again, "but my request is almost the same as his. Cut mine instead."

"We will do no such thing," I insist. "You've spent time on this. You getting what you want is fair. If anyone else in the department wanted to make sure they got what they wanted, they could have volunteered to work the budget."

He shrugs, looking back at his computer. After a minute, he frowns. "Mac has a request on here."

"Yeah. She organized the fundraiser. She was in charge of the whole thing. She deserves something out of it, too."

"Didn't she get some books out of the deal with Daniel?" he asks, and I nod. Part of the deal when Daniel shadowed her for his book was that she got a set of new novels for her classroom. He purses his lips. "Feels a little redundant to give her more books."

"She didn't want them," I clarify. "I made her fill out the form because she wasn't going to. She said the same—that she already got books and it wasn't fair to give her more."

"So why don't we take her off the list? That would bring us just under budget."

"Because I know she was excited about the possibility of more books, and I don't want to break it to her that she can't have them a few weeks before her wedding."

Ben tilts his head, regarding me. His eyes flit back and forth between mine. "You're always so concerned about her," he says quietly.

"She doesn't have anyone else," I reply just as quietly, without thinking. Ben's face softens, his brown eyes becoming still. He takes a breath, then sets his big hand on top of mine where it lies on the table, his blunt fingers curving over my own. My eyes dip to where our hands touch, then raise back to meet his.

"That's not true anymore, is it?" he asks tenderly, and I blink rapidly. My eyes fall again to our hands on the table as I slowly shake my head.

"No," I choke out, and I'm not sure if it's the acknowledgement that Mac and my relationship will change after her wedding—and has already been changing—or the warm feeling of his hand on mine that is making my heart race and my voice crack. I clear my throat and try again. "No, I guess not."

"You're never going to be less important to her, you know," he says reassuringly. I swallow audibly and nod. He squeezes my hand. "It'll be different, but different doesn't have to be bad."

Ben has comforted me before. Often. But he's never touched me like this, and I am suddenly very aware that we crossed some kind of threshold yesterday. I suddenly have a feeling akin to standing at the edge of one of those beautiful cliffs above a clear pool of water, ready to jump. Based on Ben's quickening breath, he feels it too.

I'm silent for a moment, my eyes studying how our hands look on the table, his palm completely dwarfing mine, and his short, plain fingernails contrasting against my long, pastel painted ones. I take a deep breath. "What are we doing here, Ben?" My eyes finally meet his, and there's a flicker of emotion I can't identify in them.

"I'm being a stellar friend is what I'm doing here," he says with forced lightness. I roll my eyes and bite my lip against a smile. His eyes dip to my mouth, and it looks like it takes a lot of effort for him to drag them back to meet my gaze. My breath catches at the desire written plainly on his face.

"If we pursue this, it's going to change everything." My voice is barely above a whisper.

"So?" he asks.

"What do you mean, 'so?' As you just pointed out, I'm dealing with a lot of change right now, *so,*" I emphasize the word, "forgive me if I'd like some constants in my life."

"Constant what, Jenny? Constant classroom neighbor? Constant person you call when you need to fill out a double date? Constant person to complain about your classes to?" He is getting louder and more animated, but his hand never leaves mine.

"Constant friend," I say, still quiet. "We've been friends since we started teaching."

He shakes his head slowly, as if he can't believe I haven't figured it out yet. "I've been waiting for you since we started teaching, Jenny. Maybe not constantly, but consistently. I always find myself coming back to you." His eyes drop to our hands, still joined on the table. "It's always been you." His voice is quiet now, too, and my mouth goes dry. He slips from his seat to kneel in front of me on the linoleum kitchen floor. He's about a head shorter than me in this position, and when he tilts his face up to look at me, I'm struck by the raw earnestness and vulnerability there.

"What if it doesn't work?" I ask. "What if we end up hating each other?"

He huffs. "You've hated me before. You got over it."

I scoff. "I didn't get over it. You apologized."

"I'll apologize again," he insists.

"What if it's my fault? I don't exactly have the best track record with men."

"I'll apologize anyway." He smiles, and his whole face changes, the skin at the corners of his mouth and eyes crinkling in the way of someone who smiles easily and often. He leans closer to me so our faces are only inches apart. I can feel his breath on me, sweet and inviting. He rests a hand on my knee, and I'm flooded with warmth. I'm not entirely sure I'm still breathing. "I'm not going to lie and pretend there aren't any risks here, but I can't lie and pretend I haven't wanted you since I met you anymore, either, and now that I've kissed you once, I don't want to go back to a world where I'm not kissing you all the time. Take a chance on me, sweetheart." It's somewhere between a plea and a demand, and I barely hold back a moan. My eyes find his lips, gently parted and waiting. I meet his eyes again and swallow against the dryness in my mouth. I fight against a smile, and his deepens.

I put one hand on either side of his face, and I feel him loose an exhale, like he had been holding his breath, too, and then I'm not sure who moves first, but our lips meet, and I melt into him. He leaves his hand on my knee and brings his other hand to my lower back, spreading it wide, covering most of it and pulling me closer. I shift so my knees are wide, and he presses closer still, his head tipped up to meet mine, allowing me to control the kiss. It feels right in a way not much has these past few weeks, and I want more. I move one hand to his neck and one to his chest, and he groans his approval. I press myself closer to him, seeking his warmth to match the heat pooling in my core. The fingers on the hand he is pressing into my knee curl as if he is holding himself back. I don't want him to hold back anymore; he's been restraining himself for too long where I'm concerned, so I tease my tongue between his lips and spread my legs a little wider. Then, the kiss turns urgent, as if he has been starving and my mouth is a feast finally laid out before him.

His hand moves up my leg, stopping at the hem of my dress. He draws it up an inch, and I gasp at the feeling of his hand on my inner thigh. He draws back slightly, his eyes searching mine—a silent question. I pull his lips back to mine in what I hope is a silent answer. He kisses me passionately as his hand continues its path up my thigh. The gentleness of his hand touching my leg is completely incongruous with his lips bruising my own, and it's so incredibly hot that I find myself shifting on the chair to press my center against him. He smiles against my lips as his hand answers my plea, pressing over my underwear with just enough pressure to cause me to tip my head back and moan.

"So wet," he comments mostly to himself as he kisses my neck. His hand starts a slow, torturous motion between my legs, and my hips start to move in time with his touch. I try to catch my breath, but I can't.

"Mmm hmm," I hum, chasing the friction of his palm. He moves slightly, pulling my underwear to the side and exposing me to the cool air. He places small, hot kisses along my neck and collarbone, then presses his forehead into the space at the base of my neck, breathing in.

"In my mind, I've had you on every surface of this kitchen," he mumbles into my chest, and I groan. His fingers find that most sensitive spot and start moving in lazy circles as the pressure starts to build in my core. His lips capture mine again briefly before he pulls away. "I'm going to take you out to dinner before I fuck you properly," he says, and my mind is a scrambled mess at his words and the feel of his fingers on me underneath my dress. "But until then..." he trails off as his fingers slide down to find my entrance.

"Oh, Ben," I breathe. "Yes. Please, yes."

He chuckles darkly, and I feel the vibration of it move through me. He threads one finger inside me, then another. I sigh as he curls his fingers slightly, finding a spot that makes me moan and press my chest closer to his, my hips moving in time with his hand. He uses his thumb to circle a little higher, and I'm lost to the sensation.

"You're beautiful, Jenny," he whispers. "Fucking perfect." He presses a little harder. "That's it. Use my hand, sweetheart. I want to feel you come on my fingers."

He swipes his thumb in one more circle, and I come completely undone. He wraps his other arm around my back, pulling me toward him, and he holds me as I shudder through my release.

My breath is coming in gasps, and I feel weak enough that I have to rest my forehead against his shoulder to steady myself. He slowly removes his hand, gently readjusting my underwear so it covers me again. The motion is so sweet that I melt a little farther into him, closing my eyes and breathing in the musky scent of his aftershave.

When my breathing evens out, I start to move the hand still resting on his chest down toward his belt. He catches it before I can reach for his buckle, bringing it to his lips and kissing my knuckles. I lift my head to look at him. His eyes are hooded, and the desire is still written plainly on his face, but he shakes his head slightly.

"The first time you make me come, I want to be inside you." He smirks. "And I already told you I'm taking you out on a real date before that happens."

Whatever is left of my resolve crumples. It's not that men haven't ever used this type of language with me before but hearing it from Ben is another level entirely. I'm captivated and completely turned on.

"It sounds like you've thought a lot about this," I tease.

His face becomes serious. "I've had nine years to think about this," he says without an ounce of humor.

Nine years. The revelation should feel stifling considering I haven't been with anyone with any real consistency since Kyle and I broke up ages ago, but instead, it feels like a warm blanket. Curled up. Cozy. Comfortable.

"Okay," I say slowly. "So, what now?"

"Now," he smiles in return, "you stay. We order takeout. We watch a movie and eat on the couch, and it's easy, like two old friends becoming lovers should be."

"You are very confident." I look at him skeptically, and he huffs.

He stands, pulling me up with him, his hand still resting on my lower back. "Fake it till you make it." He winks at me, and I laugh brightly.

# Chapter 17
## Present Day

Easy.

It is easy. A little, nagging part of my brain is telling me it's too easy, but my body is still zinging from the release in the kitchen, and I tell myself the rest of my brain hasn't caught up yet.

He calls a local takeout place and orders me three steak tacos and an assortment of condiments. He doesn't even have to ask me what my order is because we've had tacos together before, and he knows my preference for red meat tacos over all others.

Easy.

He turns on some quiet music. Nothing either overly energetic or embarrassingly sexy—just a quiet soundtrack to our presence in his living room. When the food arrives, he spreads out the takeout containers on the coffee table and tosses me a paper towel napkin from the kitchen. I sit cross-legged on the floor. He sits with one knee bent up and his elbow resting on top of it. I take a huge bite of one of the tacos, juice dribbling down my chin and lettuce dropping out of the crunchy shell and onto the foil packaging. I lean over the packaging for it to catch the droplets of steak juice as they fall from my chin, putting my taco down and staring uselessly at my greasy fingers. Ben laughs, then wipes at my face with his napkin. I swat him away, giggling, then wipe myself off with my own napkin. He leans over and kisses me deeply, and it feels as if he has kissed me like this several times a day, every day since we met. When he pulls away from me, his nose sweeps back and forth over mine.

Easy.

The sun starts to set as we eat, and I know the alluring thing would be to leave and promise to call him in a few days, but I don't want to leave, and I'll see him tomorrow at school, anyway. So, when we've cleaned up dinner and he insists I stay for a movie and a brownie, I sit on the couch. He turns on a mindless comedy and sits next to me, slinging his arm over my shoulder, and we both laugh at how middle-school-date-night it feels. He tucks me in closer to him, and I fold my feet under me, my knees resting on his thighs and my head falling to his shoulder.

Easy.

It's so easy that, before long, I drift off to sleep. When Ben shifts, waking me, I silently curse my ability to fall asleep pretty much anywhere after a meal.

Ben chuckles deeply. "You don't have to worry about falling asleep with me."

I stretch out a bit, then snap my eyes to him. "I said that out loud, didn't I?"

He fights a smile, nodding. "I could watch you sleep every night, all night and never get tired of it, sweetheart." He pauses, then blushes a little. "That probably sounded creepy."

It doesn't, actually. It sounds... nice. I haven't spent a full night with a guy on purpose since Kyle, and I doubt he ever had the urge to watch me sleep. I'm nowhere near ready to spend the night here, but the fact that the thought of it doesn't instantly make me recoil is an interesting new development.

He hasn't asked me to spend the night, though, and even if he did, I'd say no, so I file that away for later. Instead, I tease. "Are you going to call me 'sweetheart' all the time now?"

He shrugs a shoulder, but his eyes are twinkling. "Unless you prefer 'neighbor?'"

I grimace. "Please, never call me 'neighbor' again." My expression softens. "I like 'sweetheart.' It's... charming." But then it occurs to me exactly what it means that we will be seeing each other at school tomorrow and how tricky this could get if one of us says the wrong thing. My eyes go wide, and my lips part as I breathe in sharply.

He smiles comfortingly, his brown eyes turning warm. "I won't bring this up at school." His deep voice is reassuring, and I feel instantly at ease.

He searches my eyes, then his gaze drops to my lips. He reaches a hand to cup my face, gently bringing me closer to him. I gladly close the distance between us, and our lips meet. At first, it's a slow and sensual kiss, like sinking into hot chocolate, but when his tongue teases at my lips and I open for him, it becomes more heated. My hands snake their way over his broad shoulders, meeting behind his neck, and his lightly graze my sides, coming behind me, one hand on my lower back and one snaking into my hair.

We break the kiss when we're both breathless, our bodies still pressed together and our foreheads touching. "Jenny." His voice is airy. "I can't get enough of you."

"Every time you touch me, it's like I can't think," I whisper.

His grip on my hair tightens ever so slightly, and he nips at my bottom lip. "Thinking is overrated."

I angle my head and press my lips to his again. Our tongues tease each other. "We have school tomorrow," I say against his mouth.

"There's that pesky thinking," he grumbles between kisses. He starts to press his lips in a hot line from just under my jaw to my collarbone, and I draw myself closer to him, draping a leg over his lap so I'm almost straddling him. He moans against my skin. "I am putty in your hands, Green. But you're right. We have to work tomorrow."

"I changed my mind. I don't care about school tomorrow." I lean in and lick his earlobe. He practically dissolves under me, and I'm prouder than I should be at the effect I have on this gym-hardened man.

"If you stay here tonight, I won't be able to keep my hands off you." His protest is half-hearted.

I bring a hand to his chest and kiss under his ear. "I like your hands on me. It's not like neither of us has done this on a school night before, right? We'll be fine tomorrow."

At that, he leans backward, slightly. His hands press on my shoulders, putting some distance between us. His eyes meet mine, and his expression is serious. "I meant what I said, Jenny. I'm taking you out on a real date before anything more happens between us." Then, he cracks a smile, and his tone shifts. "I'm not some guy you've picked up at Tony's."

He's clearly joking, but I frown. "Is that what you think? That if we go any further than this tonight, I'll leave tomorrow and never talk to you again?" I'm suddenly hurt that he could even joke about that being all I'm capable of, even though I haven't shown him any different over the past six years.

He shakes his head, incredulous. "No. Not at all." He leans in to plant a chaste kiss on my lips, but my brows are still furrowed when he pulls away. His eyes are widened slightly, and his eyebrows are raised in earnestness. "I've wanted this for so long, Jenny. I want to do it right. Please, let me do it right?"

I search his face for any sign of indictment or doubt, but all I find is sincerity. My face softens. "Yeah. Of course." I drag my leg off his lap and cross my feet underneath me, facing forward. I fix my gaze on a crumb of brownie on the coffee table in front of me. "This might take me a minute to get used to. I guess I have some skeletons in my closet. Or some baggage. Demons, maybe? Pick a metaphor." It was supposed to be a joke, but it falls flat.

Ben scoots a little closer, wrapping his arm around me and pressing me into his side. "We're thirty years old. We all do at this point." He squeezes me, then adds, teasing, "Sweetheart."

I roll my eyes and shake my head, but a smile stretches across my lips, and I bury my face in his chest to inhale his musky scent one last time before I drag myself off his couch and to his front door, gathering my laptop and my bag. I pull my shoes on, and he watches me, yawning a little.

I stand, shouldering my tote bag. "Um, tomorrow, then?" I ask, suddenly feeling very uncertain.

He closes the distance between us, holding my face between his two hands, and kissing me passionately. He pulls away, his hands still on my face, and smiles. "Tomorrow."

# Chapter 18

## Four Years Ago

I WAKE UP TO my alarm blaring from the nightstand next to me and the sunlight streaming through my window at the condo. I squint and shade my eyes against the bright light as I roll over and slam my alarm to turn it off. I must have forgotten to close the blinds last night.

Last night... last night, I had gone out with a guy from a dating app. Anton. He was the definition of tall, dark, and handsome, and he was classy, too. He took me out to a swanky Italian place where we ate the most delicious fettuccini I have ever had and drank very expensive red wine. He came back here and...

I bolt up in bed, looking around my bedroom. Anton is nowhere to be found, and I sag in relief. I slept harder than anticipated, maybe because I was in my own bed for once, and I must not have woken up when he left.

And then I realize with a bang that it's Thursday, and I have to work today. I groan loudly and drag myself out of bed and over to my closet. I lay out some clothes on the bed, then slip on my fluffy robe and tie it around my waist before making my way to the bathroom. I figure I'll grab a quick shower before work to scrub the lingering garlic-and-wine scent off.

When I open my bedroom door, though, I hear voices coming from the kitchen. One is unmistakably Mac's, but the other is a deeper, male voice. I take a second to pray to everything that is holy that Mac had someone here last night, too, even though I know she hardly ever goes anywhere on school nights. I uselessly shake out my hair and swipe at the makeup I know is streaked under my eyes, then make the little walk of shame to the kitchen where, sure enough, Anton is standing behind the counter in yesterday's clothes, and Mac is sitting on one of the stools in her hot pink pajama shorts and a sweatshirt.

"Hey." I draw the word out awkwardly. They both look at me, and Anton slides a mug of coffee in my direction. I take it and add cream and sugar, pretending Mac isn't drilling holes into my skull with her eyes.

"I was going to slip out this morning before you woke up, but your roommate was already in the kitchen and offered me some coffee," Anton explains, raising his mug as proof.

I turn to Mac and smile over-sweetly. "That was so nice of you."

She smiles back in what I can only imagine is a reflection of my face—a saccharine smile that doesn't quite meet her eyes. I sip my coffee, not breaking eye contact until Anton clears his throat.

"I'd better get going if I'm going to make it to work on time today," he interjects. I'm glad he can take a hint, but wish he could have taken it about three hours earlier. "I had a nice evening, Jen."

Mac's eyes widen slightly in surprise, but I don't give her a chance to speak. I direct my sweet smile to Anton. "Me too. Let's do it again sometime."

His smile is empty, as if he, too, knows I don't mean it. He comes around the counter and kisses me on the cheek before grabbing his jacket from the arm of the couch and letting himself out.

I take a long and fortifying draw of coffee before turning back to face Mac's wrath. Her eyes are still a little wide and her eyebrows are raised. "Jen?" she asks.

I make my way around the counter to the kitchen, pulling out two slices of bread and popping them in the toaster. "Of all the things that just happened, that's where you're going to start?"

"You hate it when people call you Jen. Or, at least, you used to." She says the last part with some bite, and it takes a lot of effort not to wince.

"I still do. That man was decent in bed, but he was not a great listener." I'm trying to keep the mood light, but I know she's not going to let my jokes placate her.

Sure enough, she scowls. "Speaking of listening, you two were very vocal last night."

At that, I do cringe. It's not that I care if Mac knows whether or not I enjoyed my evening, but that I do feel bad for keeping her up on a school night. How tired I am during my day is my choice, but she didn't have a choice, and that doesn't feel fair. "I'm sorry. It was pretty good sex, and I didn't realize you could hear us."

"Sounded better than pretty good." Mac raises an eyebrow at me.

I shrug. "I may have been playing it up a little."

"What happened to our feminist duty to unabashedly and unapologetically take pleasure where we can find it and never lie about what makes us feel good?"

I narrow my eyes at her and sigh through my nose as the toast pops up behind me. I grab it gingerly and put it on a plate. The peanut butter jar is sitting open on the counter with the knife still in it, so I grab that and smear some on. When I turn around with my plate and my mug, Mac is still eyeing me from her perch on the stool.

"I honestly don't have an answer for that. This whole dating scene has me feeling less and less feminist by the day," I finally respond. I take a huge bite of peanut butter toast and chew it slowly.

Mac sips her coffee and pushes an empty plate out of the way so she can lean her elbows on the counter. "So, stop dating for a while. Or, I don't know, date the same person more than once," she suggests. I huff and roll my eyes, but she continues. "I'm serious, Jenny. All you ever do is fling around. From the sound of things last night, that's both a literal and a figurative statement. Maybe try something different for a while."

I swallow my bite of toast and chase it with a sip of coffee. "I don't know. It's not like I sleep with all these men I have dates with. Just the hot ones. And I do believe a few one-night stands is better than the zero men you bring home lately."

She tilts her head, and I don't think the sad look on her face is from the lack of sex she's had in the past year. "Is it?" she asks. I don't respond, so she continues. "Look, I'm not saying you shouldn't have a man in your life, but what about giving a guy a second date? Or, here's a wild idea, dating someone consistently for a while."

"These dating app guys aren't really built for relationships." I scrunch up my nose at the idea of it.

"What if you tried someone you didn't meet on an app?"

"Like someone from a bar? I've been down that road, remember?"

"No." She draws the word out, looking at me as if the answer is obvious. "Someone like Ben?"

I scoff and shake my head. I never told Mac we were going to go out the night of the accident. I was so engrossed in dragging Mac through her grief—speaking of statements that are both literal and figurative—that it never seemed like a good time to bring it up, and once a few months had passed, it felt too late. He hasn't made a move since then, and I don't want to crawl back to him and beg for a third shot. I haven't lost enough of my feminism to the dating scene to toss out my dignity like that.

I study her over my coffee. Last fall was rough. I had to haul her against her will to school more times than I can count. When the other teachers weren't talking about how she should be fired for not showing up and being a shell of a person when she did, they were pressing her to recall the gory details of the accident for their own edification. Ken urged her to take a sick day on the day of a faculty meeting, saying that she wouldn't be missing much with a late start. She did, and he used the opportunity to lay down the law. He told everyone to leave her alone and to stop both what they were saying to her face and behind her back. She had suffered enough, he said, and we all deserve grace from time to time.

Since then, it seems she's been able to piece herself back together. Looking at her now, I notice the faint bags under her eyes and the weight she hasn't quite gained back yet, but I know her better than I know anyone else. A casual observer would think that she has it all together, or maybe, even, that it never fell apart.

She'd be fine without me here now, and the realization hits me, but not hard. Soft, like the pins and needles of the blood rushing back to your leg after it has fallen asleep from sitting on it for too long. It's not sorrow. It's relief.

The words come tumbling out of me before I can stop them. "I think the change I need is to move out."

Mac blinks a few times, then raises her eyebrows and leans back slightly on her stool, but she doesn't seem as surprised as I would have thought she'd be, which makes me think she might have been thinking about this, too. I don't want to take any chances, so I keep blabbering on.

"I'm incredibly grateful you let me move in here after I left Kyle. I needed a place to stay, but I needed you, too, you know? And then when everything happened—"

"You stayed for me," she cuts me off. Not totally ready to talk about it, then, but that's okay. She still seems fine. "I know, and I'm so glad you did. But maybe you're right. Two twenty-six-year-old women living together isn't exactly the dream dating profile."

"You are more important to me than a million dates," I say quietly.

She's on her feet in an instant, coming around the counter and pulling me into a hug. "You're the closest thing to a sister I've got left."

"You're the closest thing to a sister I've ever had."

She squeezes harder. "Dammit, I'm not going to cry," she insists, except we are both already sniffling into each other's shoulders. "This is good for us. You know, I always tell my students not to room with their best friends for too long. It'll ruin the friendship in one way or another."

I laugh wetly. Leave it to Mac to bring her students into it. I'm pretty sure her teacher brain never shuts off. She wipes at her eyes with her fingertips, and I hold her at arm's length. "I'll start looking for a place this weekend."

"There's no rush," she says, but it lacks conviction. We both know this is the right choice.

I let her go and reach for my coffee. "You want to help?"

"As if I'd let you look for an apartment by yourself." She scoffs as if it were obvious. Then she smiles slyly. "You should ask Ben to help move you in."

My eyes roll so hard I can almost see the back of my head. "Give it a rest, will you?" I swat at her arm, and she giggles.

"Never," she says, and from the way she smiles when she says it, I'm pretty sure she's not kidding.

# Chapter 19
## Present Day

I HAD BEEN WORRIED about things getting awkward between Ben and me at school, and it turns out I shouldn't have been worried about that. Is there a word that means awkward-times-one-thousand? Because *that's* what I should have been worried about.

When I get to school Monday morning, Ben isn't there yet. Considering I roll in about ten minutes before the bell rings to let the students in the building, that's saying something. By the time I open my door to let the students in, I still haven't heard anything from him. I expect that he'll be standing across the hall, smiling at me like always, but he's not. His room is still dark, and some of his students are waiting outside the door.

My mind doesn't immediately leap to the worst, but it's only a hop, skip, and a jump to get there. Hop: Maybe he has food poisoning? We ate essentially the same thing, though, so probably not. Skip: Maybe he overslept? I didn't get home until close to midnight, so it's possible he is exhausted, but I've never known him to miss school after staying up late. Jump: Maybe he completely regrets what happened between us, and he's trying to avoid me by calling in sick and not telling me about it? Something about the way he kissed me last night makes the logical part of my brain think that cannot be the case, but I still get a little panicky feeling in my gut at the thought.

With about two minutes to spare, he comes in, outpacing the students making their way to class. He brushes past me, breathless and with a quick wave. If he had been wearing a tie, it would have been trailing behind him comically, like those cartoons who are running to catch the train. He quickly unlocks his door and enters his classroom, the students trailing in behind him.

"Woah, Coach looks like he was late to the bus this morning," Josh says, coming up next to me.

"You can say that again." I'm still looking at Ben's door, amazed at how quickly he ran in here and hoping he'll come back out in the hallway, if only for a minute to say hi.

"Do you really want me to say it again, or..." Josh trails off.

I finally turn my attention to him. "No, Josh. It's a figure of speech. You've never heard that before?"

He shrugs and walks past me, opening Ben's door and walking inside. Noah walks past me then, surrounded by his friends. Javier follows, clearly trailing him and hoping to catch his attention but not able to bust past the group. They all enter Ben's class, and the reminder of that particular messy relationship dynamic isn't doing anything good for my anxiety about my current situation with their teacher.

The bell rings to start class, and a few straggling students rush to get through the doors on time. I'm left completely alone in the hallway, trying not to gape at Ben's door. How did he go from completely captivated last night to borderline ignoring me this morning? I suppose I can't do anything about it now, though. What am I supposed to do, burst into his classroom and demand he explain what's going on in his brain in front of his students? I don't think so.

I slowly face my classroom and step toward it, taking a second to collect myself. Just before I enter the room, Ben's door swings open, and his head pops out into the hallway.

"Jenny," he says, still a little breathless.

I look at him, startled. "Yeah?"

"Hi. Hey. Hi. Just... sorry. I overslept and wanted to say hi." He smiles his crinkly smile, and I exhale, a little relieved.

"Hi," I respond, even though this greeting has already been well established.

"Okay. Gotta teach. Talk later." His head pops back into his classroom, and the door closes behind him.

I'm left once again in the hallway, alone and off-balance. I shake myself a little, then take a deep breath and get ready to start my class.

By lunch, Ben and I still have only been briefly crossing paths. If I didn't know any better, I would think he has been avoiding me, but with a weird combination of prep hours and meetings, it's not uncommon for us to see very little of each other after the first bell. Still, we usually have at least one full conversation before noon, and I would think he would make time to see me after everything that happened last night.

Lunch is my first break of the day, and I finally get a chance to open some emails while I eat at my desk. Right at the top is a message from Ken asking when we plan to have the final count and price sheet for the novels we are buying with that fundraising money.

I give myself a little mental facepalm. Ben and I never actually decided what to do about the budget overage, and my face heats when I remember exactly why we never finished.

I pull open the spreadsheet and study it for a minute. We're about a hundred dollars over budget. It would be essentially one teacher's request we'd have to eliminate, but whose? It doesn't seem fair to get rid of anyone's—even Marty's, I admit to myself begrudgingly. But what if we eliminated one copy of each novel from each teacher's request? If all the other teachers are anything like me, they put a five-copy buffer in their requests to have a few extra, so one copy less wouldn't make much of a difference to anyone. I go through the sheet, editing the numbers, and we end up about twenty dollars over budget. We can work with that amount, I'm sure.

Before I email Ken back, I want to run this by Ben since we're working together on this, so I fire off an email detailing my plan. Maybe me contacting him is also what he needs to be reminded of my existence. I don't know what I expected today, but something would be better than nothing.

I eat a few spoonfuls of my yogurt while contemplating the nagging feeling of rejection I've been getting all day, but I don't get much of a chance to dwell on it because an email comes in from Ben. *That was fast,* I think with a little smile as I click to open the message.

*Sounds good.*

My face falls. That's it. *Sounds good.* Nothing more. Not even a cute smiley or some kind of innuendo or a "Hey, sorry I've missed you today. Will you be around after school?" Nothing.

I blow out a puff of air through pursed lips. I think I'd take him being barely able to keep his hands off me in the hallway over the thorough ghosting that's happening right now.

*You know what else sounds good? Your voice saying literally anything to me, but I haven't heard it today so, I dunno, stop by maybe?* My fingers hit the keyboard a little harder than normal as I type my response. My lips form a tight line as I reread the email, but I ultimately hit the little trash can icon at the top instead of the send button. Sass isn't going to do any good, and who knows how he'd react upon seeing an email like that while teaching. It would throw me off, and that's not what I'm after.

But what exactly *am* I after? I tap my fingernails lightly against the top of the desk, resting my chin in my hands as I stare at his email. Ben and I have been work friends for a long time. We've been working here for almost a third of our lives and, sure, we've been circling around each other for almost as long, but I wasn't prepared for things to escalate between us so quickly. It feels like we crossed a threshold last night, and we didn't even talk about it. It just happened, and then we ate food and watched a movie like it hadn't.

I might be in a dry spell, but I have experience getting physical with men. Sometimes it happens like that—without warning or a lot of thought. Maybe it was an accident. We got caught up in the moment, and now he's gently trying to imply that we should go back to being flirty friends.

I bite my lip. I'm not sure that's what I want. Last night, it felt like Ben slipped into a spot in my life that was made just for him, but maybe it's for the best if nothing comes of it. Dating my classroom neighbor could be complicated, and dating a guy I've known forever could have consequences.

I drag his email to the trash, then open a response to Ken. I type out my plan for the funding, copy Ben, then attach the updated spreadsheet just in time for the bell to ring and my next group of students to file in the room.

By the time the last class shuffles out, I still haven't seen Ben. Something is definitely up with him, because that's not normal. His effort to say hi to me this morning was so minimal, it barely registers, and I'm becoming more and more certain that forgetting the whole thing ever happened is the best course of action.

When my door opens a few minutes after the last student has left, though, my heart jumps into my throat, and I sit up straight at my desk. That is, until Mac's red head pops through the doorway.

"Oh, good. You're here." She comes fully into the room and plops down in a student desk. She frowns when she sees me, then raises an eyebrow. "You look disappointed. Were you expecting someone else?"

I force myself to smile at her. "Of course not. What's up?"

She eyes me skeptically. "Everything okay?"

"Why wouldn't it be?"

Her eyebrows pinch together again, and she tilts her head to the side. "You look flustered. *And* you didn't call me last night after hanging out with Ben. Did something happen?"

I run a hand through my hair, twisting the ends around my fingers and pulling it off my neck. "We weren't hanging out. We were working." As far as she knows, anyway, and if this isn't going to be anything substantial, she doesn't need to know about the rest of it.

"Then why do you look like that?" She waves a hand up and down at me, indicating my general appearance.

"Like what?" I ask as my door pops open again. For a second, I'm grateful to whomever it is for even temporarily saving me from this conversation, but when Ben leans through the half-open door and Mac's lips twist into a devilish smile, I fight the urge to groan out loud.

"Oh, sorry. I didn't mean to interrupt." Ben waves awkwardly when he sees Mac sitting there. He starts to back out of the room.

"You're not," I say quickly and without thinking about it, but by the way Mac is clearly trying to keep a straight face, it would have been better for both of us if I let him go. He looks skeptical, but steps fully into the classroom and lets the door close behind him.

There's something about his presence that instantly relaxes me, and I feel tension slide out of my shoulders and a little smile play on my lips. He leans against the wall next to the door, trying to play it casual, but that lean does other things to my insides I'm not proud of.

So much for going back to being just friends.

Mac is looking between us with her eyebrows lifted, her shoulders shaking slightly with repressed laughter. "I feel like I'm the one who's interrupting," she manages to choke out.

I turn my attention to her, raising an eyebrow. "Did you need something, Mac, or did you come here for a laugh?"

She shifts in her seat. "I did need something, actually. Two things, to be exact. I wanted to know if I could cash in that rain check on our run this week. Wednesday?"

"Wednesday should work." I feel my face soften at the request, even though I know from her tone that she's buttering me up for a bigger ask.

Sure enough, she clears her throat again and straightens a little in her seat—a sure tell that she's about to drop a bomb. She glances at Ben, then back at me. "Great. The second thing is that a couple of Daniel's friends are coming in from New York this weekend. They needed some time away, I guess, and they haven't seen Daniel since he came out here two

years ago, so they're going to spend the next two weeks here before the
wedding doing some Chicago tourist stuff with their kids." She pauses
and looks back and forth between Ben and me again, drumming her
fingers against her thigh.

"A two-week Chicago vacation? That's a long trip," Ben speaks up
from his post by the wall.

"Yeah, well, they're old family friends, so they have a lot of money and
leisure time, I guess."

"That sounds fun," I say tentatively. There must be a reason why she's
nervous about this, but maybe by the way she keeps looking at Ben, she
doesn't want to say it in front of him.

"It should be." She sighs a little and rubs her palms on her slacks. "I
haven't met them yet and little kids kind of freak me out."

"Really?" Ben asks, pushing off the wall and sitting in a student desk
near Mac. I send up a prayer of thanksgiving to the entire universe that
he's no longer leaning against that wall as he keeps talking. "They're just
miniature people. Treat them like you would anyone else, and they'll love
you."

Mac raises an eyebrow at him. "Are you some kind of child-whisperer
or something?"

"He kind of is, actually." It's out of my mouth before I can stop it. I
press my lips together uselessly and make a mental note to figure out why
I can't keep my mouth shut.

Ben blushes adorably and shifts his eyes to me. He grins, and I immediately melt. I am definitely in trouble.

Mac clears her throat, and I snap my attention back to her. She raises
her eyebrows in question. It takes me a second before I remember what
we were talking about, and then I realize she's waiting for an explanation.

"His niece and nephews were at dinner the other night, and he seemed really comfortable with them," I offer. Mac's eyes start to sparkle at the mention of Saturday's dinner. Fully aware that Ben and I have a lot to sort out before I loop her in on any of this, I give her a pointed look. "You said you needed something?"

She straightens up again, as if she's just remembering her mission here. "Right. Yes. We are having a dinner party for them on Saturday at seven, and I wanted to know if you could be there." She smiles her best "pretty please" smile, but then we both see Ben sag a little in his seat. She angles herself toward him. "I'd love it if both of you came, if you're free?"

Ben perks up a little at that, eyeing me from across the room. His expression is subtly questioning, as if he's waiting for me to make the first move. "Uh," I say. "Sure. I mean, I can't speak for Ben, but I'll be there."

Mac claps her hands and wiggles a little in her chair. Then we both look at Ben, who is still looking at me.

"I can't think of anywhere else I'd rather be," he says, his gaze heating. I swallow audibly, unable to look away.

Luckily, Mac doesn't seem to notice. "Perfect!" She jumps out of her seat excitedly. "I'm so glad. I have to go home now, but I'll see you both this weekend."

"Don't forget our run Wednesday," I say as she puts her hand on the doorknob. I know she forgot as soon as she got up the courage to ask me about dinner, but I'm not letting her off the hook.

"Wednesday! Yes. Can't wait." She checks that Ben's back is to her, then wiggles her eyebrows suggestively at me. I try to keep my face neutral as she waves and walks out of the room.

Ben lets out a long breath and scrubs a hand back and forth through his hair. He stands, too. "I have conditioning," he says, but he makes no move to leave.

"I know you didn't come in here to bum an invite to Mac's impromptu dinner party." I raise an eyebrow, and he drops his hand to his side.

"I most definitely did not. I came to ask you to dinner on Saturday." His eyes darken and his voice turns husky. "A real date. Like we talked about."

This knocks the breath out of me completely against my will, and his gaze drops to my parted lips. He takes a small step closer to me. "Ben," I breathe. Then I shake my head ever so slightly. "No." The word is small and uncertain, so I stand and come around to the front of my desk to try again with more conviction. "No. You don't get to ignore me all day and then come in here all hot and ready for whatever you're suggesting." I point my finger at him as I say it to add an emphasis I'm not entirely feeling.

To his credit, Ben looks shocked. "What do you mean, ignoring you?"

"Are you serious? You ran in here pretending to be late to avoid me this morning and haven't said more than ten words to me all day."

"Pretending? Jenny, I overslept."

I huff in disbelief, and he takes another two steps toward me. I can feel the heat radiating off him from this close, and my resolve starts to crumple even further. He lifts his hands as if he's going to touch me, then thinks better of it and drops them back to his sides.

"I overslept," he continues, his voice almost a whisper, "because I couldn't stop thinking about you all night. I couldn't sleep, thinking about how your lips fit perfectly against mine and how your skin felt so soft when I touched you. And I was avoiding you today because I knew if I came anywhere near you, I wouldn't be able to keep my hands off you. You're living rent-free in my head twenty-four-seven, Jenny, and I like it way too much."

I inhale sharply, and his attention falls to my lips again. He's larger than life in front of me, and I don't want anything else in my view but him. "We can't do this here," I murmur, trying to retain some sense of control.

"No, we can't." He takes a step back and runs a hand through his hair again. "Hence my staying out of your way."

"Surely there is some way to be professional while we're here and..." I trail off, not sure how to word the rest.

"And unprofessional when we're outside of school?" He ridiculously leans into the word "unprofessional," and I burst out laughing.

"Something like that," I say between laughter.

He chuckles. "Just give it some time. This is going to take some getting used to for both of us. We'll figure it out. But I meant what I said, Jenny." He keeps saying my name, and every time, it sounds like chocolate rolling off his tongue. "I don't want to go back to a world where I'm not kissing you all the time. I'll all in on this if you are."

He looks at me expectantly, maybe even a little hopefully, and I feel utterly off balance for the second time today. All in? What does that mean? I haven't been all in on someone since Kyle, and that was a disaster. My eyes widen slightly, and I swallow hard. A flicker of concern crosses Ben's face, and he slowly closes the distance between us, as if moving quickly would spook me. He gently places a hand on my cheek and waits until my eyes meet his. "That was a lot. I'm sorry. I just want you to know that what you thought was me avoiding you was me... well, it was me avoiding you. But not for the reasons you think." When I don't say anything, he frowns and leans a bit closer. "Are you okay?"

"I think," I start, then take a deep breath. I want to be honest with him, but it's hard to think about anything with his warm palm on my cheek. I try again. "I think I really want this to work, and I think I'm really afraid that it won't."

His entire expressions softens with relief. "It'll work, Green. I can promise you that."

I feel my mouth stretch into a wide smile, even as I shove the little part of me that is screaming that he can't possibly promise that down into the basement of my brain and shut the door on it. "Okay," I say.

He leans in and kisses my forehead, then meets my gaze again. "I do actually have to go to conditioning, but I will call you tonight. We have a date to figure out." He winks, and I giggle.

"A dinner party totally counts as a date if you pick me up and take me there." My eyebrow ticks up in challenge.

He drops his hand from my face and tips his head back and forth, considering. "A dinner party I pick you up for counts as a date if it is followed by ice cream, just us," he counters.

"Now you're speaking my language." I laugh with relief.

"It's a date, then?" He backs his way toward the door, keeping his eyes on me the whole time.

"It's a date."

# Chapter 20
## Present Day

THE NEXT MORNING, BEN is waiting in the hallway with his smile like normal, and while he keeps our conversations throughout the day short, it feels a lot better than it did yesterday. On Tuesday night, he calls me to say goodnight, and my insides do flips at the sound of his voice on the phone. The call is interrupted by Mac, however. She drops by with an armful of portfolios and a box of wedding favors that need to be assembled. I, of course, had forgotten about that particular calendar invite, but I let her in all the same, pouring a glass of wine and wisely deciding not to mention how haggard she looks.

Wednesday comes and goes with the same normalcy, and I'm glad the weather looks nice enough for Mac and me to go for our run after school. Based on how droopy she looked when we finished assembling favors last night, I think she might need this run as much as I do. When she comes into my classroom at the end of the day with her gym bag, I'm happier than I should be that she's ready to go and not going to cancel on me so she can go home to Daniel or do other wedding-related tasks.

We change into our running clothes in the faculty bathroom, and when we get back to my classroom to drop off our school clothes, Ben is just leaving his room.

"Enjoy your run, ladies," he says. "The offer stands if you want to stop by the weight room and lift with me."

Mac wrinkles her nose. "No thanks. I'm not trying to smell like a gym all night."

"And smelling like outside is better?" I ask.

Ben chuckles as he locks his classroom door. "I'm going to win you over to the dark side yet, Green."

"You won't have to work too hard, Coach," I tease. "I liked lifting, but if it's a choice between that or a run with my bestie here, the redhead wins."

"Fair enough. I'll come back to it when your schedule isn't so full. Have a good run. I'll... uh... talk to you later?" He says it more as a question and glances at Mac and back at me, probably not quite sure how professional he has to be in front of her. I haven't told her much because I haven't been able to ask Ben what he wants me to tell her, and she's been consumed with wedding details, anyway. Come to think of it, she didn't give me crap about him last night, which is unlike her.

"Yeah, later," I say, unlocking my classroom door and holding it open for Mac. She enters as Ben walks away, and I take an extra second in the hallway to note how good his ass looks in his gym shorts. I'm still looking in his direction when I walk into the room, so I jump when I all but run into Mac directly in front of me. Her arms are folded, and she's glaring at me.

"I was standing right there. You both talked to me, and I responded. So why did I feel like the ultimate third wheel, and if there is finally something serious going on between the two of you, why am I only finding out about it now?"

My eyes go wide, and I take a step back, bumping into the door closing behind me. I pull it shut. "Uh... Well, there have been some developments. Let's start this run," I suggest before she can get a word in. "I'll tell you. I promise. Just not here."

She narrows her eyes at me. I'm stalling, and she knows it, but she nods once and passes me out the door. I trail behind her, trying to decide quickly what I can safely tell her and hoping she's not too angry that I haven't mentioned much to her yet.

Once we are outside, I start my running watch, and we begin our run at an easy pace. As soon as we are off school property, she glances sidelong at me. "Spill it."

I sigh. "You know we kissed," I say slowly. She gives me an impatient look, like I had better get to the good stuff fast. I roll my eyes. "Okay, fine. I went back there on Sunday to work, which we did as I'm sure you know, because Ken probably went over our plan for your money with you."

"Mmm hmm," she mumbles, still clearly annoyed.

"Right. Well, we kissed again." I reach up and smooth away some flyaway hairs that are in my eyes. She lets out a small, frustrated noise as if she's certain I'm not telling her everything, which I'm not. "And maybe some other stuff, too," I admit.

"What other stuff?" Her face is turning redder than our easy pace would suggest it should be. She's angry, and even though she's my best friend in the whole world, I find myself wanting to keep at least some of this close to the vest.

"Just other stuff. Look, he and I haven't had a chance to talk about this. It's still new and, honestly, I'm not sure what it even is yet." I pause to breathe, then I admit, "I want to sort it out before I get my hopes up." I haven't exactly thought about it that way, but as soon as I say it, I know it's true. It's what has been nagging at me since Sunday.

"What do you mean, you don't want to get your hopes up?" Mac frowns. "Ben has been interested in you since the day we met him."

"As you keep reminding me." I take a deep breath and let it out slowly. "It's a lot of pressure. I'm me and he's... well, he might be the nicest guy I've ever known."

"What do you mean, you're you? You're the best."

I laugh humorlessly. "Damn straight I am. When it comes to friends, anyway. When it comes to relationships, I'm a disaster. Don't bother telling me otherwise," I say over her when she begins to protest. "My emotionally abusive high school boyfriend of ten years cheated on me, and I followed that up with a string of no-substance one-night stands between spells drier than the Sahara Desert. Ben is commitment personified."

"You don't want commitment?"

"I do." I pause. "I'm not sure I'm capable of it."

Mac is silent for a few beats. When she speaks again, she's so quiet, I almost can't hear her over the cars zooming by us on the street. "You are. You've just been so committed to me for the past five years that you haven't been able to commit to anything else."

I stop dead in my tracks. Mac goes a few more paces before she realizes she's left me behind. She stops, too, and faces me.

"My commitment issues have nothing to do with you," I insist.

She shakes her head slowly. "Come on, Jenny. You think you can hide all this from me, but we lived together. We work together. Ben and I work together, too, you know. I may not know the extent of it, but I know you turned him down at least once because of Ellie. Because I needed you."

"How—"

"He told me." She spits the words out like she has been holding them in her mouth for too long and they've gone sour. "He and I are friends, too, you know. He was worried about you. We both were. That night he carried you out of the bar? He slept on the couch. He left your door cracked open so he could hear if you puked again, and he stayed there. When I woke up, he left. By the time you moved out, we had a plan to talk to you about it. That's when he told me about the night of the accident. You were supposed to meet him for dinner. But after, it was man after man after man, and we were both so sick of watching you self-destruct. And then you got your own place. You either pulled it together or got better at hiding it. I was never quite sure, but Ben moved on, and I met Daniel and..." she trails off, raising her shoulders in a shrug.

I stand there, dumbfounded, blinking at her and trying to process all of this. She knew and never told me? *She knew?* "Why am I just hearing about this now?"

She throws her arms up in frustration and yells, "You never told me either, Jenny. We're best friends. I thought you would tell me eventually, and then you never did. You kept all these secrets, and now you're keeping more. Why?" Her voice cracks when she hurls the question at me, and I take an involuntary step back.

I run a hand through my hair again, wiping away some sweat. "Shit, Mac." Now I'm yelling, too. "You were in pain. You had no one, and I wanted to be there for you like you were always there for me. Ben's just another guy. Guys come and go." I wave my hand frantically back and forth in the space between us. "We stay."

"That's exactly what I'm saying, though." She says it as if she is beyond exasperated. "Some guys are forever. Daniel is forever for me, and I want you to have that, too, if you want it."

"And you think that's Ben for me?" I ask incredulously.

"You're the only one who doesn't see it!" She slaps her legs with her palms in her anger. "But you have to want it, Jenny. And not only that, you have to believe you're worth it."

I stand there like an idiot, my mouth open while I stare at her. Her nostrils flare slightly, and I see tears start to well up in her eyes. When she blinks, they fall, mixing with the sweat on her cheeks. "Why didn't you tell me?" Her voice is quiet again, and she makes no move to brush the tears away.

I take a deep breath, feeling my own tears start to prick the corners of my eyes. I don't know how to get her to understand the deep-seated fear that I'm going to mess this up or run away like I always do, and that she'll be disappointed it didn't work out. Or that my mom will call to chastise me the day it's over, just like she's always done. Or that the feel of Ben's hands on my back and his lips on mine fills me with so much happiness that I don't know what to do with the extra that overflows every time I see him.

Whoever thought happiness would be so miserable?

I lift my hands from my sides and drop them again. I don't have words to convey any of this. The hurt written plainly on her face lodges a pit in my stomach, but I'm going to have to live with it for now. There is no way to convince this woman, who has always believed in me unconditionally, that I'm not always as amazing as she seems to think.

Her shoulders sag as she wipes at her cheeks. She takes a deep breath and kicks a rock with her shoe. "I think we've gone far enough out. Let's head back."

It's no use pointing out that we've done less than a mile and we usually do three. I start running alongside her back to school.

The rest of the run is silent except for our breathing. It might be my imagination, but Mac seems to pick up the pace the closer we get to school. When we get back inside, we pass her room first. She unlocks it, then rests her hand on the doorknob. She doesn't look at me or move for a moment, so I wait.

"You're still coming Saturday, right?"

My heart breaks at how helpless she sounds. "Of course." I try to infuse as much apology into my tone as I can. "I'm here for you, Mac. Whatever you need."

She doesn't say anything. She just nods and enters her classroom, closing the door softly behind her.

# Chapter 21
## Three Years Ago

"Jenny!" A deep voice comes from behind me as I make my way to my car after what has been a very long day. My students were impossible. One of them managed to stick a pencil into my ceiling, and another shot a rubber band at my face. It was an accident, but it still hurt. At one point, I thought about looking at my calendar to see if there's a full moon today, but then got distracted and forgot.

I groan inwardly. Today is about to get longer. I turn around to face whoever is calling for me.

It's Ben, and he jogs the last few steps to close the distance between us.

"Hey, what's up?" I try to keep the terseness out of my voice, but I'm not sure how successful I am.

"I don't want to keep you," he starts. I wasn't very successful, it seems. "Do you have a minute?"

I open the passenger side door and toss my bag inside. I lean against the open door as I face him. He looks excited and sincere. It's almost the same expression he had when he asked me out right before the accident, and it occurs to me that he might have noticed that enough time has passed and we're all mostly recovered now. Maybe he's going to ask me out again.

I swallow hard and meet his brown eyes. When I moved out of Mac's condo a little under a year ago, I decided to clean up my act. I deleted all the dating apps and limited myself to drinking wine only when we went out, and only two glasses, tops. While my remaining scraps of pride have prevented me from asking Ben for yet another chance, there's a part of me that has known for a while now that if he asks again, I'm going to say yes.

I'm thrown by the possibility and by his presence here, next to my car, waiting patiently for me to return to the conversation. I give him a little smile, suddenly feeling nervous. "Yeah, of course."

His grin is wide and warm, and it makes me lightheaded. "I need some advice," he says, "about a girl."

Is this it? Is he pretending to ask advice about a girl, but actually asking about me? "Aww." I smile broadly. "Who?"

My heart rate speeds up as he rubs his hand back and forth through his hair, resting it on the back of his neck. He's blushing, and it's so charming that I'm having a hard time concentrating. "I was thinking of asking out Natalie."

I blink a few times and force my smile to stay plastered on my face. "Natalie?"

"The girls' basketball coach."

"Oh," I say, pretending to realize who he's talking about and hoping it covers up my surprise enough that he can't tell how thrown off I am. "Right. Natalie. You want to ask out Natalie, and you need advice about how to do it? Or where to take her?"

"Not exactly." He looks uncertain all of a sudden. His shoulders tense, and his smile turns tentative. "This sounds stupid now that I'm here."

I tilt my head. "We're friends." Just friends. "You can ask whatever you need."

An unrecognizable expression flashes across his face, but it's gone too quickly for me to identify it. "Good friends, right?"

"I'd say so." The initial shock is starting to wear off, and now I'm genuinely curious about where this is going.

"Good enough friends that you'd tell me if I were making a huge mistake by asking her out?" His eyes widen a little, and his expression is hopeful. Something tells me he's maybe hoping I'll say this is a mistake, but it's a gut feeling, and my gut was dead wrong a few minutes ago when I thought he was going to ask me out, so I tell it to shut up.

"I think it's a great idea. She seems nice, and you deserve someone nice." I try to infuse as much genuineness into my voice as I can. He does deserve someone nice. He has made no secret over the years that he wants to settle down with someone and start a family. Now that I think about it, I'm positive this is why he's not asking me out again. He's realized I'm a mess, and he wants someone who has her shit together—someone who is wife material, not someone who has spent the better part of the last few years drowning her emotions in wine and sex.

The same unrecognizable expression flickers across his features again, but then he smiles, and it's gone. "Great. Okay. Thanks, Jenny." He turns to go back into the school.

"That was it?" I ask. "You ran all the way out here just for that?"

He stops and faces me. "Yeah, that was it. It felt important at the time, but like I said, it sounded stupid as soon as I got out here."

I laugh lightly, though it feels disingenuous. My phone buzzes in my pocket. I take it out to look at it and try not to groan when I see it's my mom calling. I show him the phone and roll my eyes. He shrugs and turns back to the school again, his steps quickening.

"Good luck," I call after him, pressing the green button and bringing my phone to my ear. He doesn't turn around again. He raises his hand above his head in a wave and hurries back toward the building. "Hi, Mom," I say. This long day is about to get longer.

"Hey, honey," she replies, and her voice shakes a little. She hasn't called me "honey" in years, and I frown.

"You okay?" I walk around to the driver's side of my car and get in.

"I'm okay. I just wanted to..." she trails off, and I remain silent. She sniffles. "How are you doing?"

My eyes follow Ben as he continues to make his way into the school. "I'm fine. It's been a weird day."

She chuckles cynically, and I'm taken aback by the sound. "Funny. I've had a weird day, too." She pauses, but before I can ask her what's going on, she asks, "Boy trouble?"

Across the street, the muscles in Ben's back ripple as he pulls open the heavy door at the entrance to the school and disappears behind it. I haven't talked to my mom about dating since the critical show she made over Kyle and me splitting up, but over the phone, I hear the sound of my mom's sniffle again, and there's something about it that makes me want to open up to her a little. "Maybe. I don't know. I thought a guy was interested in me, but I guess it's not the right time for us."

My mom is silent for so long that I start to regret telling her that much. She takes in a loud breath. "Well, keep trying. You'll find someone eventually."

I straighten in my seat, surprised at even this minimal amount of support, even if she sounds like she's just too tired to critique my love life. "Yeah. Sure."

I've given her all I'm willing to give, and she must know it, because she says, "Well, I just wanted to say hi. I'll talk to you later." She hangs up without waiting for a response.

I pull my phone away and frown at it for a minute, then I glance at the door where Ben disappeared. I shake my head, taking a deep breath as I tell myself today must be a full moon. There's no other explanation.

# Chapter 22
## Present Day

WHEN MY BUZZER SOUNDS at exactly six-thirty on Saturday evening, I curse my seemingly impeccable ability to always be getting ready at the wrong time. My hair and makeup are done, but I am still in my fuzzy robe. I stand there uselessly for too long, and the buzzer sounds again. I push the button to let him in, then pop the door open and run back into my bedroom. I hear Ben's footsteps outside the apartment door, then a light knock.

"Come in!" I yell. "I'm just finishing up."

I hear the door open, and Ben steps inside, closing the door behind him. "Are we going to be late?" he calls.

"If I know Mac, this thing actually starts at seven-thirty, and she told me seven so I wouldn't be late. She always does that for important stuff," I call back. "Have a seat. Make yourself at home."

My heart flutters a little as I pull on a lacy black bra and matching underwear. I don't want to make assumptions about what is going to happen tonight, but I want to be prepared. I look at myself in my full-length mirror and bite my lip. I'd much rather go out into the living room right now, just like this, to see the look on his face instead of dealing with the new tension between Mac and me, but I know this night is important to her, and I'm sure if I did that, we wouldn't leave this apartment tonight.

I smile at the thought as I pull on a form-fitting, sleeveless, dark purple dress. I add nude, strappy sandals and dangling silver earrings. I fluff my long brown hair one more time to loosen the waves I curled into it then check myself in the mirror. Satisfied, I take a deep, fortifying breath and step out into the living room.

Ben is sitting with an ankle crossed over his knee and his arms stretched out over the back of the couch, but as soon as he sees me, he's on his feet. He's wearing dark jeans, a light blue button-down shirt, and a navy blazer. The top button of his shirt is unbuttoned, showing a hint of collarbone. His blond hair has clearly been combed and styled. He brings a hand up to run through his hair but thinks better of it and lets it fall to his side.

"You are stunning." His voice is husky and about an octave lower than normal.

"You clean up pretty well yourself, Coach." I try to lighten the mood, but he shakes his head slightly, unable to take his eyes off me.

"I'm not Coach tonight, Jenny." He says my name like it's something precious that could break if he's not careful with it. The sound of it sends shivers down my spine. He takes a step toward me, then another, until he is close enough that I can smell mint on his breath. "Tonight, I'm Ben." He reaches out a hand to cup my cheek, and my eyelids flutter. I lean into the warmth of his palm.

"Ben." His name escapes from behind my lips in a moan.

His fingers curl into my hair as he lets out a little contented sigh. "Will I mess up your makeup if I kiss you?"

"No," I breathe, and an instant later, his lips are on mine. It's a deep kiss, slow and languid, and when he pulls away, I'm left with the promise of more to come.

He reaches for my hand, threading our fingers together and bringing our clasped hands to his lips. He kisses my knuckles. "What are the ground rules for tonight?"

"Ground rules?" I ask. My heart is still pumping from that kiss and the feel of his palm pressed against mine.

"Do they know about us?"

Us.

"Oh." I clear my throat and try to get my heart rate under control. "Mac does, sort of, which I assume means Daniel does, but can we play it cool? She's..." I trail off, not wanting to divulge too much about our fight earlier this week. I look down at our hands to avoid his eyes, suddenly feeling the weight of being stuck between Mac's ire and the nagging fear that I won't be able to see this through. I squeeze his hand and settle on something close enough to the truth. "She's been rooting for this for a long time, and I don't want to steal her show."

He chuckles and kisses my cheek, which you would think would be less sensual than the sultry kiss we just shared, but I gasp a little at the contact. He hums a low, approving noise, and my knees go weak. I lean into him slightly, and he loops an arm around my lower back. "That might be difficult," he whispers next to my ear. He nips my earlobe, and my body molds to his.

"It will if you keep doing that," I whisper. He hums again as if he's accepted a challenge. I take a deep breath and step back, separating our bodies but leaving our hands clasped together. I smooth my free hand over my dress, straightening the hem a little. When I meet his eyes again, they're blazing, but he is grinning playfully.

"I promise to keep my hands mostly to myself." He snickers.

I roll my eyes. "I suppose that's the best I'm going to get?"

"It is."

I sigh, but I'm also teasing. "Okay, then. Let's go."

I grab my purse and a bottle of wine, and we walk hand-in-hand to his car. When we get there, he opens the door for me and kisses my cheek again before I get in. After he starts the car, he threads his fingers through mine again, and that's how we drive the fifteen minutes to Mac and Daniel's new house. Once we get there, though, he reluctantly drops my hand, and the air is cold against my skin in his absence.

Daniel answers the door, and his face breaks into a wide and mischievous grin when he sees how close we're standing. He looks past us and notes Ben's car sitting alone in the driveway. "You came together."

I roll my eyes and push past him through the door. "Settle down, Evans. Gas prices are high, and you had to buy a house on the other side of town."

"Sure." He shakes Ben's hand, a knowing look on his face. "Hey, man. Welcome to the house."

Ben looks around, clearly impressed at the high ceiling and the gorgeous chandelier hanging in front of a grand staircase. "This is a great place," he says.

"Let me introduce you to everyone, and then I'll give you a tour." Daniel motions toward where I hear voices coming from the kitchen. We all walk toward the back of the house where the kitchen and living room are. These rooms are no less impressive than the front room. They are open and spacious and more furnished than the last time I was here. Some of Mac's knickknacks from her condo are carefully placed throughout, but the rooms mostly look like they came right out of a home and garden magazine. Knowing Daniel, he probably hired a magazine editor to style this house for him.

Mac is standing on the stove side of her giant kitchen island wearing her favorite black dress she stole from me a few years ago. She borrowed it to wear on her first date with Daniel and said she needed to keep it for good luck. It looks better on her, anyway.

There is a striking woman sitting at the island. She looks as if she is relatively short, though it's hard to tell with her sitting down. She has curves for days, and the tan dress she's wearing hugs them as if it were tailored for her. Remembering what Mac said about their finances, it may have been. Her platinum blonde, almost white, hair falls in loose waves to her shoulders, and jewelry sparkles on her wrists and her ring finger. Behind her is a man who is equally striking. He's incredibly tall—probably a few inches taller than Ben—and he has a full, rust-colored beard and long hair pulled into a sleek, dinner party version of a man bun. He's incongruously dressed in tailored navy slacks and a pale green button-down shirt. He's holding what looks like an IPA in one hand and gently rubbing circles on the woman's upper back as if it's the most natural thing in the world. He almost doesn't look aware that he's doing it.

Mac comes from around the island, a wide smile on her face that only half meets her eyes, and I can't help but wonder if she's faking her smile because of me or because of the stress of having Daniel's friends here. "Ben! Jenny! Seven-thirty, right on time," she says, slightly too cheerfully. I shoot Ben an I-told-you-so look, and he huffs a small laugh. Mac doesn't notice as she continues. "This is Brandon and Katie. Brandon has been friends with Daniel since they were kids. Brandon, Katie, this is Jenny and Ben. Jenny and I have also been friends forever, and Ben works with us."

"You're the best man?" I shake Brandon's hand.

"Guilty as charged. You're the maid of honor?" He smiles, showing a row of perfectly straight, pearly white teeth.

"That's me." I put the bottle of wine on the counter. Mac takes it and sets it next to one that is already open.

Ben jumps in to shake hands. "I'm a lowly wedding guest," he jokes.

"Me too." Katie laughs. It's a twinkling sound that matches her jewelry. "We can hang out while these four do their wedding duties."

Mac tries to hide a wince as Daniel comes behind her and places a hand on her lower back. She relaxes into him slightly, and with all this casual touching around me, I'm suddenly wishing I hadn't told Ben to keep his hands to himself. Judging from the hard set of his shoulders, he's thinking the same thing.

"You want the tour, Ben?" Daniel asks. Ben nods, looking relieved to have something to do other than watch these well-established couples get indifferently handsy. Brandon offers to go with the guys. As they walk toward the front rooms, I make my way around the island to pour myself a glass of wine, noting that Katie doesn't have one, either.

"Do you want some?" I ask.

She shakes her head, her hair falling over her cheeks. She tucks it back behind her ear. "No, thank you. I don't drink."

I stop pouring and put the bottle down. "Oh. Do you mind if I do?"

Her eyebrows shoot up, and she leans backwards ever so slightly. "People don't usually ask me that. Thank you for being so considerate. No, I don't mind at all."

I smile warmly and nod, taking a long sip. I don't know what I expected, but it does nothing to calm the heat that started building with Ben in my apartment. I'm glad he's not in the room right now.

Mac is standing awkwardly to the side of the island. I notice her hands are empty, as well, so I grab another glass and pour her one without asking. It's a sort of olive branch, and I hope she understands as she takes it from me. When I look at her hands, I notice her nails are painted a pale pink. She must feel like this dinner is important; she never paints her nails. She also takes a long sip from her glass, then puts it carefully down on the island. Katie's blue eyes flick back and forth between the two of us.

Mac, never one for an awkward moment, sets her glass on the counter and excuses herself to make sure the sleeping bags are set up for her visitors upstairs. Katie and I stare at each other for a moment before she scrunches her nose. "I've seen enough desperate pulls from glasses of wine to know what they look like. Are you two okay?" she asks.

I look to where Mac has disappeared, but she doesn't seem to be coming back any time soon. I didn't want to talk about any of this tonight, but I know this is one of those scenarios where being honest would probably break the tension. I suppose being the sacrificial lamb is worth it for Mac, considering how important this is to her, and I desperately want to make things right with her. I sigh, then shrug. "Well, I think she's nervous you won't like her, and I'm here on what I'm pretty sure is a first date with a man I've known for almost ten years."

Katie looks completely stunned. Her eyebrows pinch, her lips purse together, and then she bursts into laughter. She doubles over in her seat and smacks the counter lightly a few times with her hand. Mac comes back in then, looking at me as if she's nervous I broke her guest. After a few moments, Katie straightens up and dabs at the corners of her eyes with her knuckles. "Whoo. Okay." She addresses Mac first. "Honey, I'm not some Daniel gatekeeper. He's allowed to marry whomever he wants, and he doesn't need my permission to do it. I told him every single day of his last relationship to run as far away from her as he could, and he never listened. But, for what it's worth, I could tell in the first five minutes how perfect you are for each other, so we are going to get along just fine. And you." She turns to me, then shakes her head incredulously. "I don't even know where to begin with that."

Mac's eyes are wide as she looks back and forth between us. I shake my head slightly and take a sip of my wine.

A loud crash comes from the front office, and Katie's shoulders immediately slump inward as she tips her face up to the ceiling and groans. "We can continue this after I deal with my son." She hops off the stool, and I immediately notice that she is, in fact, very short. She has that larger-than-life mom presence at the moment, though, that makes her seem imposing even to me.

Before she can even take two steps, Ben comes half-jogging into the room with a foam football in his hands. He smacks it with his palm as if he's going to throw it. "Go long, Mason," he calls, and a little dark-haired boy about seven years old comes running into the room.

Mac looks horrified, but Katie puts her hands on her hips. "No. Mason James, you do *not* go long. Ben, I am not your mother, but you should know better than to play football in someone else's house. Outside, both of you."

I hide a snicker behind my wine glass as Ben sags, looking for all the world like a boy who was just chastised by his mommy. He ruffles Mason's hair. "Let's go outside, buddy," he says. Mason walks quickly outside through the French doors off the kitchen, and Ben follows.

"Bedtime in ten minutes!" Katie calls after them, and Mason whines something incoherent.

"They've known each other for like five seconds," Mac murmurs to me in awe, her eyes following Ben and Mason outside.

I'm a little surprised she's talking to me, but I try not to show it. "I'm telling you, he's a child-whisperer," I reply as Katie returns to her seat at the island.

Brandon and Daniel saunter back into the kitchen, and Katie shoots daggers at them. They both look sheepish and say, in unison, "Sorry, Katie." Assuaged, Katie nods once and takes a sip of her water.

Mac gapes at her, smiling smugly. "Oh, you need to teach me that little trick," she says eagerly.

Katie shoots another glare at the guys who cower even more. "I'd love to."

Once Katie sheathes her dagger-eyes, conversation flows easily between us until Katie excuses herself to drag Mason to bed. Apparently, their two-year-old daughter, Christine, is already asleep upstairs.

Once Mason is tucked in, Mac and Daniel lead us into the dining room, where the long table has been set beautifully, with fresh-cut flowers and candlesticks lining the center runner. Katie and Brandon sit across from Ben and me, and Daniel takes his seat at one end of the table. Mac lays out a cheese plate, then sits at the other end. We all load up our plates with some of the cheese, then snack for a bit. After a few minutes, Ben puts his hand on my knee under the table, and I shift ever so slightly closer to him. Katie catches the movement and smiles into her hand.

After the cheese, Mac brings out a beautiful tray of honey-glazed salmon fillets and a dish of perfectly prepared asparagus. We pass everything around the table, and Ben's hand comes to rest on my knee again. I risk a look at him only to find he's already looking at me, a soft smile playing at his lips and candlelight sparkling in his eyes. He takes a bite of salmon while still looking at me, and there's something so indecent about it that my cheeks turn red. I shift my eyes to my own plate and completely avoid Katie's knowing stare across the table.

"So, Mac," she says after a minute, her voice a little dreamy. "Has planning your wedding been everything you've ever imagined?"

I stiffen and turn my attention to Mac. She smiles joylessly, the color leaching from her skin. "It has been an experience," she says meekly. At that, Daniel stops eating and lifts his eyes to her, his brow pinching. She tries to recover by immediately adding, "I've been so busy with the start of school, too, so it feels like there's never enough time."

"Why didn't you have a summer wedding?" Katie's blunt question catches Mac off guard, and she coughs into her hand.

"Oh, well." She wipes her hands on her napkin in her lap, then fidgets with her sister's ring under the table. "Daniel and I met in the fall two years ago, and we got engaged in the fall a year later. He thought it would be a good idea to get married around the same time." He's staring at her across the table, but she's looking down at her hands.

"Fall weddings are beautiful," I try, but Mac curls further inward.

Katie looks back and forth between Mac and Daniel and clears her throat. "When Brandon and I got married, I felt like I wanted to crawl into a hole during every single appointment." She looks at her husband and smiles at a shared memory. "I begged him to elope."

He meets her eyes, then raises an eyebrow as he takes a sip of his beer. "The way I remember it, I was ready to take you to the courthouse that day, but you said, and I quote, 'But then I wouldn't be able to wear my dress.'"

She shrugs. "It was a great dress."

Mac droops even further, as if she wishes the seat could envelop her completely. "My dress is..." she trails off, poking at the fish on her plate. I look from her to Daniel. He glances at me, concern clearly written on his face. I speak up again. "Her dress is beautiful, but it's not turning out quite how she expected."

Mac shoots me a grateful look and sits up in her seat. Daniel, who has turned his attention back to his salmon, is still frowning.

Katie swivels her head to look at Mac, then Daniel. She looks back down at her plate and pushes her asparagus around with her fork. Then, as if she can't help herself, she says, "I can't imagine not liking my dress." She puts her fork down and lifts her head, focusing on Daniel. He raises his eyes to her, and they exchange a silent conversation while Mac stares soundlessly at her lap. I can see the muscles of her right forearm moving slightly, and I know she's fidgeting with her ring under the table again.

After a few moments, Katie wisely turns the conversation away from weddings and Mac recovers, but Daniel quietly studies her from across the table off and on for the remainder of dinner. For the first time, I wonder how much Mac has talked to him about her distaste for the wedding planning process and her fear of attention, and if this is the first time he's registering how much she hates it.

After the main course, they serve a delicious chocolate mousse. Ben's hand stays on my knee through it all, and once he starts closing and opening his fingers lightly on my skin, I'm having a hard time concentrating. Luckily, shortly after dessert, Katie lets out a huge yawn, then sheepishly looks at us. "I'm so sorry. We were traveling all day."

Ben and I take that as our cue to leave. Mac walks me to the front door as Ben hangs back to exchange phone numbers with Brandon.

"That was a great dinner party," I reassure her.

She smiles an exhausted smile. "It was." She yawns into her hand as Ben joins me at the door. "Thank you for coming."

"Thanks for having us," he says, and something about the way he says "us" has my stomach doing flips all the way out the door and to the car.

When Ben starts the car and the dashboard lights up, the clock reads ten-thirty. He pinches his mouth together as he backs out of the driveway. "I don't think there are any ice cream places open." The regret is almost palpable in his voice.

"Hmm," I hum. "I couldn't eat another bite, anyway." I reach over and thread my hand through his, and he shoots me a sidelong glance. "Doesn't mean this wasn't a date. Felt a lot like a date to me."

He kisses my knuckles, and I can feel him smile against the skin of my hand. I lean my head on his shoulder, and he plants a quick kiss on my forehead. "Let's get you home," he whispers. I let my eyes flutter closed, enjoying the feel of him next to me.

# Chapter 23
## Present Day

BEN PARKS IN AN empty spot in my apartment parking lot and leaves the car running. He shifts in his seat to look at me, dropping my hand in the process. The lack of physical contact is jarring. His brown eyes glisten gold in the yellow light of the streetlights illuminating the parking lot. My fingers itch to touch him so badly, I almost can't stand it.

I take a deep breath. Only one way to find out if he wants to stay or go. "Do you want to come up?" My voice is more tentative than it ever has been.

He's quiet for a moment, his eyes burrowing into me. "Do you want me to?"

"I really do," I say, laughing breathlessly. He grins and immediately turns the car off. We walk hand-in-hand to my apartment, where I let us in, closing the door carefully behind us. I drop my purse on the small table by the door. I take off my earrings and put them next to my purse, then slide off my shoes and tuck them under the table. Ben has kicked his shoes off and is studying me with a crooked smile.

Suddenly, I feel self-conscious. "What?"

"I couldn't take my eyes off you all night in that dress, but there's something about you making yourself comfortable as soon as you get home." He shakes his head slightly, then closes the distance between us, placing his hands on my hips. He kisses me deeply in that same way he kissed me while we ate tacos on the floor of his living room last weekend. It feels like he's been kissing me like this every day since we met.

He pulls away, and his eyes search mine. "I have some questions." His voice is ragged.

"Questions?" I ask, intrigued.

"Yeah."

"Okay," I say slowly.

He swallows hard, and his hands tense on my hips. His fingers press little half-moons into my flesh, and my entire consciousness zeros in on the feel of it. "The most important one is…" he trails off and swallows again. "Do you want this?"

"Yes," I reply without having to think. "God, yes."

He looks like he's holding something back. He bites his lip, and my insides ignite. "There's no going back from this, Jenny."

I inhale sharply, and he blinks, his face carefully neutral. He is trying not to sway me with his expressions, and the thoughtfulness is so sweet. I sigh. "I know. I think…" I pause. I take in a tentative breath before I continue. "I think I've wanted this almost as long as you have." It's the first time I've admitted it out loud, and the relief is palpable. I release my breath quickly, only to gasp again when my eyes meet his and see the desire plainly written there.

"I was hoping you'd say that." He smiles a wicked smile that completely changes his features. I've never seen this side of him, and it's positively indecent. I want him so much I can't stand it. I fist his shirt in my hand to pull him closer, but he shakes his head.

"No, Jenny. I said questions." He emphasizes the S, the gleam in his eyes deepening.

"Okay." I arch an eyebrow. "What else?"

"I have waited so long for this. In my mind, I've had you a million different ways, but I want this to be perfect for you. I want to know what you like."

I know how long he's waited, but I'm not going to make this easy for him. Where's the fun in that? "That's not a question," I taunt.

"You're right." He leans slightly closer. "Do you want to be in control of this, or do you want me to be?"

The question catches me off guard, and I feel a little lightheaded. He senses it and draws closer, sliding his muscular thigh between mine. It doesn't make me less lightheaded, but it keeps me steady. I'm completely enveloped by his large frame and his powerful legs and arms now. I feel safe. Completely. I can sense how good it would feel to give up and let him lead, and I'm so turned on by the idea of it. "You," I breathe. He grins devilishly, as if this were exactly the answer he wanted.

"Okay." He traces a line slowly down my jaw with his thumb, and I shiver. "I have more questions, but I'll tell you what. For each answer you give me, I'll choose an article of clothing to remove." He catches my chin between his fingers and tilts it up, his grip firm enough that I can't move, but not hurting me. Never hurting me. His other hand settles on my hip again, and I lean into the pressure. "Are you going to be a good girl and answer my questions?"

My mouth goes dry. Is this what he meant by being in control? Because if so, I want more. I try to nod, but his grip tightens on my chin.

"Say it, Jenny."

"Yes," I whisper.

He moves his hands to my wrist and removes my watch, placing it on the table with my earrings. "Do you like being on top or bottom?"

"Top."

He grins wildly as he takes off his blazer and tosses it to the ground. He moves to press into me again with only a few thin layers of fabric between us. I moan, biting my lip, but he asks another question quickly.

"Gentle or rough?"

I think about his strong, blunt fingers inside of me, pressing deeply and drawing pleasure out of me. "Um..." I say. I can feel my cheeks heating, and my eyes slide away from his.

"Sweetheart." His voice is quietly reassuring, and it brings my attention back to him. "We can stop this any time if you're uncomfortable."

I shake my head quickly, swallowing hard. "No, I... No one has ever asked me this stuff." It's usually fast and heated, and I've never had anyone care so much about what I want before. I press my palm into his chest, feeling his muscles flex against my touch. It grounds me. I meet his eyes and say, "Not rough. But not gentle either."

He leans in and kisses under my ear. I shiver. "Perfect," he murmurs as he gently bites where he kissed.

"Yeah," I whisper, my fingers threading through his hair. "Like that."

I can feel him smile against my skin, his breath hot and tickling my ear.

"Don't I get some clothes for that?" I ask.

He pulls back and meets my gaze. "So impatient," he croons, but I smile, waiting. Without breaking eye contact, he slowly starts unbuttoning his shirt. I watch his fingers deftly undo his buttons, and when his shirt hits the floor with his blazer, I finally get to look at his bare chest. It's magnificent. It's the torso of a man who spends hours each day on his body, and I want to touch it, so I do. I trace my fingers over the slight dips and ridges of his muscles. His breath starts to speed up.

I meet his eyes again. "More questions?" I'm trying to be as coy as I can be.

"Two more." He runs a hand up my leg and pushes the hem of my dress up an inch. "Do you want me to touch you, or do you want to touch yourself?"

"You mean—"

"I mean," he interrupts, "I know it's hard for women to come without some extra stimulation. And you're going to come for me, sweetheart. So how do you like to be touched? By me, or by yourself?"

"Oh," I breathe. My chest is brushing against his with every breath, and I'm acutely aware of the steady ascent of his hand on my thigh. My dress is suddenly itchy and too tight. I need it off, so I choke out an answer. "Both. Either."

"Good girl," he says again, and lifts my dress over my head.

His eyes burn through me as they take in my matching black lace undergarments. His gaze is almost feral as he traces a hand down my bra strap and over a nipple with a delicious amount of pressure. He twists it gently between his fingers over the fabric, then harder. I gasp.

"Hmm," he hums. His other hand reaches between my legs, cupping me with only the fabric of my underwear between us, but somehow the layer is too thick. He rubs back and forth a few times, and I can't help the movement of my hips against him. "You're so wet," he murmurs. He lowers his forehead to mine, as if needing support. "Fuck, Jenny."

"You had one more question, I think?" I ask quietly, playing with the buckle on his belt.

He squeezes his eyes shut as if afraid of the answer. "Are you sure you want this?" he asks, and my heart skips. This man. This kind, caring, sexy man. So sure, yet so vulnerable in his desire to make sure I'm ready. He's perfect, and I'm not worthy.

I undo his belt buckle and deftly unclasp the button of his jeans. "Yes, Ben. Yes."

And then his lips are on mine, bruising and urgent. I manage to slide his jeans down his hips, and they pool on the floor. He steps out of them, then grabs my ass, lifting me off my feet. I wrap my legs around his waist. He moves us to the bedroom, never once breaking the contact of our lips.

He gently tosses me on the bed and climbs over me. His hands skate over my skin, leaving trails of heat in their wake. He plants hot kisses down my collarbone, dragging my bra strap down my shoulder and out of his way. He tugs me up and reaches behind me, undoing the bra clasp. He pushes me back into the mattress and pulls away to watch as he slowly slides my bra down my chest and off my arms, exposing my breasts. His eyes rake slowly over my chest, then his palm covers one of them, squeezing artfully as his lips meet mine again.

A small moan escapes me, and he hums approval against my mouth. His hand again skates down my waist. He hooks a finger under the waistband of my underwear, then he grabs it and pulls. I kick my feet beneath me to wriggle free, and my panties join my bra on the floor. He again stops to look at me, now naked before him, and his desire is evident both in his eyes and his cock straining against his boxers. I reach for his underwear and tug. He springs free, and he slides his boxers off and to the floor.

We both take a minute to look at each other in the dim light filtering in from the living room. I feel a little thrill at the sight of him. His body is sculpted, and the way the light is hitting him, he looks like a god.

"You're flawless," I say, my fingers desperate to touch him again, but wanting to let him look his fill. "I can't believe it's taken us so long to do this."

He smirks, an eyebrow ticking up. "Not for lack of trying."

I can't hold back anymore. I reach up and circle my hand around his cock, pumping a few times. He moans and almost collapses on top of me, rolling to the side. I shift to face him, slinging a leg over his hip, my hand still circling him. His fingers find my clit and press down, then they're at my entrance and push inside. I gasp for air, my mouth finding his. His other arm presses on my back, pulling me closer to him.

Our hips move in time with our hands, and the tip of him slides through my wetness. "Jenny." My name sounds like a plea on his lips.

"I'm on the pill, and I've been tested," I say quickly. "If you wanted to—"

"Tested. Yes. Me too. Shit, we should have talked about that before we started."

I pull myself on top of him, forcing him onto his back. He drags his fingers out of me, eliciting another moan. "It's okay." My lips find his as I line up above him. "I mean, is it? Is this okay?"

His hands find my hips, and he gently pushes me down onto him. "Sweetheart, this is better than okay." It takes a few times, but when I'm fully seated with him inside me, I groan at the luscious fullness. I rock back and forth tentatively. He reaches up and pinches a nipple, which causes my hips to buck involuntarily. He makes another approving noise, so I do it again and again as his hand trails down my torso and his fingers find my clit. He circles in time with the thrust of my hips, his eyes never leaving mine.

The pressure builds in my core, and I lean forward, capturing his lips. My tongue sweeps into his mouth, and his meets it, matching the circles of his fingers. My nipples graze his chest, and the sensations become almost unbearable.

"I'm going to..." I lose my train of thought, my breathing ragged.

"Yes, Jenny. Come for me, sweetheart." His fingers find a little more pressure, and I come undone. He wraps both arms around me, holding me close as he thrusts a few more times, then he follows me, emptying himself inside of me. The thought of it sends more shudders through my entire body.

He holds me on top of him for a long time, until he softens, and I shift so I'm lying on my side next to him, our legs still tangled together. He rolls his head, and his eyes find mine. He kisses me deeply, then pulls away and starts to slide off the bed.

As soon as his feet hit the floor, I sit bolt upright. He twists to face me, frowning. "Are you okay?"

A little panicky feeling rises from the pit of my stomach. "Don't leave," I choke out. "I mean, don't go home. Stay. Please?"

His face softens, and he reaches a hand to cup my face. "I'm just going to clean up. I'm not going anywhere." He kisses me again, and the panic dissolves.

He gets up, and I hear water running in the bathroom, then he's back next to me, like he promised. I take my own moment in the bathroom, then go straight back to the bed. He tucks me into his side, wrapping me in his warmth and pulling the covers over us. "Not going anywhere," he murmurs again, and he strokes my hair lazily, almost as if he doesn't realize he's doing it, until we both drift off to sleep.

# Chapter 24
## Two Years Ago

THREE DAYS. THREE FULL sleeps and wakeups. Three long school days. And I can't get the feel of dream-Ben's lips and hands out of my head. It wasn't even real.

We were at the pumpkin patch together, sure, but we were decidedly *not kissing*.

My brain hasn't gotten the message. It thinks about that dream-kiss unexpectedly, sending shockwaves of desire through me at very inopportune times. I have lost track of what I'm saying more often than I care to admit over these past few days because dream-Ben is pushing his way into my thoughts. I keep telling myself the kiss wasn't even real, but I'm finding myself just as often wondering if a real kiss would be as Earth-shattering as the dream one was.

I've been completely avoiding him in the hallway. I'm terrified that if I saw him, I'd either blush so hard I'd set fire to the building, or I'd grab his shirt and pull his lips to mine right there in the middle of a hallway packed with students. Better not to see him at all than risk either scenario.

I've made it to Wednesday without seeing him at all. It's not a huge feat, considering his classroom is on the other end of the hallway and we don't have the same off periods, but I'm bound to run into him pretty soon. But as I sit at my desk halfway through grading a paper, and I find my fingertips gently touching my lips as if I can feel his still on me yet again, I realize I'd better deal with this soon.

I always tell my students there are no stupid questions, but it feels stupid to ask whether I want Ben. Based on the kiss that's not even real that has been invading my head since Saturday night, I think it's safe to say I do. My heart rate picks up slightly at even the silent admission. I scrub my eyes with my palms, then lean my elbows on my desk and rest my chin in my hand. I'm still holding the pen I was using to grade papers, and I can feel it press against my cheek. It makes sense I'd be a little nervous. We flirt with each other often, and there has been quite a bit of push and pull between us for a long time. It's just always felt like that next step into an actual relationship has gotten further and further away with each year we've known each other, with each misstep and near miss.

We're both single now, though. I've figured out a thing or two about myself and what I want. I'm basically watching Mac fall in love before my eyes. I want that, too.

I want that with Ben.

The realization hits me like a ton of bricks. I want that with Ben. *I want that with Ben.*

I push my rolling chair away from my desk and make to stand up, but before I can, Mac comes crashing into my classroom looking like she's seen a ghost. I drop my pen on the desk and fly to my feet.

"Holy hell, Mac. What happened?" I rush to her and practically force her into a student desk as I slide into the one next to her.

She stares at a spot on the floor in front of her, putting her feet on the bottom rung of the chair and pulling her knees as close to her as she can. She rests her forearms on them, her shoulders slouching so far they practically meet. I've seen this before—she is intentionally trying to make herself as small as she can so she can fade away.

"They were..." She is breathing so hard, she can hardly get the words out. "Talking about me. Marty... and Edgar... and Ben."

I'm back on my feet before I can even think about it. "Ben?!" I explode. Mac grabs my wrist and forces me back into the chair. I'm ready to commit murder without hearing more and trying desperately not to flash back to myself standing in the entryway of my apartment, listening to Kyle talk to another woman about me. This is about Mac, not me, and she clearly needs to get it out, so I wait until she can tell me what she heard.

"They picked up right where Marty left off in the meeting last week. Commenting on my demeanor. Marty..." She swallows heavily and starts to fidget with Ellie's ring on the pointer finger of her right hand. "Marty said this was just like when I needed Ken to stand up for me after Ellie."

I grind my teeth together so hard it hurts. "That's not what happened."

She waves a hand and shakes her head, and my stomach sinks, knowing that's probably not even the worst of it. "I know. Apparently, they and their toxic masculinity don't accept the ways people process grief. They never did, but that's not all of it. He suggested there's something going on between Daniel and me. He asked Ben about it."

It doesn't matter that there *is*, in fact, something going on between Daniel and her. Those assholes don't get to talk about it behind her back. It's none of their damn business. "Pricks."

"I didn't hear what Ben said," she offers meekly, as if she knows his participation in this will hurt me.

It does hurt me, but watching Mac on the verge of a panic attack because of him hurts more. "But he was there."

"He was there. He was laughing."

I'm on my feet again without even realizing it. "I'll kill him," I grind out, but before I can, my door opens.

Daniel comes in. Mac insists she can't see him anymore. She's clearly beyond upset, and he holds his hands in fists at his sides as if he could grip the air to hold himself back from sweeping her into his arms and making everything okay. Mac storms out, and Daniel is left looking at my door shutting behind her like a deflated balloon.

I know I say things. I know I try to remain calm and help, but I'm too busy seeing red to process much of what's going on. When Daniel asks me what happened, I give him a shaky rundown. He oscillates between unadulterated fury and defeat, but he mostly looks like a sad puppy.

"I'm going to go see her. It doesn't have to be like this. Those fucks don't get to define her or us." He's clenching and unclenching his fists at his sides, and that snaps me out of my rage for a second.

"No. That is a terrible idea," I say quickly. He eyes me skeptically. "Look, I know you two have been playing tonsil hockey or whatever, but I've known her almost my entire life. Do not push her. She'll only dig in further. Give her some space. She'll come around."

He narrows his eyes at me, shoving his hands into his pockets. "You're sure?"

"I'm sure. And if she doesn't, I'll personally see to it that she gets her head out of her ass, okay? But I need you to trust me. You going there or calling her will make it worse right now."

He considers me, then he nods once. "What are you going to do?" he asks.

I purse my lips, looking him up and down. I'm not normally in the habit of sharing information with Daniel Evans, but he looks so discouraged that I feel bad for him. "Give me your phone. I'll give you my number, and we can keep in touch if we hear anything from her."

He pulls his phone out of his pocket. I punch my number in, then send myself a text. He sighs. "You didn't answer my question."

I hand his phone back to him. "I can't leave without trying to find Ben. But don't you dare tell her if she calls you. She doesn't like it when other people fight her battles for her, but this is personal for me, too."

He nods curtly again, then turns to leave. He rests his hand on the doorknob and, without looking back at me, says, "Thanks, Jenny."

"Don't get used to it, Evans," I caution. "I'm still not sure if you're good enough for her."

His shoulders sag slightly with his hand still on the doorknob. He continues to face the door as he says, "I'm not. But I'm trying to be."

My heart breaks a little as he pulls down on the doorknob and lets himself out into the hallway. *You probably are if you're thinking like that.* Part of me wants to rush after him and reassure him, but I have bigger fish to fry. I'll deal with Daniel's broken ego later.

I take a few breaths and wait until I know Daniel is out of range, then I square my shoulders. The dream-kiss is still scorching me, but in a blistering and painful way, and I shove it so far down into the recesses of my brain that it won't be coming back up any time soon. I don't date men who talk about women behind their backs. I made that promise to myself a long time ago. I swing my door open and stalk down the hallway.

When I get to Ben's room, his lights are still on. Good. This is going to feel so much better in person.

I fling his door open, hard. He's sitting on the edge of his desk as if he's waiting for me, which throws me a little, but I recover quickly by yelling, "What the actual fuck, Ben?"

"I screwed up. I'm sorry." He holds his palms out. That throws me, too. I was expecting more of a fight. I *need* more of a fight. He isn't going to get off that easy.

"Yeah, you fucking did. What the hell happened in there?"

He presses his palms into the edges of his desk and leans slightly forward. "We were all hanging out after conditioning. Marty was back on his bullshit, and you know how Edgar is when Marty is around. He'll agree with anything Marty says."

"Apparently, so will you." I spit the words at him, and he leans back as if they hit him in the chest.

"That's not fair. I should have stopped them, but I didn't add anything."

"Silence is compliance. You're right, you should have stopped them."

"I know. I made a mistake."

"She's your *friend*!" I cry. "Doesn't that mean anything to you? Or are you just a sheep following whatever herd you're closest to?"

"I said I made a mistake," he repeats, grinding the words out as if he's trying not to lose his cool. His fingers curl around the edges of the desk underneath him.

"She was finally feeling stable. You saw her at that meeting. Her old spark was back, standing up to Marty like that. She's allowing herself to fall for someone. I, for one, am not going to let you ruin that for her. And you assholes have to go and talk about her behind her back, suggesting she can't do her job—which she does circles around all of us, by the way—and insinuating private things about her love life."

"I didn't say any of that." His tone has turned eager, and his knuckles are now white.

"You didn't say *anything*. That's the problem."

"I made a mistake, Jenny." His brown eyes meet mine, pleading, but he must see something in my face that makes his turn cold. "It was a mistake. You've never made a mistake before?" His eyebrow ticks upward slightly in challenge, and with just that motion, my mind is filled with fuzzy memories of bowls hitting walls, a dive bar bathroom, a rainy night in his car, an orange car crumpled and bleeding and a hospital waiting room. A man, and a man, and a man, and, through it all, Ben, and Ben, and Ben.

I blink rapidly, hoping the tears I can feel starting won't betray me yet. I lower my chin and glare at him as hard as I can. To his credit, he winces.

"How dare you." My voice, to my surprise, is quiet and steady. "How dare you suggest that the choices I've made that affect only me are the same as the one you just made that crumpled a woman who has been crumpled enough."

He regards me, his expression hardening again. He is silent for a long moment before he takes a breath that rattles slightly. "You're kidding yourself if you think your mistakes haven't affected anyone but you."

A little breath makes its way through my lips that are parted in surprise. His eyes dip to them as if he can't help himself, but they fall all the way to the floor just as quickly.

I don't know if he's insinuating that I've affected him or Mac or both, but I don't stick around to find out. I turn on my heel and stalk out of the room. He doesn't try to stop me.

My tears mercifully wait until I've made it back to my classroom. I sit at my desk with a box of tissue as they fall, unfettered, down my cheeks.

After a few minutes, I've calmed a bit, and I see a shadow of someone passing by my door. He slows as it comes to my room but, ultimately, he continues on down the hallway.

*It's for the best*, I try to tell myself. I say it in my mind over and over again until I half-believe it, even as my fingertips reach, without my permission, to lightly touch my lips again.

# Chapter 25
## Present Day

"I'm not buying it, Miss Green," Cecily practically shouts from her seat in the corner. "How could Viola fall in love with Orsino after seeing him like twice?"

This is not where today's discussion of *Twelfth Night* was supposed to go, but I'm not surprised the topic comes up. It's always one of the students' major issues with the play. "Good question—"

"She was royalty, right?" Kayla interrupts me.

I blink a few times, my mind pivoting again. "She was the daughter of an aristocrat."

"So, basically royalty," she confirms. I decide it's not worth splitting hairs about it, so I motion for Kayla to continue. "Weren't all marriages among the wealthy pretty much arranged? Maybe she sees that Orsino is rich and hot and figures it's better him than some dude her dad hooks her up with," she suggests. I stifle a laugh.

"She doesn't say anything about that, though," Jayden chimes in. "She just says she loves him right off the bat."

"Yeah, it's not right. Olivia says she loves Cesario right away, too, and Cesario is a woman." Diego scrunches his nose as if the very thought is disgusting.

"We don't tolerate homophobia in here." I shoot a warning look at Diego, who slouches his shoulders a little. "And you have to remember that Olivia has no idea Cesario is actually Viola."

There is an eruption at this. Cries of, "It makes no sense!" and "How could she not know?" bounce around the room. Apparently, my lesson about suspension of disbelief made zero impact.

Ana is raising her hand patiently, so I shush the students and point to her. "Yes, Ana. Thank you for raising your hand," I add pointedly.

"Isn't love at first sight Shakespeare's thing? I mean, we all read *Romeo and Juliet* last year. It was the same as far as them falling in love," she says quietly.

I nod, but before I can expand on that, Diego jumps in. "Yeah, and we didn't believe it then, either."

"Do you believe in love at first sight, Miss Green?" Jayden asks.

I narrow my eyes at him, trying to decide if he's trying to get me off track so they don't have to discuss the play anymore. I glance at the clock and note that the period is almost over. I decide we can afford a little venture into real life. "No, I do not."

"How long do you think it takes?" Cecily wants to know.

"To fall in love?" I ask, and she nods.

*I've had nine years to think about this.* Ben's voice rumbles through my thoughts. I fight a shiver, my eyes widening slightly in surprise.

How long does it take to fall in love?

Nine years?

I look around at my students' eager faces and swallow. No time for that right now. "I think it depends on the person," I finally say.

"That's not an answer," Jayden grumbles.

For once, I'm thankful for a disgruntled student to get me on much more solid ground. I look at him incredulously. "It's not a science, Jayden. Every person and every couple are different."

Jayden shrugs. "Minimum, then. How long do you need to know someone to fall in love at minimum?"

"I don't think there's a time limit on it." I'm quickly losing my grip on this discussion, which is what I get for allowing them to get me off course.

"Okay, so if you don't believe in love at first sight, then why are you making us read this?" Diego waves his book in the air.

"It's *fiction*," I laugh. "I don't have to believe it! And neither do you. You just have to enjoy it."

"No one enjoys Shakespeare, Miss Green," Kayla adds in her best know-it-all tone.

"I have centuries of evidence to prove that statement wrong, Kayla." I arch an eyebrow at her as the bell rings to end class. "But we'll have to save that for tomorrow. Have a good day, everyone!" I call as they pack up their things and file out of the room.

About two seconds after the last student leaves, my door opens again. I expect to see a student who left something behind, but Ben slides through the door. I see a student from my next class peek in as the door is closing behind him, but he sees Ben and does a U-turn. In their eyes, the only thing worse than one teacher in a room is two, I suppose.

"Hey." He smiles his crinkly smile at me, and I take in the sight of him. I never thought I'd see the day that I thought a man in khakis and a polo looked so good, but here we are.

"Hey," I return, smiling slightly. "How are you?"

His gaze turns a little heated as he looks me up and down. "Better now. I missed you last night."

Good grief, this man is going to ruin me. I decided to spend *one night* alone in my apartment. It wasn't even really a decision; he had conditioning and then a Monday coaches' meeting until late, and I was so tired from our weekend of barely sleeping that, by the time he called me on his way home, I was having a hard time keeping my eyes open. Still, I regretted it last night as I was falling asleep in my cold bed, and I certainly regret it now with the desire on his face stifled, but still plainly there.

"Yeah?" I smirk. The door pops open behind him, and another student pokes her head in but, upon seeing Ben, pops back out to wait in the hallway.

"Yeah. I don't have anything after school today. I was wondering if you wanted to come have dinner and watch the game with me at my place."

"What game?"

His eyes twinkle. "Do you actually care what game?"

I raise an eyebrow, pursing my lips against a smile. "No, I do not. You aren't going to try to persuade me to go lifting with you instead?"

His eyes burn into me as he says, "Not tonight."

"Right. Okay, then. I'll see you after school." I start straightening some papers on my desk to avoid his gaze, hoping he'll take the hint. He can't be allowed to carry on like this if I'm expected to teach another class in three minutes. Thankfully, he turns and opens the door wide, holding it open for the students to come in. "Enter, scholars! What are we studying today?"

Begrudging grumbles of "Shakespeare" and "some play" drift through the open door as the students shuffle in.

"Oh no. Miss Green is *still* torturing you with Shakespeare?" He grimaces.

"Hey, do not undermine my lesson, Coach," I bark from the whiteboard where I've started erasing the last period's notes to prepare for this class.

"Wouldn't dream of it." He winks at me as he shoves a doorstop under my door to keep it open for the remaining students, then disappears into the hallway.

I stop by my place after school to pack an overnight bag—just in case—with a vague plan to leave it in my car so he doesn't think I'm assuming anything. I check myself in the mirror in my bedroom, tilting my head at my reflection. I'm still in my olive-green trousers and off-white blouse from school. I look good, but after a long day of teaching, the clothes are uncomfortable.

I worry for a second that showing up in a t-shirt and leggings would be too casual considering we've just started... whatever this is. I haven't gotten to the t-shirt and leggings phase with a guy since Kyle, so I don't know how long one is supposed to wait for that. I chew on my bottom lip and debate texting Mac for advice, but ultimately think better of it. Our conversation on our run left such a sour taste in my mouth that I'm not eager to start again.

"This is stupid," I mutter to my empty bedroom. "He's seen you in leggings before." I quickly change into black leggings and a baggy Leade Park Lightning t-shirt that I tie at the waist high enough to show a little skin. I pull my hair back into a ponytail, slide on some comfy white socks and my shoes, and I'm on my way.

When Ben answers his door, he's wearing an old college sweatshirt and—God help me—a backwards blue baseball hat and gray sweatpants. I almost turn into a puddle right on the spot. I never truly understood the appeal of these micro tropes in all the smutty novels I read until this very moment. My mouth practically waters at the sight of him, the way his sweatpants hang low on his hips, barely hiding a slight bulge and, somehow, making him look even more fit than he does in slacks or jeans.

He breathes a sigh of relief, which brings me back to reality. "Oh, good," he says, some of the tension leaving his shoulders.

I pinch my brows together and look behind me, then back at him. "Were you expecting the cops to come take you away or something?" They should, though. The sweatpants-and-backwards-hat combo on this man should be illegal.

"No." He laughs lightly, then sweeps a demonstrative hand in front of himself, as if I needed any help noticing his outfit. "I didn't know if we were, you know, casual like this."

"Oh." I let out a laugh with a nervous edge as I push through the doorway. "Yeah, well. I don't usually wear school clothes one second longer than I have to." I shrug, pretending like I didn't just spend twenty minutes on the same conundrum.

He shuts the door, then turns to look at me again. I hear the unmistakable crack of a bat hitting a ball, then tinny, television-speaker cheering and a sports announcer coming from the living room.

I raise an eyebrow. "Cubs, I take it?" I ask, raising my chin in the direction of his blue hat.

He nods and grins, then silently crosses the distance between us. He brings a hand to the back of my neck, and his lips meet mine. His tongue teases against my own, and I run my hands over his chest as my eyes flutter closed. I press myself closer to him, just as he breaks the kiss. My eyes open and meet his. "And I ordered pizza," he says, his tone teasing.

"I don't think there are four sexier words in the English language." His eyebrow raises in challenge. "I bet I could find some." He is still pressed against me, and I can feel the hardness of him through his sweatpants.

I tap my chin with a finger, pretending to think. "Maybe, 'And I made spaghetti?'"

He laughs his deep belly laugh, pulling away from me, but threading his fingers through mine as he pulls me into the living room. We sit on the couch, and I immediately curl my knees up against his side. He wraps an arm around them, pulling me close. "How about, 'I love your meatballs?'"

I giggle. "That sounds weirdly dirty."

"I didn't know dirty was an option. That changes things." The heat pooling between my legs has me hoping it's only a half-joke.

"Dirty is always an option."

His dark eyes meet mine, and his lips part slightly. He moistens them with his tongue, and I'm about ready to jump on top of him when the doorbell rings. "Hold that thought." His voice is husky and, when he stands, I smile slightly as he adjusts himself before going to answer the door.

He comes back and deposits a pizza box on the coffee table in front of me. I open it as he goes to get some plates and napkins for us from the kitchen. It's half cheese and half what looks like all the meats known to man. I smile up at him as he hands me a plate and sets a pile of napkins next to the pizza box.

"Thanks for sacrificing half your pizza for me," I say, grabbing a slice of cheese.

He stands in place, tilting his head. "Nothing I do for you is a sacrifice." I pause with the slice halfway to my mouth. "I want to acknowledge how sweet that was, but I also really want to eat this pizza," I admit.

He laughs so fully that I can't help but laugh, too. He grabs a slice from his half and takes a huge bite as he sits next to me on the couch. I take my own bite, too, trying to chew and smile at the same time.

By the time we're done, there are two slices of mine and zero slices of his left. I glance at him out of the corner of my eye and vaguely wonder where he puts all that pizza, but I'm no stranger to the hunger of an athlete. I haven't been running as much as usual lately, but when I'm logging high-mileage weeks, I can easily eat just as much as he can, maybe even more.

We sit there for a while, our feet resting on the coffee table and the soft noises of the baseball game in the background. Ben is looking at the television, but the straight line of his shoulders and the set of his jaw have me thinking he's not actually watching the game.

I take his empty plate from his lap and put it on top of mine, then I put them both on top of the pizza box. I move to the floor, where I kneel in front of him, squeezing myself between his knees. He looks down at me but doesn't move his arms from where they rest on the back of the couch. I bite my bottom lip as I slide my hands up his thighs to grip the waistband of his sweatpants. I tug down, and he lifts his hips to help me. He springs free, and I pull the sweatpants down to his ankles. I kneel on top of them, ensuring that he's going to stay where he is, and press myself between his thighs. His eyes are hooded but are locked on me as I reach a hand to circle his length. He lets out a low moan as I pump my hand a few times.

I lean closer, planting a kiss on one inner thigh, then the other. Then, I press a kiss to just under the tip of him. He breathes in sharply. My eyes meet his and I raise an eyebrow in question. He nods once, and that's all the signal I need. I open my mouth and take him in, my hand covering where my mouth can't yet reach.

His hips buck slightly, but from the small movements, it's clear he is trying not to hurt me. He moves one of his hands from where he's gripping the back of the couch down as if he's going to grab my hair, but then rests it next to him. I reach my free hand for it and press it to the back of my head, not breaking the rhythm of my mouth.

He shakes his head slightly, putting his hand back on the seat of the couch. "Take off your shirt," he chokes out. I stop my movement, slowly dragging my mouth all the way off him. He tips his head back and groans.

"Those are four pretty sexy words," I tease as I lift my shirt over my head. He strokes himself as he watches me. My eyes follow the motion of his hand, and I reach back to unclasp my bra, letting it fall to the ground. He kicks his sweatpants all the way off, and they join the pile of clothes, too. I kneel in front of him again, and he shifts so he's sitting a little straighter. As I take him in my mouth, he wraps one hand around my ponytail and bends slightly closer to me so his other hand can graze my nipple. I moan around him, which makes him tighten his grip on my hair and buck further into me.

My other hand skates down my torso and into my leggings, where I start slow circles between my legs. I sigh around him.

"Yes, Jenny. Touch yourself," he commands. Those are also four sexy words, and I'm all too happy to oblige, feeling the pressure build as he reaches the back of my throat with his cock.

Suddenly, he pulls out of my mouth with a pop. I cry out, frowning up at him. "I'm going to come, sweetheart," he explains.

I am breathing heavily as I continue the circles between my legs. His cheeks are flushed, and his hand still rests on the back of my head. "Come in my mouth," I whisper, my heart racing and pressure building.

His pupils dilate slightly, which turns his brown eyes dark with desire. He grips my ponytail tightly. "I think you found the sexiest four-word combination," he murmurs as he thrusts back into my mouth. I moan in pleasure as I take all of him and thread two of my own fingers into me. His thrusts become erratic and strong, and he squeezes his eyes shut. "Jenny, I..." he trails off.

"Mmm hmm," I encourage around him. As if that were all he needed, he shudders and pulls my head as close to him as he can, emptying himself into my throat.

After a few moments, he lifts me up and lays me down across the couch cushions. He pulls my leggings and underwear off as one and tosses them aside along with his hat. He wastes no time pushing his blunt fingers into me, and I gasp. His thumb circles a bit higher, and I squirm in pleasure at his touch.

"It's... you don't have to..." I can't get a whole sentence out.

He shakes his head sharply, cutting me off. "You come every time," he insists, pulsing his fingers in and out of me as he skates a hand up my torso to cup my breast.

"You win," I breathe. He chuckles as he applies more pressure, pinching my nipple delicately between two of his fingers, then flicking it with his thumb. I come completely undone, and he stills inside me as he drops his forehead to my shoulder and brings his hand behind my back, holding me tightly while his thumb continues circling me, drawing out every last bit of pleasure from my body.

He removes his hand, then turns his head, kissing my neck. I lean into him. He kisses up my jaw until he finds my lips. He kisses me deeply, then rests his forehead against mine. He presses his eyes closed. "I don't want to spend another night without you."

He opens his eyes and searches mine. From the pleading look on his face, I know he's not only talking about tonight. He wants some level of commitment, and this is his way of broaching the topic, but I'm not able to think past the satisfied buzzing in my limbs and the steady, consistent feeling of his body on top of mine.

"I brought a bag. It's in my car," I say, my breathing still ragged.

He must understand, because after a moment, he lifts himself off me. He reaches for his sweatpants and pulls them on. "I'll go get it."

I start to sit up and grab my clothes, pulling them on as well. "I can," I offer.

"No." His voice has the slightest edge to it, which stops me in my tracks. He clears his throat and tries again, his voice softer this time. "I've got it." He leaves and I hear him grab my keys off the front table, then I hear the front door open and close.

I finish getting dressed again, then sit back on the couch, my hands clasped in my lap and a little uneasy pit in my stomach. Thankfully, though, when he comes back in and tosses my bag into the corner, his smile is wide and genuine. When he practically crawls over the couch cushions to kiss me passionately again, the little pit dissolves, and I melt into him, relishing in the way our bodies fit perfectly together.

# Chapter 26
## Present Day

WE DON'T SPEND ANOTHER night apart during the week and into the weekend, but we don't talk about commitment or the status of our relationship past that one little hint on Tuesday night, either. We alternate between staying at my place and his, spending our evenings cuddled on the couch watching a movie or a game, and spending our nights tangled together between our sheets. He fits so perfectly into my life, I sometimes have a hard time remembering he first kissed me just two weeks ago.

All has been blissfully quiet on the wedding front, as well. Maybe too quiet. I keep meaning to talk to Mac, but by the time I leave school, her lights are off, and all my free time has been spent with Ben. I vaguely wonder if Daniel took a hint after Mac's clear distress over the wedding at the dinner party and took some tasks off her plate. I genuinely hope she's relaxing in these last few weeks before the big day, which is why she doesn't need me as much.

On Sunday night, Ben is at my place. We're both squeezed into my tiny kitchen, making Chicken Marsala. He's monitoring the chicken in the pan, and I'm slicing mushrooms. I finish that up and turn to toss the mushrooms into the pan with the chicken and wine, and I run straight into Ben's back.

"Sorry," I mumble, an errant mushroom slice falling to the floor. I move around him and dump the remaining mushrooms into the pan.

"Too many cooks in the kitchen." He taps me with his hip, and I laugh.

"Wasn't a problem at your place."

"My kitchen is a lot bigger than yours." He points his tongs at me.

"Your whole place is a lot bigger than mine." I wipe my hands on the towel next to my sink.

He rests the tongs on the edge of the pan, and for a moment, the only sound is the chicken sizzling on the stove. I face him to find he's already looking at me, his brows lowered slightly and his expression serious.

"Move in with me."

My eyebrows raise, and my eyes widen. I involuntarily try to take a step back, but I bump into the counter, and in a moment of pure comedic timing, my phone rings from where it's sitting in the living room.

I curse under my breath and cross the room in about two steps to look at my phone. "I want to talk about this." No, I don't. "It's Mac, though, and I haven't talked to her in a while."

He scrubs a hand back and forth through his hair. "Yeah, take it." He takes the tongs from the edge of the pan and pokes at the chicken.

I hit the answer button before it goes to voicemail. "I'll be right back," I say. He nods silently, his eyes not meeting mine. I sigh quietly and bring the phone to my ear while walking to my bedroom and shutting the door. "Hey, Mac. What's up?"

I expect her to give me crap because I know she hears me talking to Ben as I answer the phone, but she doesn't. She just says, "Hey" so warily, I'm immediately concerned.

"Everything okay?" I sit on the edge of the bed.

"Yeah," she says a little weakly. Everything is clearly not okay. "Are you all set with your dress?"

"I'm picking it up from the seamstress on Tuesday after school," I reassure her.

"Great. I also don't have your RSVP."

"Oh, sorry. I figured you knew I was coming, being the maid of honor and all." I'm teasing, but she doesn't laugh.

"Right, but I need to know if you are using your plus one. I'm calling everyone who hasn't responded tonight. The caterer needs the final count tomorrow." Her tone is flat and not at all inquisitive like it would normally be with a question about who I'm bringing to a wedding. She's not fishing for information about Ben like she usually would; she's really just after the RSVP. My heart breaks for her for about the millionth time during this whole process, and, though the sound of her voice has me aching to tell her about this past week with Ben, I can tell she's withering and probably doesn't have time right now.

I pinch the bridge of my nose. "No, I won't be bringing anyone." We haven't talked about it, but I assume I'll be bringing Ben, and he's already invited.

"Okay, thanks Jenny," she says in a clear dismissal. I try not to let it sting too much, telling myself she probably has about thirty more of these calls to make tonight.

"No problem," I reply, but she's already hung up. I drop my phone away from my ear and stare at the screen. It bothers me that I can't fix this for her. I can't swoop in and make this process easier for her or make her have more fun with it. It bothers me even more that she's all but stopped talking to me about it.

*Less than two weeks*, I tell myself. She'll be married then, but hopefully, I'll at least have my best friend back.

I toss my phone on the bed and leave the bedroom. Ben is already sitting at the table, a plate in front of him and one in front of my seat. As soon as I sit down, he digs into his food.

"How's Mac?" he asks around a mouthful of chicken.

"Miserable." I shake my head while I cut a piece for myself and use my fork to pop it into my mouth. "She's working on the last RSVPs, which is probably the worst part of the whole thing."

He swallows his food. "What did she need you to do?"

"Nothing." I also swallow my bite. "She just wanted to know if I needed my plus one."

He stares at his chicken while he cuts it into small pieces, then puts his knife down next to his plate. "What did you tell her?"

"I told her I didn't need it." I take another bite. It's delicious and practically melts in my mouth.

His eyes snap to mine. His grip tightens slightly on his fork. "You told her you didn't need it?" The words are clipped.

I frown. "You're already going, so I don't need it. I figured it'd be weird if I brought someone else." I try for a joke, but when he simply nods and turns his attention back to his food, I ask, "Is that okay?"

"I guess I thought you would have explained that to her. That you're bringing me." He doesn't lift his eyes from his plate, and my frown deepens.

"It didn't feel like the right time. She's stressed and unhappy, and we haven't had a chance to talk about you yet. I don't know why it matters—"

He puts his fork down on the table a little too hard and finally meets my eyes. "She's your best friend, Jenny. You two tell each other everything. When was the last time you didn't tell her about a guy you were seeing?"

I blink silently, then put my fork down, as well, the chicken suddenly tasting sour. "She doesn't know everything about every guy I've been with, Ben. Most of those guys weren't worth talking about."

"That's the point. That's why it matters." He's louder now, and I startle in my chair. "I want to be worth talking to her about, and you don't think I am."

I'm angry he made me jump, so I decide two can play at that game and raise my own voice. "This doesn't have anything to do with us. I'm looking out for her. She can't see past her to-do list, and she hates it. You didn't hear her sounding absolutely defeated on the phone just now. She's tired and cranky, and now is not the time."

"Don't you think she'd be less tired and cranky if she could have a normal conversation with her best friend about a guy?"

"You don't know her like I do," I insist, and he huffs a frustrated breath. I frown. "Can't you trust me on this one?"

"I don't know what I can trust you about, Jenny. Here I am, asking you to move in with me, and you can't even tell your best friend that I'm your date to her wedding. This whole time, I thought you were all in. Like I am."

"Damn, Ben. Slow down. It's been like two weeks."

He goes completely still, his eyes boring into mine and his fingers curling inward slightly where they rest on top of the table. "It's been nine years."

It's not exactly a revelation. We've circled around each other for almost that long. He's wanted me for that long. But I guess I didn't realize he's been falling for me for that long, too.

When I don't immediately respond, his brown eyes turn colder than I've ever seen them, and it feels like the warmth has suddenly been sucked out of the room. "What did you think we've been doing these past weeks, Jenny? Was it just sex, like with the past men you've been with? Is that all this was for you?"

"That's not fair." My voice is barely audible, but I straighten in my chair. I've never let anyone slut-shame me before, and I'm not about to start now.

He studies me intently, his expression carefully neutral and his eyes still cold. "Sometimes I think you don't give one single shit about yourself. I guess it's true what they say. You can't love someone until you love yourself." Love? But he barrels on before that can sink in. "You're worth more than sex, Jenny. You're worth the whole damn package, and I have wanted to show you that since the day I met you. Since Kyle..." he trails off, shaking his head in dismay. "I should have known you never saw your worth when you kept going back to that piece of shit."

"Fuck, Ben," I breathe. "Low blow."

"You cared about him more than you cared about yourself. You care about Mac more than you care about yourself. You think she's worth more of your time and energy than you are. You dragged her through her grief, you dragged her back to Daniel when she needed you to, and now you won't even tell her about me because she's a little stressed. The whole time, I was trying to get you to notice that you deserve to be taken care of, too. But you don't believe that. Mac can't take care of you like I can, Jenny. Those other guys can't take care of you like I can. I want to give you all of me. Forever. You either think you're worth that, or you don't. You either want it, or you don't. But I'm not going to keep watching you bring home guy after guy because you think you're not worth more than a nice dinner and a decent lay. I'm not going to keep watching you put Mac first because you think she's more important than you are."

I gasp in protest, but he doesn't let me get a word in. "I'm yours. I always was. I thought you were finally ready to be mine, but I guess not." He stands, then, his chair scraping harshly against the floor. "I'm not going to sit here and watch you push away everything that could be great because you don't think you deserve it. I'm not going to watch you hide behind Mac and her feelings anymore." He pauses, his eyes boring into me. "You keep putting her first and taking scraps for yourself. Those other guys? They're the scraps." Then, he lowers his eyes to the table, pushing his fork and knife into a perfect parallel. "You get to be the protagonist of your own story, Jenny. You deserve a happy ending, too."

He doesn't wait for me to respond, which is just as well, because I don't have words. He abruptly walks to the door, opens it, and leaves, shutting it carefully behind him.

# Chapter 27
## One Year Ago

I HAVE SPENT THE better part of a year avoiding Ben Allouer as much as I can. I don't care that he apologized to Mac. I don't care that he bodyguard-blocked Daniel-freaking-Evans in the aisle of the Leade Park High School auditorium after Daniel's ex-fiancée showed up wearing that giant ring and throwing Mac for a loop. I don't care that he has casually tried to contact me at least weekly, either conveniently running into me after school or emailing me some random article or meme he thinks I'll enjoy. I don't care that Mac, too, has begged me, also at least weekly, to forgive and forget, quoting all sorts of writers and philosophers and proselytizing on the power of forgiveness.

I. Do. Not. Care.

Frankly, I never told her what he insinuated when I confronted him, and even if I've been able to take a hard look at my past self and admit Mac has not escaped my escapades completely unscathed, when I look at the larger picture of my entire life, no one—*no one*—gets to suggest that Mac isn't a top priority in most of the decisions I make. Certainly not Ben-gossip-behind-her-back-Allouer. And, if some of my choices stung his fragile ego in the process, well, too damn bad. I also don't remind her it was easier for her to forgive him than it would be for me, though by the way she keeps trying to persuade me, she probably knows. I hope there is a special place in Hell for men who gossip like spineless cowards, and as far as I'm concerned, Ben has a seat there waiting for him.

So, when Mac comes into my classroom after school, her new sapphire-and-diamond engagement ring glinting in the overhead lights, to remind me that the first wrestling tournament of the year is this weekend, all I can do is blink uselessly at her and say, "I don't care."

She sighs and sinks into the nearest student desk. "Yes. You do."

"I really don't," I insist.

She rolls her eyes. "It's tradition that we go to at least one meet a year. You're free this weekend. I'm free this weekend. Daniel is free this weekend, and he's never been to a wrestling meet. Let's go."

"No." I fold my arms and lean back in my desk chair, pursing my lips.

She brings her lower lip out in a pout and widens her eyes. "Please?"

"That might work on Daniel, but it is not going to work on me. I'm not going."

Her face immediately goes from pout to frown. "It doesn't work on Daniel."

I raise an eyebrow at her. "There's got to be something that works on Daniel," I say suggestively.

She giggles mischievously. "There is, but it probably won't work on you."

I wince and make a gagging noise. "Ew. Do not tell me more."

"That's what you get for trying to change the subject. Come on. Don't make me go alone."

"You just said you're bringing Daniel!" I throw my hands wide, then slap my thighs in exasperation.

"But he's not my wrestling meet buddy!" She mimics my gesture. "You are. If you don't go with me, the whole time I'll be sitting there thinking about how much I wish my bestie was with me."

I scowl at her. Her pouting might not work on me, but bringing our friendship into it definitely will. Judging by the smug smile she's fighting, she knows it.

"You're manipulative, you know that?"

She claps her hands giddily. "Yay! Okay, I'll pick you up at noon tomorrow!" She stands and leaves quickly, not giving me any time to change my mind. I, on the other hand, bang my head lightly on my desk and groan.

Noon comes fast, and when Mac texts that she's outside, I toss a school sweatshirt over my leggings, remind myself that I don't care what I look like, and run out the door.

When I get in the back seat of Mac's car, I watch in the rearview mirror as her eyes flick to the dashboard clock. "You weren't even dressed when I pulled up, were you?"

"You know better than to pick me up right on time, bestie." I emphasize the last word to remind her of why I'm even here right now. She shrugs and backs out of the driveway. Daniel, wisely, keeps his mouth tightly shut.

When we arrive, the gym is chaos, as it always is during wrestling meets. I'm relieved, because it means Ben probably won't see us and I can sneak out toward the end unnoticed. The relief is short-lived, though, because Ben looks up from where he's watching two wrestlers on the other side of the gym and finds us almost immediately upon walking in.

His face lights up completely, and I can see from here how his eyes crinkle at the corners when he smiles. Mac raises her hand over her head to wave dramatically.

"Do you think he sees us?" Mac asks.

"I think everyone sees us." I reach over to grab her arm and shove it back to her side. "Put your hand down. You look like a fool."

"I look like a fan," she protests, and Daniel chuckles, looping an arm around her back and pulling her to his side.

"Only a fan would have spirit shoes like those," he teases into her ear. She scowls at him and playfully swats at his arm.

"Good to know I'm not the only one who thinks those shoes are ridiculous," I say. Mac makes a small noise in protest, but I start climbing the bleachers. "If you two lovebirds are done getting handsy, let's find some seats."

They follow me up a few rows and we all sit together, but Daniel ends up sitting between us, making it hard to talk. So much for needing her wrestling meet buddy.

It wouldn't be so bad with the two of them if they didn't constantly have to be touching each other. He either has his hand on her knee or her lower back. Once, he even tucks her hair behind her ear and leans closer to whisper something that has her cheeks going almost as red as her hair.

They leave me with nothing to do except watch the wrestlers and their coaches, which also wouldn't be so bad if my eyes didn't keep finding Ben against my will. He's such an enigmatic coach, and it's hard not to watch him—the way he gets animated when one of his wrestlers makes a good move, the way he jogs up and down the length of the gym to check on different team members, the way his face lights up when one of his kids wins. I might be angry at him, but I can admit that he's good at what he does, and it's clear from the way the kids listen and respond to him that he's a great role model for them.

Daniel gets up to go to the bathroom about halfway into the meet, and Mac slides over to sit next to me. She sits without saying anything for a while, cheering every so often when one of the LPHS kids gets their hand raised in the air. She doesn't take her eyes off the mats as she says, almost too quiet to be heard over the crowd, "You're softening up."

"I am not." I'm immediately defensive.

She glances sidelong at me, then back to the mats. Ben is leaning over, his green-and-gold tie dangling in front of him and his hands resting on his knees as he shouts something to one of the kids on the mat. It's a few seconds before I realize she's still looking at me. I sit straighter and shift on the hard bleacher seat.

"You are." She tilts her head. "It's okay, you know. You don't have to stay mad at him forever on my behalf."

"I'm not entirely mad on your behalf," I say, then we both cheer as the kid who Ben was yelling at clearly wins his match. "I'm mad on my own. He..." I trail off, then shift in my seat so I'm looking directly at her. "He said some things."

She purses her lips and narrows her eyes, studying me. "I'd ask you what things, but if you haven't told me yet, you're probably not going to."

I nod curtly, swiveling so I'm facing the mats again. Ben's eyes meet mine, and his face softens slightly. He dips his chin, acknowledging me, then turns back to his work.

"Were they true things?"

"What?" I ask, facing her again.

"The things he said. Were they true?"

*You're kidding yourself if you think your mistakes haven't affected any-
one but you.*

I flash back to drunk nights at Tony's, Mac's near-constant concern
about me, and the one-night stand that was the catalyst for me moving
out of the condo like I do every time I replay his words in my head. She
might have a point, but I say, "Doesn't matter if they were true. They
were hostile." She has me pegged, but what Ben said was deliberately
hurtful, and I'm not letting him get away with it.

"So what?" she asks, and my jaw drops.

A little offended noise escapes me. "What is that supposed to mean?"

"It means that you tend to get the most angry at hard truths people hit
you with, and you're so stubborn that, by the time you admit to yourself
they were right, you've dug your heels in so hard, you're not going to let
it go."

My face goes from confused, to offended, to incredulous in the span of
a few seconds, and she huffs. I force my expression to go neutral. "Okay.
I'm angry. So what?"

"Do you remember Doc O'Connell?"

I lean back and blink at the rapid change of subject. "Our junior
English teacher?"

"Yeah."

"Of course, I remember him. That asshole almost had me thinking I
wasn't good enough to study literature in college."

"Mmm," she hums noncommittally. "You remember not shaking his
hand at graduation?"

"I walked right by him on the stage." I smile fondly at the memory.
High school Jenny was a firecracker.

"All because he said... what was it?"

She knows exactly what he said, but I play along, wanting to see where this is going. "He called my writing 'self-indulgent.'"

"Mmm hmm." She turns her attention to the mats again, clapping for one of the LPHS kids. "And have you read your high school writing since then?"

I narrow my eyes at the side of her face, but she doesn't look at me. I take a deep breath. "I have."

"Any particular words come to mind when you did?"

"I get it. He was right, but, honestly, what an awful thing to say to a teenager. All they are is self-indulgent. What does that have to do with anything?"

She finally meets my eyes. "I've known you a long time, Jenny. I've learned how to tell you what you need to hear without you blowing up in my face, and I also know that you only stay angry at other people for this long when they tell you something you aren't ready to hear. I don't need to know what it was"—she holds her hands up, palms out, then returns them to her sides on the bleachers—"but, I think that if you've considered whatever he said and can admit that it had some truth to it, you should let it go."

I don't say anything. She's dropping some pretty hard truths right now, but she's right. I'm not mad at her. I could never truly be mad at her.

"I wasn't wrong," I say after a moment. Daniel comes back and sits on the other side of Mac this time, his full attention on the matches. He was gone for a long time. I have a sneaking suspicion she asked him to leave, and he didn't actually need the restroom.

She laughs softly. "I'm sure he deserved the majority of your ire."

"I won't apologize. Apologies are an admission of guilt."

Ben's gaze meets mine again across the crowded gym. Mac's eyes flit between the two of us, a smug smile on her face. "I don't think you have to. Just talk to him."

I consider the conversation for the rest of the meet. As we are leaving, Daniel and Mac spot a student from her class last year. They peel off to talk to her, leaving me alone.

*Just talk to him.* Mac's voice intrudes through my thoughts. I roll my eyes and groan inwardly. It seems simple enough, but I don't want to. Staying angry at someone is easier than making up, and even though I don't have a real reason not to find him anymore, it'd mean admitting he wasn't entirely wrong.

Better to get this over with now, I suppose. I wander around a bit, but I don't see Ben anywhere. I figure he's probably in the locker room with his team, except I see a bunch of his wrestlers standing around waiting for their rides. I head back to the gym, thinking maybe he is there helping clean up from the meet, but as I walk down the half flight of stairs leading to the narrow passageway to the gym entrance, I see him. He's talking to a very short, very cute brunette in the passageway. He's leaning his back against the wall casually, his arms folded and a huge, happy smile on his face. I can only see the back of her head, but she's bouncing slightly on her toes, and I hear her giggle echo off the cinderblock walls. He pulls out his phone and hands it to her, and she starts typing something into it.

He doesn't take his eyes off her, and it takes me a second to realize that's noteworthy. I'm so used to him seeking me out in every room we're in together that, when he keeps his eyes fixed on the woman in front of him, I suddenly feel the breath knocked out of me.

Even though I've been cold-shouldering him for an entire year, every time we were in a room together, he still managed to find me, nod to me, smile at me. For all that time, I barely acknowledged him, but he still did it. Unfailingly. Until now.

Only an absolute moron would think he'd continue to seek me out indefinitely while I more or less ignore him. Am I an absolute moron? I definitely feel like one at the moment. Do I want him to smile at me like he's smiling at that woman in front of him? Surely I do not, or I would have tried to talk to him before now. Right?

He doesn't look at me, though, and I've been standing there in the dimly-lit corridor for far too long. I turn around and walk slowly away, trying to make as little noise as possible.

I don't get far before I hear him call, "Jenny," behind me. My relief is stunning in its completeness, which should be a revelation, but I keep walking, hoping he gives up. No luck. I hear his footsteps jogging to catch up with me. He slows to my pace when he reaches me, the scent that's distinctly him—a mix of gym and sweat and aftershave—comes along with him.

"Jenny, hey," he says, and I have a fleeting hope that his breathlessness is from his little jog and not from his conversation with that woman. I stop and turn to him.

"Oh, hi. I, uh... I didn't see you there." If my brain could facepalm itself, it would. Hard.

"I'm glad you came. We missed our cheering squad last year."

"Yeah, well..." I trail off, toeing a piece of tape stuck to the floor.

"I know. Look, I'm sorry, Jenny." He scrubs a hand back and forth through his hair. "Really sorry. I wasn't thinking and—"

I hold up a hand to stop him, meeting his eyes. "We both said and did some things we didn't exactly mean. Let's leave it at that."

He studies me for a moment, then nods once. "Friends again?"

I swallow. "Yeah. Friends."

We don't know what to say after that, but neither of us moves to walk away. I shift my weight to my other foot and break the silence because one of us should. "So, who was that you were talking to?"

He smirks knowingly. "I thought you said you didn't see me there."

I raise an eyebrow and fold my arms, waiting. He caves. "Her name is Faith. She wanted to say congrats after the meet." As he speaks about her, his face breaks into a brilliant smile, and his cheeks turn a little pink.

He's got it bad. And, honestly, he deserves this. He hasn't dated many women since I've known him, and certainly not one who has made him smile this easily and broadly. I may not be able to get my feelings under control, but what Mac said was right. Ben dropped a hard truth a year ago when he suggested my choices don't only affect me and I'm done doing things that could potentially string him along. Ben deserves to be happy, and there's no guarantee I can ever make him smile like that.

"She's cute." A corner of my mouth tugs up, and despite the laws of physics, his smile broadens.

"You think so?"

I shrug. "The back of her head was, anyway. You should ask her out."

He tilts his head, looking at something on the wall behind me and considering it. "I think I might."

"Yo, Green," Daniel's voice booms from up the half-flight of stairs to the building entrance. "You want to go to Tony's?"

I raise my eyebrows at Ben in question.

"Maybe I'll meet you there. I want to... uh... make a call first."

I keep my face completely neutral as I shift my gaze to his shoulder. I swallow again, my mouth suddenly dry. "Okay. Good luck."

"Jenny," Mac sings my name impatiently from up the steps.

I roll my eyes at Ben, who chuckles. I turn to call up to them, "Coming!" and by the time I turn back around, Ben is already walking away, his head down, smiling at his phone screen.

# Chapter 28
## Present Day

I TAKE A SICK day on Monday. I'm not physically sick, but I have limits. Ben would probably avoid me all day anyway, but getting dumped on Sunday and potentially running into the guy at work—or even the simple knowledge that he's on the other side of my classroom wall—on Monday is too quick of a turnaround for me. I tell myself this is exactly why I avoided dating Ben for so long, but the part of my brain that calls me out on my own bullshit is raising the red flag on that one loud and clear.

I know avoidance does not fix anything, and I also know that I can't take Tuesday off, too, let alone the rest of the year, but the way I see it, that's Tuesday's problem. Today, I wallow.

I spend most of the morning trying not to look at my phone. When I look at the clock and see that school started about an hour ago, I risk a glance. Maybe Ben feels bad when he notices I'm not there and sends me a quick message to check in? Or maybe Mac doesn't see my car in the parking lot and is worried about me since I didn't want to bother her with more intense stuff last night, so she has no idea why I wouldn't be at school?

Nope. Nothing.

I toss my phone on the couch cushion next to me harder than I have any right to. It's not my phone's fault I have no one in my life anymore.

According to Ben, it's entirely my own fault. I certainly don't think that's fair.

I draw the hottest bath I can stand, grab another smutty romance novel from the stack on my nightstand, and get in. The scalding water feels punishing instead of comforting, and I give a little frustrated sigh through my nose. Even my bath has turned against me.

I stubbornly sit in the water until it's cold, reading my novel and doing everything I can not to think about Ben. Except, when I get to a particularly sexy scene, all I can think about is how much better my time with him was than whatever this nonsense is on the page. The positions they're in seem to defy gravity, and it requires far too much thought to figure out how they're even doing what the author says they're doing, which does not help pull me out of reality. I toss the book aside and opt to stare at the wall instead.

By the time I get out of the tub, I'm hungry. A quick glance at the clock tells me it's almost lunch time. If Mac were here, she'd bring me cheeseburgers just like we always do when one of us gets dumped. Well, now it'll only be when I get dumped, I suppose, given her soon-to-be-changed marital status. Not to mention, it's my own stupid fault she isn't here with a greasy bag of cheeseburgers, because I dragged my feet telling her anything of consequence about Ben and me, and now she doesn't even know.

These are revelations I don't need right now, so I decide if Mac can't bring me cheeseburgers, I'll have someone else do it. I pull up a food delivery app, order way too much food for any one person, and wait.

The food arrives, and I flip through some movies while I eat. My algorithm is all rom-coms since that's all I ever watch, which seems like a cruel joke from the universe, so I settle on bad daytime television. Eventually, I curl up under a blanket and fall asleep on the couch.

When I wake up, the sun is almost setting. The school day is long over, so I risk another check of my phone. Nothing.

I could, of course, call Mac and spill everything, but I don't want to bother her. I could also call Ben and say... I don't even know what I'd say, so I'm not doing that.

*You get to be the protagonist of your own story.*

"Ugh, Ben, get out of my head," I groan, scrubbing at my eyes. "What does that even *mean*?"

I should probably cry, but right now, I'm angry. I'm angry at Ben for kissing me in the first place. I'm angry at Mac for folding in on herself despite every way I've tried to keep her from doing so for as long as I've known her.

I can get in my time machine, too, and get angry at Kyle for being—how did Ben put it? A piece of shit? Yeah, that about sums it up.

I huff. Ben was right about at least one thing last night. Kyle had me feeling like I wasn't worth his time, but it was the other way around.

Ben was right.

I stretch my legs out in front of me and roll onto my back, covering my eyes with my hands and groaning. This feels like the scene where I replay every little thing he said in my head and have some kind of epiphany, and I don't want to do that right now. What he said *hurt*, and that's not something I'm going to forget about just because he was right about the objective truth that Kyle was a jerk and the other guys in my life have never been able to make me happy.

Sure, I was happy for those few weeks with Ben, but I was happy with Kyle at first, too. At least, as happy as a high schooler can be in a relationship—all awkward glances and nervous first times. People change. Their needs and desires shift, and before you know it, you're moving in two different directions, a fraying rope between you pulled too tight, tethering you to each other only until it snaps and whips back to hit you in the face.

I practically launch myself off my couch and start to clean up the fast-food wrappers that are still strewn out across my living room. Dwelling on this isn't going to change anything. I hurt Ben, Ben hurt me, it's over. It was fun while it lasted. This is Mac-level brooding, and I don't need it.

The thought of Mac sends a pang of regret through me as I toss the wrappers in the garbage. I walk back to the couch and flop down on it, glancing at my still-silent phone. I open it up and hover my thumb over the call button next to her name. Maybe Ben was right about this, too. Maybe she's waiting for me like I'm waiting for her. Maybe what she needs is a normal friend talking about normal things. Maybe that's what I need, too.

Without thinking too hard about it, I push the call button.

She answers after the third ring, and, even though she sounds flat and tired, I let out a breath I didn't realize I had been holding as soon as I hear her voice.

"Hey," she says.

"Hey," I respond.

"Jenny. What's wrong?" She's immediately her former self, concern and energy and care in her voice. And it only took one word from me for her to know something was up.

I sigh deeply, the sound catching on a lump in my throat. "Kind of a lot, actually," I start.

"I'll be right over. Should I bring cheeseburgers?"

She's been my best friend practically as long as I can remember, and she still is. I just needed to reach out. I laugh, surprised at how harsh and wet it sounds. I wipe my cheeks, and my fingers come away wet. "Cheeseburgers would be great." I don't tell her I already had cheeseburgers for lunch. It doesn't matter. They'll taste better with her, anyway.

# Chapter 29
## Present Day

MAC BRINGS CHEESEBURGERS AND wine. We set up on the floor of my living room without having to talk about it. It's easy, and I can almost feel my heart cracking wide open with both pain and relief. I haven't even taken a bite before I see tears hit the bun of my cheeseburger.

"What happened?" Mac asks, tilting her head and studying me.

I don't want to cause her more pain or stress, but it feels like a dam has broken in my chest, and there's nowhere for it all to go but out.

"I don't know if I'm more upset about losing Ben or losing you." And there it is. The words hang there for only a second before I burst into tears. Mac grabs my cheeseburger off my lap and sets it on the floor, then she scoots next to me and throws her arm around my shoulders.

"I don't know if I'm more upset about this wedding or losing *you*." She's crying as much as I am now. "I knew eventually you'd have to focus more on yourself than on me, and I wanted that for you. I did. I just didn't expect it to feel this lonely."

I look at her incredulously, then raise the back of my hand to her forehead. "Are you ill?"

A laugh-sob wracks her body as she swats my hand away. "What are you doing?"

"You must be sick as hell if you think you'd ever lose me. I had myself convinced you didn't need the stress of my love life on top of everything else. I've been right here this whole time, so worried about you that I didn't know what to do."

She sobs again, and I get up to grab the tissue box from the kitchen counter. Then, I turn back and grab a bar of chocolate from my pantry for good measure. We each grab a few sheets of tissue and blow our noses in unison, which sets off a fit of teary giggles from both of us. Once the laughter subsides, she lowers her eyes and picks at a piece of the carpet.

"I needed my friend, Jenny." She meets my eyes. "I wanted to know things could be normal between us even when I'm married, but you were avoiding me."

I swipe at my eyes with my wad of tissues and sigh. "Would you believe me if I told you it came from a place of love?"

"I would," she says tentatively. "Would you believe me if I told you whatever Ben said to you probably did, too?"

I frown. "You talked to him?"

"No, but I saw him in the hallway today. I don't think I've ever seen a man look so much like a sad puppy. What happened?"

I take a deep breath and let it out slowly. "He was so mad I hadn't told you every little detail about us that he walked out in the middle of dinner last night."

She scrunches up her face as if this is not at all what she expected me to say. "That doesn't make sense."

I laugh bitterly. "There was a little more to it than that, but the moral of the story is that he wanted to be worth talking to you about."

She nods knowingly. "Because you never bothered telling me anything about the men who meant nothing to you."

"Apparently being included in our friendship is a badge of honor or something," I joke.

"Or it proves to him you want him to stick around, because if I know about it, it's real."

My gaze falls to the carpet, and I rub my toe against it, feeling the rough grooves of the threads against my foot. "It sure felt real, even if I didn't tell you about it." My voice is small, and Mac throws her arm over my shoulders again.

"Tell me about it now, then."

"It's too late." I almost sob again, but she laughs and shakes her head.

"Oh, sweet Jenny. You're always late. Why should now be any different?"

I laugh harshly and roll my eyes. She's not wrong, so I tell her everything, and by the time I'm done talking, I'm crying so hard I couldn't continue even if there was anything more to say. Mac, to her credit, doesn't press for more or try to insist all isn't lost. She just listens. In all our years of friendship, she knows that's what I need now. That, and her, next to me, with cold cheeseburgers and wine on the floor of my apartment.

She spends the night, and I drive into school the next morning on her tail. When we get out of our cars, she immediately links her arm with mine and walks in solidarity with me all the way to my classroom. Luckily, Ben is nowhere to be seen.

"You going to be okay today?" She tilts her head, her eyebrows pinched together.

"Yeah. My plan is to hide in here like a troll and then run out of here as soon as I'm sure he's at conditioning to pick up my dress from the tailor."

She eyes me warily. "Okay. But if he tries anything, you let me know. I'll beat him up."

I snort. "You couldn't hurt a fly."

"Ah." She holds up a finger. "That's where you're wrong. I may not be able to inflict physical damage, but I can lecture him to death, and a lot of people think that's actually more painful."

The image of Mac lecturing Ben has me cackling, and it feels good. She winks at me and starts to leave, but before she can get out the door, I call out, "Hey, Mac? Thanks."

She looks over her shoulder. The bags under her eyes are apparent, and she looks gaunt, but she was willing to put all that aside for me, and I'm relieved we can fall so quickly back into our old routine.

"You don't have to thank me for being your friend, Jenny. You needed me. I'll always be here when you need me."

I smile a little, and she returns it, then she leaves.

By some miracle—or by the sheer willpower of two people avoiding each other—I don't see Ben all day. I glance at my desk calendar and do a quick calculation. I only have to avoid him for about 155 more school days. Totally doable.

I contemplate emailing Ken and asking him for a room change, but that would require more explanation than I'm willing to give my boss at the moment. I know Mac would feel comfortable with something like that, but he and I have never had that kind of quasi-father-daughter relationship they've got going on.

One day down is a small victory, though, and when I also don't run into him on my way out of the building, I find myself feeling a little lighter as I walk to my car.

The victory, however, is short-lived. My phone buzzes inside my bag, and when I pull it out and see *Mom* across the top, I groan and smack my forehead against the steering wheel. How does this woman always find the absolute worst times to call me?

I bring my phone to my ear with my head still resting against the steering wheel. "Hi, Mom." I can barely hide my annoyance.

"Hi, honey. I was driving out by your school, and I thought you might want to come to dinner with me."

"Oh, I can't." I know I don't sound too disappointed, but I don't have the energy to care what she thinks about me today. "I have to pick up my dress for Mac's wedding."

"That's okay. I can wait."

I press my head even farther into the steering wheel. My brain can't think of an excuse fast enough, so I concede. She tells me where to meet her, and I swing by the seamstress's shop on my way there. By the time I slide into the booth across from my mom, I'm beyond exhausted. She checks her watch pointedly, making it clear she's been waiting a while. Even though I told her I needed to pick up my dress first, the woman makes me feel like I'm here at the wrong time.

She finally looks up at me. "You look awful, Jen."

That's how she starts. No greeting, no questioning why I look like someone chewed me up and spit me out, no empathy or sympathy or concern. Just a negative comment on how I look.

Maybe Ben was right about this, too. Maybe I am worth standing up for myself.

At any rate, I've had enough. I slide right back out of the booth and stand up. Her mouth makes an O-shape, and her eyebrows shoot up her forehead. Or they go as far as they can for someone who has had so much work done over the past few years.

"It's Jenny," I say through clenched teeth.

She leans back in her seat a little. "What?"

"My name is Jenny. You don't have to like it. You just have to call me it."

"You're leaving because I called you Jen?"

I let out a sigh so deep I may have pulled it from the foundation of the building. "No. I'm leaving because I've had a shitty couple of days, and I'm too tired to do this with you right now."

She frowns the frown of the chemically enhanced, and I feel vindicated that I've forced my mother to make two facial expressions in the span of five minutes.

"Do what with me?"

"Listen to you talk about how I eat too much or not enough, or about how I'm not pretty enough, or I don't know how to hold on to a guy." My voice betrays me on the last part, and her expression softens.

She waves at the seat across from her. "Sit, Jen." When I raise my eyebrow at her and stay standing right where I am, she closes her eyes. "Jenny," she says.

"I hope that wasn't too painful for you," I mutter as I slide back into the booth.

She opens her eyes and studies me, but I refuse to cower under her scrutiny anymore. I sit, straight-backed and with my hands clasped tightly in front of me on top of the table. My expression is carefully neutral.

She purses her lips, then starts speaking cautiously. "I had no idea you felt this way. Why didn't you ever say anything?"

"I did, Mom. You didn't listen."

She waves this away, and an anger rises from my belly and into my throat, but she says, "You mentioned your name once or twice, but you never said anything about the rest of it."

I bark a laugh. "What else would you call criticizing my food choices or taking Kyle's side over mine—"

"I did no such thing."

"The week we broke up, we were here, at this same restaurant." I'm yelling now, and I don't care who hears. "Mac was here, and you told me he was a 'sweet boy.' The best I could get out of you was, 'Oh, that's too bad' after I told you he *cheated on me.*"

She stares at me and says nothing for long enough that I smack the table with the palm of my hand and move to get up again.

When I've reached the edge of the seat, she says, almost a whisper, "Your father cheated on me. When I was pregnant with you."

I go completely still. I carefully slide my gaze to her, worried that if I move too fast, it'll spook her. She has never spoken about my father before. Not once in thirty years.

"He told me I was fun before I got pregnant, and he wanted someone fun again. I kicked him out that night, and I never saw him again."

"Shit, Mom," I breathe, sliding back to the center of the booth. "That's awful."

She nods and swallows hard. Then, her eyes meet mine. "I wanted you. Desperately. I figured I didn't need him. That we'd be enough for each other. And we mostly were." She swallows again. "If I ever made you feel like you weren't enough for me, I'm deeply sorry. I guess we all have our demons to fight before we can truly love."

She's quiet for a long time, and I know that's probably all I'm going to get from her. I'm not going to let myself hope that this means things will get better between us, but for the rest of dinner, we chat about various topics. She doesn't once criticize me or suggest I'm not living up to her standards. We simply enjoy each other's company.

It's a start.

# Chapter 30
## Present Day

I haven't heard anything from Ben all week. It's almost as if he left LPHS and works somewhere else now. 152 more days to go before I can request a room change and stop hiding, I suppose.

By Saturday night, I've opened and closed the text thread to Ben so many times, I've lost count. I don't know what to say to him, and even if I did, I'm not sure I'm ready to say it.

The sun is just lowering past the tops of the trees outside my window as I'm about to curl myself into bed and hope for sleep to take some of the stress away. Before I can close my eyes, my phone rings from the nightstand. I've long-since lost the little skip in my heart at the thought that it could Ben, so I drag the phone by its charging cord to the top of my comforter to see who is calling.

When I see Daniel's name, I answer so quickly that I fumble the phone as I'm bringing it to my ear. "Is Mac okay?" I sit straight up in bed.

"Uh, yeah. Hey, Jenny. Mac is fine, but we've had an idea and we could use your help. Can you come over in about two hours? And dress nice?"

I take a few deep breaths, willing my heart to slow down and my brain to process what he's asking. "What's going on?"

I hear some scratching noises as Daniel's phone transfers hands, then Mac's voice comes through. She has clearly been crying. "We want to get married tonight. At our house."

My head is reeling. "Tonight? At your house?"

"Yes, Jenny. Keep up. You have your officiant's license still, right? Can you come officiate? Just something small. It doesn't have to be a huge thing. We have our marriage license already since the wedding was supposed to be next week, so we can do it privately. Please?"

I rub my hand hard over my temples. "Of course I can, Mac. Are you sure this is what you want?"

"I haven't been more sure of something since you were dragging me into a university auditorium two years ago."

I hear Daniel grumble something about her seeming pretty sure the night they got engaged, and she laughs. It's a pure sound—one I haven't heard from her in a while—and it's clear to me that this hare-brained plan has already lifted a huge weight off her.

I let her know I'll be there in two hours, then hang up and set a timer. I might show up at the wrong time for everything, but I will not be late to my best friend's wedding. I don't get ready right away, though. Instead, I sit at my desk in my sweatpants and grab a pen and some paper. I've made some poor choices when it comes to Mac this year, but I can at least do this. I shake the image of Ben from my head and start writing.

I pull up to Daniel and Mac's house exactly two hours later. Daniel said dress nicely, so I'm wearing a simple, capped-sleeve, black dress that falls to my calves. There is a slit up the side to my thigh that allows me to move easily. I paired it with black, strappy heels and some simple silver jewelry. My long hair is curled in loose waves, and my makeup is dark enough to hide the bags under my eyes from not sleeping this past week. It has been surprisingly difficult to adjust to sleeping alone after only one week of Ben's warmth next to me.

I shake away that thought as I look up at the house. I take a deep, fortifying breath and walk up to ring the doorbell.

When the door opens, I'm greeted by both Katie, who looks stunning in a shimmery charcoal bodycon dress, and the scent of fresh flowers. It's so strong that it nearly knocks me back a few steps.

"Is Daniel opening a flower shop in here?"

Katie rolls her eyes. "You'd think so by the look of it. Come on in." She opens the door a little wider, and I move past her, completely floored by what I see. There are white roses on almost every available surface. Some are in vases surrounded by candles, some are laid out artfully, and, on the front table, there is a beautiful bouquet of them next to a single white rose boutonniere.

My jaw drops as I slowly turn to Katie. She shrugs. "Daniel put me to work."

"You did this?" I am completely amazed by how extravagant yet tasteful it all looks.

"I'm a bit of an artist, so I guess he thought I'd have an eye for it." She shrugs again.

"You certainly do. But... why?" My eyebrows pinch together as I do another sweep around the room.

"Believe it or not, Daniel loves a grand gesture."

"This must have cost him a fortune," I breathe as I look around the room again.

Katie chuckles. "Their endless money is harder to get used to than you'd think, isn't it?"

My eyes are still wide as I turn to her and nod. "Do you know what happened to prompt this?"

"That idiot finally talked to his fiancée and figured out what her problem was," a deep and booming voice comes from the hallway. Brandon appears behind his wife, rolling his eyes. "She was terrified of the ceremony. Didn't want people staring at her."

My gaze flits between Brandon and Katie, suspicious. "He finally talked to her, or you both stepped in?"

Brandon looks at Katie, his eyebrows raised. She tilts her head to the side. "I may have suggested he open his eyes and get his head out of his ass."

Something about Katie tells me her suggestions are more like orders, and I can't help but be impressed. And then a little pang of guilt zings through me at the thought that I should have stepped in long ago. I know Mac better than anyone, and even I thought she'd get over her fear of being the center of attention for her wedding.

Thankfully, Brandon interrupts my thoughts before I can go too far down that rabbit hole. "So. Here we are. Rushing around last minute while he..." He trails off and looks around. "Where is he, anyway?"

"I'm in here," Daniel calls from the direction of the living room. He appears in the entryway, dressed in a crisp navy suit and a light pink tie. He checks his watch. "I just finished setting up. Mac should be coming down any minute."

As if on cue, Mac appears at the stop of the stairs in an ivory sun dress, her makeup done and her hair curled. I'm impressed; usually she needs me to help her get ready. But instead of the pang of sadness I would have felt a week ago, I am so happy for her, I could burst. I'm not leaving any room for sadness today.

She smiles at us as she descends the stairs carefully in her high-heeled shoes. "Okay, everyone. Let's get this show on the road."

# Chapter 31
## Present Day

LUCKILY, I HAD BEEN at least thinking about my maid of honor speech these past few weeks, so by the time I'm standing at the end of the makeshift aisle Katie littered with rose petals and lined with candles and fabric, I feel mostly prepared.

Katie sits, bouncing their daughter, Christine, on her lap, and Mason sits next to Brandon. There's no music or fanfare, just Mac entering on Daniel's arm, carrying her bouquet on slightly unsteady feet either because of her high-heeled shoes or because of her nerves. Daniel stops at the end of the aisle farthest away from me and faces her. "I know you hate being the center of attention." He clasps their hands together between them. "I know you've been dreading our wedding, probably since the day I proposed, but you only wanted to make me happy, so you did what you always do. You took it upon yourself to take care of me, to do what you thought I wanted. But all along, all I've ever wanted is for you to be happy."

She drags her eyes away from him and looks around the room, taking in the flowers, and candles, her green eyes wide. "Oh, wow," she whispers. "This is amazing." I can almost feel her relief from where I'm standing, and, impossibly, my smile widens. Daniel cups her face with his hands and kisses her deeply. She lifts her free hand to circle his wrist, a grin breaking through.

The kiss goes on long enough that I interject. "Hey, you two. Save some for the ceremony." Daniel pulls away and shoots me a look, but I shrug. Daniel offers Mac his arm again. She takes it, and they begin their walk down the aisle.

They reach me and face each other. Seeing them there, I'm suddenly so overcome with emotion that I can't speak. A lump rises in my throat, and tears threaten to fall. Mac looks at me, tears already trailing down her cheeks. I blink, letting my own drop, then sniffle.

Daniel shoots a glance between the two of us and fights an amused sigh. "I knew this would happen."

"If you're asking me not to cry, you're asking too much, Evans," I say quietly.

"This is everything I've ever wanted." Mac fights a sob.

Daniel's expression immediately softens, and he leans forward as if to kiss her, but I can't let that happen again or we'll be here all night. "Dearly Beloved," I say loudly, and he straightens. I continue. "We are gathered here today to witness the marriage of Mackenzie Milcrest and Daniel Evans. I'd ask if anyone opposes this union to speak now or forever hold their peace, but if anyone says anything, I'll personally take you down, so let's skip that part." There is hearty laughter from both Katie and Brandon as I shoot a mockingly threatening look at them.

"I would like to take a moment of silence to remember those who cannot be with us today." I pause and glace at Mac. She looks back at me, her expression both sad and grateful. I lower my voice to almost a whisper. "I know Ellie would have loved this."

Mac shakes her head, a tear falling down her cheek. She chuckles. "No she wouldn't have. She would have made fun of me for getting married in my living room." Her gaze meets Daniel's. "But she would have loved you."

Daniel smiles sadly, and I pause for a beat before I continue, raising my voice a bit. "Mac has been my best friend for almost as long as I can remember." I turn my eyes to her. "And Daniel... well..." I hold back a chuckle. "He's okay, I guess."

"High praise from Jenny Green, believe it or not," he mutters.

"When Mac met Daniel, they seemed to be an unlikely pair. She, a hardworking, dedicated, introverted teacher. He, a famous, wealthy writer who lied about his name." Daniel shoots me a warning look. "I'm kidding. They were damned perfect for each other, and everyone knew it. They belong together, these two, and I'm proud of the part I've played in their relationship."

I raise my eyes to those assembled again, and this time, I snag on an empty chair. "Mac and Daniel have taught me that falling in love is one of the bravest things two people can do." I swallow heavily, and against every rational fiber of my being, I find myself wishing Ben was here. Another tear threatens to fall, and I wipe it away quickly. "They both had to overcome some pretty deep scars, but they helped each other heal. Opening up those scars from the past can be painful, and the willingness to see that pain, to work through it and stitch each other back together... that's bravery. That's love." I shift my attention back to Mac and Daniel, who only have eyes for each other. "Someone said to me the other day, 'We all have demons to fight before we can truly love,' and that has stuck with me. She was right, of course." Then I roll my eyes a little. "But I think there's more to it than that. I think finding love is about fighting those demons together, and I know Mac and Daniel will continue to fight like hell for each other."

Mac looks at me, tears lining her eyes again, and her face fixed in a smile wider than I've ever seen from her. I glance at Daniel, who clearly cannot take his eyes off Mac. Yeah, they'll fight like hell for each other. I'll always be in her corner, but I'm glad she has him there, too.

I walk them through the vows, then the exchange of rings, which Brandon produces from a pocket in his suit coat. I read most of it from a page I hastily printed from the internet at my apartment, but no one seems to mind.

"It is my absolute pleasure to be the first to introduce you to Mr. Daniel Evans and Ms. Mackenzie Milcrest-Evans." I grin at them both. "Kiss each other, you fools."

They do, and the family of four erupts into applause so loud, it sounds like thirty people. Mason whoops from his seat, and I follow suit, unable to help myself.

Daniel breaks their kiss, then leans in to kiss her forehead. He takes her hand, and they face everyone. "There's food and drinks in the kitchen. Everyone, help yourselves. Let's celebrate!"

Mason makes a beeline to the food with Brandon and Katie close behind. Mac pulls Daniel into the next room, and I'm left standing there with my papers still clutched in my hands.

Feeling a jealous pang at the realization that I'm the odd one out, I grab a glass of champagne off a table near the open patio door and head outside. The air is pleasantly cool, finally, and the setting sun is painting beautiful colors across the sky. I take a deep breath and sink into one of the outdoor couches on the patio.

"You don't strike me as the type not to eat food that's offered to you." Katie comes around and sits next to me. She's holding a plate in one hand

and her toddler in the other. As soon as she sets Christine down, she immediately wobbles off to explore.

"I'm not." I laugh lightly. "I needed a minute."

"Stomach in knots?" She scoops up some vegetables on her fork and takes a bite.

"Something like that," I murmur. Christine toddles back and puts her little chubby hands on Katie's knees, leaning in and opening her mouth. Katie stabs a carrot and holds it out for her to bite. Happy, she wanders away again.

"It was a beautiful speech. Hard to believe you threw that together in a few hours."

I huff. "I've had a few years to think about what I wanted to say and some experience winging it in front of people."

Katie nods, impressed, then takes another bite of her food. "I can't help but think you may not have just been talking about her and Daniel, though." She smiles smugly as she watches Christine sniff at a flower.

I give her a sidelong look. "And?" I ask, taking another sip of my champagne.

"And..." she trails off, chewing and swallowing her food. "I was surprised not to see Ben here with you."

It figures she'd get right to the point. I take a deep breath, then let it out quickly through puffed cheeks. Some quiet music starts playing in their outdoor speakers. From the way Mason is dancing erratically, the same song is playing through the indoor speakers as well.

"Remember how I said we've known each other a long time?" I ask.

"That was a particularly interesting detail." Katie raises her eyebrows.

I purse my lips and look upwards at the darkening night sky. "He's seen a lot of my worst moments. Some of it was really bad. I'm the type of person who screws these things up."

"Hmm," Katie hums as she chews, then swallows. "What about all that stuff you just said about healing each other's past pain?"

"I never said I wasn't a hypocrite." I shrug, and she laughs.

"I've been married for almost six years now—and let me stop you there because I see you doing the math. Mason was born before we got married, and, yes, he's Brandon's."

"None of my business."

"It's a point of contention for us. Not the paternity; the waiting so long to get married." She sighs. "Regardless, I've been married for a bit, and the thing I've found about love is that it doesn't matter how or when you meet. If you love someone long enough, you're inevitably going to find out all their deep, dark secrets. The love part of it is when you keep choosing them anyway."

That hits like a punch in the gut. Ben has definitely seen some of my darkest moments—*the* darkest, really—and he chooses me. Again and again and again.

I don't have time to dwell on it before Mac squeals behind me. "Jenny!" I twist around to see her, a glass of champagne in her hand. I stand, and we meet halfway to each other, hugging as if we haven't hugged in a million years. "Jenny, that was so beautiful."

"You're beautiful. You're my beautiful, wonderful friend, and I'm honored to have been a part of this at all. I'm so happy for you." I squeeze her tighter. I mean it. The jealousy has been replaced by a budding hope that her life is all happiness from here on out.

Mac holds me at arm's length and glances at Katie. "Can I steal her for a minute? We need her to sign some papers."

Katie smiles. "Of course. I have to wrestle this one into bed, anyway. Come on, squirt." She sets her plate aside and picks up a giggling Christine, sweeping her back into the house.

Mac leads me back to the office where the marriage license is. Daniel and Brandon are there, too. We all sign it, and the guys make their way back to the kitchen. Mac lingers, so I do, too.

She toys with the corner of the marriage license, wiggling it back and forth on top of the desk. "I wanted to say thank you. I know this was last minute."

"Last minute is a bit of an understatement."

Mac winces, still playing with the items on the desk. "Yeah, I don't know how he did all of this in only a few hours. I started crying and told him I wanted it to be done today, and... poof."

"He really came through for you. I wish I had been the one to suggest it a long time ago."

At this, her eyes snap to mine. "It's not on you to fight my battles for me. I've spent years of my life trying to get students to advocate for themselves. I should have taken my own advice and spoken up."

I tilt my head to the side. "Why didn't you?"

She rolls her eyes. "I don't know. It mattered so much more to me that Daniel was happy. He made such a big deal about having a big wedding, and then my mom got all teary about that dress over the phone. I lost myself a little. I'm not proud of it, but we all do stupid stuff in the name of love, I guess."

I smile a little sadly. "I guess we do."

She pauses, chewing on the inside of her lip. "How are you doing?"

"Don't you dare worry about me on your special day, Mac. I'm fine."
I scowl at her.

She presses her lips into a thin line as if she could physically hold the
words back, but then they tumble out, anyway. "Ben should be here."

It's my turn to start playing with things on the desk. I grab a pen and
start twirling it in circles with the tip of my finger. "Well, he's not."

I can feel Mac's eyes on me, but she doesn't say anything for a long
moment, and neither do I. "I'm still your best friend, Jenny. When you're
ready to talk about it."

I roll the pen back and forth and nod, but I don't say anything. I take
a deep breath and let it out, proud of myself that it's only a little shaky.

"Why don't you stay here tonight?" she suggests. "Katie, Brandon,
and the kids are spending the night again, and we set up some air mat-
tresses in the empty bedrooms. We can hang out, like old times. Plus a
few more people."

When I look up, her green eyes are full of hope, and to be honest,
another lonely night at my apartment after this beautiful ceremony feels
like twisting the knife that has been lodged in my chest for the past week.

I smile a real smile. "Lucky for you, I stashed a bunch of clothes in one
of the closets up there a while ago for just such an occasion."

# Chapter 32
## Present Day

ONCE THE KIDS ARE asleep, we all change into pajamas and play card games into the wee hours of the morning while we finish off the champagne and sit on the living room floor. Mac's relief is palpable as she leans back into Daniel. The tension that has been lining her face for the past few weeks is gone, and her smiles are genuine again.

Katie and Brandon sit without touching, and though there doesn't seem to be a lot of tension there, it's clear something is going on between them, though no one asks, and they don't offer any information.

Eventually, we all make our way to our respective rooms. I plug my phone into the spare charger they keep in their kitchen on my way upstairs. No one is going to be calling me tonight, anyway, and I'd like one night to go to bed without staring longingly at a blank message screen.

The next morning, I hear little footsteps run past my door at what feels like an ungodly hour to be awake. I check my watch and, sure enough, it's seven in the morning. I scrub my eyes with my palms and roll over, but I know I'm not going to go back to sleep. I slide myself as carefully as I can off the air mattress as it bounces back and forth with my weight and grab some clothes to change into out of the closet that I had claimed as my own a few months ago. I pull my hair into a ponytail and make my way to the kitchen.

When I get down there, I'm greeted by a bleary-eyed Brandon, his hair falling around his shoulders in waves I'd kill for, and a slightly more awake Katie, each with a cup of coffee in their hands. We nod in silent greeting as Katie passes me and goes to the television to turn on cartoons for the kids. I pour myself some coffee, add milk and sugar, and take eggs, vegetables, and cheese out of the fridge. I go about making omelets for everyone, cracking every single egg they have into a huge mixing bowl.

"Need any help?" Katie asks, coming back into the kitchen. She sits at the island, warming her hands on her mug.

"No." I grab a whisk and start mixing. "This is kind of my thing. Or, at least, it was when I used to spend the night at Mac's condo."

I pour some of the egg mixture into a pan heating on the stove, sprinkle on vegetables and cheese, and grab a spatula. "Will the kids eat vegetable omelets?" I ask.

Katie snorts, and Brandon shakes his head in dismay.

"Scrambled eggs?" I suggest.

"I like scrambled eggs," Mason shouts from the living room.

"Scamby eggs!" Christine's little voice chimes in.

"Coming right up," I call back as Mac and Daniel finally pad into the kitchen with us. They look like they didn't sleep much, and I hide a wry smile behind my coffee mug.

Mac walks over to the stove and inhales deeply. "I love it when you stay over," she says dreamily. I chuckle, flipping the omelet and sliding it onto a plate. I deposit it on the island and start the next one.

We get food and coffee in front of everyone. The kids sit at the table while the rest of us sit or hover around the island, scooping bites into our mouths and taking turns eyeing the kids from where we chat pleasantly.

"What will you do about the wedding next weekend?" Katie grabs a refill on her coffee and sits back down. Brandon remains standing near her in case one of the kids needs something.

Mac and Daniel look at each other and share a private smile. "I think we're going to go ahead and have a party anyway, just without the ceremony," Daniel says.

"And without the dress." Mac grimaces, and we all laugh.

Katie's eyes go practically heart shaped as she croons, "Oh, your first marital compromise. How sweet." She shoots Brandon a pointed glance, and he quickly looks away.

Someone's phone starts dinging rapidly as several messages come in quick succession. Everyone glances at their own phones, and I pat my pockets looking for mine before I remember I left it charging on the counter last night.

"It's me." I grab it, pulling it off the charger and unlocking the screen. There are several messages from two unknown numbers.

*Hi Jenny. I hope this isn't weird.*

*This is definitely weird.*

*This is Ashley, Ben's sister. The other number is Chloe. We were a little surprised not to see you at family dinner last night, so we stole Ben's phone and found your number.*

Chloe: *For the record, I told her this was a terrible idea.*

Ashley: *I'm the lawyer here. Let me worry about what goes on the record and what doesn't.*

With each message that comes through in rapid-fire, my frown deepens.

Chloe: *You'd think a lawyer would be more concerned about an invasion of privacy.*

"Are you okay? Is something wrong?" Mac asks.

I look up at her. "I'm not sure. It's Ben's sisters, and they're arguing with each other on a text chain that somehow includes me."

In an instant, Mac is by my side and Katie jumps off her stool to join us, both of them reading over my shoulders. The guys exchange wary glances over their mugs.

Ashley texts next: *Anyway, we missed you.*

Then Chloe sends: *Mom mostly missed your meatballs.*

Ashley: *Ben is sad.*

Chloe: *Really sad.*

"Are you going to respond to them?" Mac asks, her chin practically leaning on my shoulder.

"Doesn't look like she needs to. They're doing a fine job of carrying on this conversation all by themselves." Katie arches an eyebrow, her head peering around my upper arm.

Ashley: *On the off chance you're sad too, we're all going to the pumpkin patch in about an hour, and we thought maybe you'd want to come.*

"This might be the weirdest thing that has ever happened to me," I mutter. Mac chuckles.

Chloe: *This is admittedly not a well thought out plan.*

Ashley: *Please come. We won't tell him you'll be there if you don't want. We hate seeing him sad like this.*

We all wait for a bit, but the messages stop.

"Is it my turn?" I ask.

"Maybe?" Katie leans back to look at me. "What are you going to do?"

Mac is practically vibrating on the other side of me. "I love the pumpkin patch," she says slyly.

"This isn't about the pumpkin patch." I shoot her a sidelong glance, setting my phone down on the counter and backing away as if it is going to attack me.

"I want to go to the pumpkin patch!" Mason calls from the table.

"Patch! Patch! Patch!" Christine beats her little hands on the table in time with her exclamations.

Brandon chuckles. Katie pinches the bridge of her nose and sighs a sigh so deep it feels like it comes from the tips of her toes and out her mouth. "I guess we're going to the pumpkin patch," she mutters, but the kids hear her and cheer.

Mac looks at me expectantly, one side of her mouth turned up in a bad attempt at hiding a giddy smile. "You coming?"

My heart leaps into my throat and starts pounding so hard, I'm surprised everyone can't hear it. "What if he doesn't want to see me?" I whisper. "What if..." I trail off and swallow. "What if that was my last chance?"

Once I've given voice to the fear, I feel tears prick my eyes and fall down my cheeks. I quickly wipe them away. Katie's shoulders fall slightly as she covers her mouth with her hand and gives me a look of pure pity.

Mac, however, nudges my phone toward me. "Only one way to find out."

# Chapter 33
## Present Day

GETTING OUT OF THE house with five adults and two children is absolute chaos, but somehow, in an hour, everyone is dressed, snacks are packed for the kids, and we've impossibly found two pairs of child-sized shoes after a ten-minute search.

Brandon drives Katie and the kids, and I'm tucked in the backseat of Daniel's car, my hands pressed tightly between my thighs as my right foot bounces uncontrollably. It's a quiet ride, but Mac makes sure to shoot me a few reassuring glances in the rearview mirror. Each time, I smile tightly, but I can't get control of my heart rate, so I mostly keep jiggling my foot to take the edge off my nervous energy.

When we arrive, the kids run to the entrance ahead of us, then stop in their tracks. "Woah," Mason breathes, taking in the vast field of pumpkins, the corn maze, and the petting zoo in front of him. Mac shoots Katie a quizzical look.

"City kids," she says by way of explanation.

Mac practically rubs her hands together in glee and steps out front to lead the way. "You all are in for a treat."

As we walk through the field of pumpkins, I can't help but scan in every direction, but I don't see Ben or his sisters. I had texted them that I would be there, and with getting everyone out of the house, it's been well over the hour they said it'd take for them to arrive. Maybe they did tell him, and he decided he didn't want anything to do with me. Maybe we're late. It would figure I'd show up at the wrong time for what feels like the most important moment of my life. My shoulders sag a bit at the thought, and Mac reaches out to rub my arm comfortingly.

"He'll be here," she says reassuringly.

Just then, I hear a squeal to my right and turn to see Ben lifting Caleb onto his shoulders. Caleb is holding a small pumpkin, and Brody is jumping, trying to reach it. They're all laughing as Ben twirls Caleb this way and that, evading Brody's reach.

I freeze. My heart feels like it's going to squeeze into itself as I watch the easy way Ben interacts with his nephews, and I'm not sure what I find more attractive—the bulge of his muscles as he lifts and twirls Caleb, or the absolute dad vibes he's giving off.

Even my ovaries want him. I silently tell them to shut up.

I don't know what Ashley and Chloe were talking about. He looks plenty happy to me. He doesn't need me ruining his fun. I turn toward Mac, shaking my head. I don't have the words to tell her I can't do it, but she seems to understand. Her hand is still on my arm, and she gives it a little squeeze.

Before I can say anything, Mason takes off running in their direction. Katie straightens as if she had been leaning down to talk to him. She comes to stand next to us and shrugs. "Kids, am I right?"

"Hi, Ben!" Mason shouts. He looks around at the sound of his name, his eyes finally landing on Mason. He stiffens a little but smiles warmly at him.

"Hey, Mason. Funny seeing you here." Ben's deep voice carries across the rows of pumpkins, and I suppress a shiver. He lifts Caleb off his shoulders and sets him on the ground.

"Mom said we'd see you here. She said we were looking for you." Mason reaches their little group. Ben's eyebrows pinch together, and he looks around, presumably to find Katie.

"Hi, I'm Mason," he says to Brody. "Want to play?" The boys, including Caleb, run off through the field just as Ashley, Amelia, and Chloe come into view. Ben squints into the distance, slowly surveying the field when his eyes land on me and widen. I'm frozen in place, only able to take little sips of air, my heart pounding uncontrollably in my ears.

Mac gives me a little shove, and my feet start moving stiffly, as if I'm not controlling them at all. Ben glances at his sisters. Chloe shrugs and Ashley winks. Ben shakes his head slowly, but his face softens, which I choose to take as a good sign.

I stop about five feet in front of him, and I suddenly wish I had taken the ride over here to think about what to say, because I'm at a loss for words. My breath is sucked straight out of my lungs. He looks fantastic, and my heart skips over itself, ultimately lodging itself in my throat.

I've missed him more than I even admitted to myself.

We are close enough that I can smell his aftershave and the slightest tang of the gym. He must have been lifting before he came here.

"Hi." I'm so grateful my voice doesn't squeak that I smile.

He smiles back, though it doesn't meet his eyes, and I find myself longing to see the corners of his eyes crinkle. "Hi."

The feel of his gaze and the sound of his voice finally addressing me is enough to make my knees weak. A simple, two-letter word, and I'm pudding. Unbelievable.

He takes a step toward me, then another, as if he can't help himself.

I let loose a breath. "You, uh, look good." As soon as I say it, I cannot believe this is how I choose to start this conversation.

"It's good to see you. I wasn't sure you'd ever come out of your classroom."

I swallow. "I wasn't sure you wanted me to."

"Of course I wanted you to." He says it so quickly, like he didn't even have to think about it, and I'm taken aback.

"You did?"

His eyes suddenly turn sad. "I meant what I said—"

That is all it takes to light a fire in me. "Oh, you did, did you? You meant all those things you said to me before you *walked out of my apartment*?" I have to fight to keep my voice down. I see Ashley and Chloe exchange looks, and I feel Mac come up behind me, ready to get me out of here if I need.

He sighs and reaches up to scrub a hand through his hair. "Will you just listen?" He leans slightly forward in earnest. "I meant what I said when I said I'm yours. I was frustrated, but I wasn't ready to pack it in."

I study him, my frown deepening. "You sure have an odd way of showing it."

His eyes fall to a spot on the ground. "Yeah. I see that now." Then, his eyes meet mine again, and there is an earnestness in them that wasn't there before. "I made a mistake. I shouldn't have walked out on you. I'm sorry."

I desperately search for words to respond, but I don't have any. This feels so unlike any apology I've ever been given that I'm not quite sure what to do with it. It's so honest and pure, without the expectation of any reciprocation. Just a man who knows he said some things he shouldn't have and saying he was wrong.

Mac nudges me with her shoe, and I roll my eyes. "Well, you weren't entirely wrong, and I'm sorry, too," I admit begrudgingly, "but if you felt you made a mistake, why didn't you come talk to me this week?"

He raises his arms and lets them fall again in a helpless gesture. "A part of me was hoping you'd see I was right. That you're worth all this and more."

"Look, Ben—"

"I love you, Jenny." He shakes his head incredulously. My jaw falls open and my eyebrows raise, but he continues. "I'm in love with you. I think I have been since we met, or soon after." He waits for a beat, but I stand there, words floating just out of my reach. "You don't have to say anything right now. I had to say it because I can't hold on to it any longer, but you don't have to. You're it for me. If it's not you, it's no one. Not anymore. And I'm such an idiot, I'd probably wait nine more years for you to figure it out."

"At least you're a self-aware idiot," I mumble, and my hand flies to my mouth as soon as it's out, but Ben tilts his head back and laughs harder than I've heard him laugh in a long time. His laughter makes me smile, and I shake my head, lowering my hands. "I'm sorry. My mouth works without the permission of my brain."

He takes another step toward me and reaches out as if he's going to touch my jaw or brush some hair away, but he doesn't. I wish he would, and I find myself taking an involuntary step toward him.

"I love your mouth and your brain," he says softly. "I love all of you, Jenny." His eyes sparkle in the sunlight, and there is still a smile playing at his lips.

More than anything, I want to kiss those lips. And I think—no, I know—that I'd be more than happy for his to be the only lips I kiss for the rest of my life.

"I love you, too, Ben." It's almost a whisper, and he leans forward as if he didn't quite hear me, or he isn't sure he can believe his ears.

His smile fades, and his expression is so open, so earnest, it hurts my heart to look at it for too long. "Is that your mouth working without the permission of your brain again?" His eyes search mine.

I shake my head. "No. I've had a long time to think about it. I'm sick of thinking about it."

His brown eyes burn into me, and my cheeks grow warm. "I know everyone is watching us, but I'm going to kiss you now."

A little, relieved laugh escapes me. "Finally," I tease, and before I can say anything else, his lips are on mine and I'm being wrapped in his strong arms, pressed close to his body. I melt deeply into him, soaking in his warmth as he kisses me deeply. There are some cheers and laughter, and I think I hear Ashley mutter, "I told you so," but I'm too busy kissing Ben to care.

I pull away suddenly and narrow my eyes at him. "I'm not moving in with you, though. I need to do this on my own time."

He smirks, his brown eyes never moving from mine. "You do everything on your own time."

"Yeah, and if you want to be with me, you'd better get used to it." I raise an eyebrow in challenge.

"I'd be happy to be on your time for the rest of my life."

It took me nine years to realize what was right in front of me the whole time, and when my lips find his again and he sighs into me, I make a silent promise never to make him wait for me again.

# Epilogue
## Three Months Later

IT ONLY TOOK US about three months before we moved in together, or, as Ben likes to say, it took us *nine years* and three months. Every time he says it, I roll my eyes good naturedly, swat his arm, and he grabs my wrist, spins me into his chest, and kisses me. His kisses are always a mix of I've-waited-so-long-for-this and this-is-how-it-should-always-have-been, and I can never get enough.

That next step has happened slowly, and then all at once—I kept leaving things at his place, staying there more and more often, until all my things were there, and I never left, and we decided it was silly to keep paying rent on my apartment.

It's new, but it's easy. Everything with Ben is easy, and the simple feeling of never having to push or pull anymore is intoxicating.

Mac, however, comes up with this idea for a date jar, where we each put slips of paper for date ideas and randomly pull one out once a month. Whatever is on the slip of paper, we have to do, all four of us, together. No questions asked. She says she comes up with this idea because she is bound and determined that our relationships will never lose their spark, and our friendships will last a lifetime, but I know her well enough to know she's desperately trying to do something fun to recover from wedding planning. So far, we've been to a cooking class where Daniel set off the smoke alarm; horseback riding where Mac gripped the reins so tight in fear, her hands were claws for days; and ballroom dancing lessons where Ben literally and figuratively swept me off my feet. The man can dance, apparently.

We trade off possession of the jar each time, and it's our turn to host date jar night, which is when we pick a slip out of the jar and make plans for when to carry out the activity we draw while eating a simple dinner. I stand in front of the mirror in the bathroom, curling my hair. When I set the curling iron down, Ben comes up behind me and wraps his arms around my waist. He bends down to rest his chin on my shoulder and looks at us in the mirror.

"You're beautiful," he says into my neck, kissing the skin under my jaw. My eyes flutter closed as I lean into him. I twist in his arms to face him, our lips meeting. He lifts me so I'm sitting on the counter, threading his fingers into my freshly curled hair and pressing himself between my legs.

The doorbell rings, and he breaks the kiss with a groan, resting his forehead against mine. I giggle. "You really should have known Mac would be right on time."

"We will continue this later," he promises, nipping at my bottom lip. I slide off the counter, and we walk hand-in-hand to greet Mac and Daniel at the door.

We lead them to the kitchen, where the jar sits in the middle of the table. We all sit.

"I think it's Jenny's turn to draw," Mac says, and the guys nod dutifully.

I frown. "I drew last time, remember? I laughed so hard at the idea of Evans ballroom dancing that I couldn't even tell you what was on the paper."

"Hilarious," Daniel grumbles.

"See?" I wave a hand at him. "It's someone else's turn."

Mac picks up the jar and holds it out to me. "That's not how I remember it. Is that how you remember it, Daniel?" She says it through gritted teeth. Daniel avoids looking at me and shakes his head. I pinch my eyebrows together and look at Ben, who shrugs, the picture of casual nonchalance.

"Pick a slip, Jenny. I'm hungry, and I can smell your meatballs." She wiggles the jar at me.

"Okay," I say slowly as I reach my hand in the jar and draw out a slip.

"Read it," Mac insists.

"Will you calm down?" I shake my head and open the slip of paper. Daniel finally looks at me, and Mac is smiling from ear to ear. Ben leans forward, clasping his hands together on the table. "Why are you all being so weird?" I ask, looking back and forth between each of them in turn.

"What does it say?" Ben smirks playfully, his brown eyes sparkling in the light hanging over the table.

My eyes linger on him. "It says..." I finally look at the slip of paper in my hand. I inhale sharply, blinking rapidly.

"Well?" Mac's voice shakes me out of my shock.

"It says, *Will you marry me?*" I look at Ben, who has moved his hands and, in their place is a small box. I shake my head ever so slightly. "Ben..."

He slides the box toward me. "Open it."

My hands are shaking as I pick the box up and flip the top open. Only, there's not a ring inside. There's another slip of paper. I glare at Ben. "Is this some kind of sick joke?"

He chuckles warmly, the corners of his eyes crinkling. "Read it."

I pull the paper from the fold where the ring should be and unroll it. *I'm ready when you are. Take your time. I'll wait for you.*

I carefully set the paper on the table, stand, and walk over to him. He leans back in his seat enough that I can swing a leg over him and sit on his lap, facing him. His broad hands grab my hips, holding me steady. I cup his face with my hands and kiss him.

When I pull away, he sighs. "What do you think, Green? Maybe another year or two—"

"Or now." I shrug. Mac lets out a little squeal.

He leans back a little, eyebrows raised. "It's only been three months."

"It's been nine years and three months," I correct him.

His smile could light up the entire room. "I was hoping you'd say that." He shifts me so he can reach into his pocket and pulls out a gorgeous solitaire. He slides it on my finger, then holds our hands together, pressed to his heart. "We can do this whenever you're ready," he whispers, and, maybe for the first time ever, I feel like I've finally shown up at the right time.

# A Note About Setting

LEADE PARK IS NOT a real place, and Leade Park High School is not a real school. It is a combination of all the Midwestern places I've encountered and all of the schools in which I've worked. I tried to keep it as realistic as possible while also keeping it completely separate from any real place. Any likeness to a real town or school is purely coincidental, and is most likely a result of my deep love of—specifically—the quirkiness of each school in which I've worked and—more generally—all things Midwestern.

Not ready to leave Leade Park? Sign up for Allie's newsletter for free bonus chapters and behind-the-scenes content at https://alliesamberts .substack.com.

# Acknowledgments

The second book is no less daunting than the first. In fact, it might be even more so because you feel you have something to live up to. As always, there are so many people to thank in an endeavor this huge, and never enough time or space to do so. Thank you to every single person who has had any involvement in taking this book from my brain to the printing press. I truly could not have done this without you.

Thank you, first and foremost, to my husband. Thanks for hanging out with the kids, taking the nighttime wake-ups after my late-night writing sessions, acting out gym scenes, and telling me—without a doubt—that this book is better than the last. (I'm still trying to decide if I should be offended by that or not.) You're always my first (and favorite) reader. I love you.

Major thanks to my alpha readers, Jillian and Alexis. Thanks for reading this halfway through when I was pretty sure it was too boring to continue writing, spitballing ideas, helping rewrite parts, and then reading it again and again. When I say I couldn't have done this without you, it's literal. This book would not exist had you not been there to tell me to keep going.

Thanks, also, to my beta readers, Sandy, Elizabeth, and Stefanie. Your comments helped improve this story, and your unending faith in me helped keep me going. Thanks, also, for being as obsessed with Ben as I am.

I would be remiss if I didn't thank my editor, Cindy Ray Hale, and my cover designer, Jillian Liota of Blue Moon Creative Studio. I'm so fortunate to have professionals who know what they're doing to help make this book into the best version it can be.

And, maybe most importantly, thank you to my family—my mom, dad, and brother. I was nervous to tell you I was starting this author journey, but you all didn't even blink. Thank you for teaching me to live my dreams, and thank you for believing in me.

Finally, thank you to my readers. I had no idea how my first book would be received. Your love for it encouraged me to do it again.

As always, I hope I didn't forget anyone. If I did, please forgive me. And thank you, thank you, thank you.

# Also By Allie Samberts

The Write Place

The Write Time

Leade Park #3, coming soon

# About the Author

Allie Samberts is a romance writer, book lover, and high school English teacher. She was voted funniest teacher of the year for 2023 by her students, which is probably her highest honor to date. She is also a runner, and enjoys knitting and sewing. She lives in the Chicago suburbs with her husband, two kids, and a very loud beagle. You can follow her on Instagram @alliesambertswrites, read her blog at alliesamberts.substack.com, and get other updates at www.alliesamberts.com.

Made in the USA
Las Vegas, NV
27 January 2024

84972231R00177